ISLAND ROMANCE

"Let me show you how different I am," Cole drawled huskily.

He claimed Carla's lips, rubbing across them in slow motion with a coaxing intensity that made her wild with yearning.

She'd never been kissed like this before. It was amazing . . . it was awful . . . she felt eager . . . she felt appalled.

When Cole finally released her, his breath was ragged and his hands were shaking against her arms, knowingly aware that Carla had tried to resist him. "What am I going to do about you?"

Carla was at a loss. "I don't know."

Cole's gaze met her sable eyes. "So Darnell Farrell hurt you, and now you think every man is going to treat you the same way he did. Well, Carla, take a good look. I'm Cole Richmond, not Darnell Farrell. If you think you're going to confuse the two of us in your mind, then maybe it's time you made me kiss you again. . . ."

ISLAND ROMANCE

SONIA ICILYN

BET Publications, LLC
www.msbet.com
www.arasbesquebooks.com

ARABESQUE BOOKS are published by

BET Publications, LLC
C/o BET BOOKS
One BET Plaza
1900 W Place NE
Washington, D.C. 20018-1211

First Printing: April, 1999
10 9 8 7 6 5 4 3 2 1

Printed in the United States of America

For my daughter, Parissa, the smartest kid I know

ONE

"His grandfather never missed a meeting," the bespectacled, confused-looking Caribbean woman complained with a polite cordial smile marring her face, her feet stumbling over rocks and stones as she led the way ahead. Hastily introducing herself as they plodded along, she added, "We just don't know how to take the young Mr. Richmond."

"When did he take over the Linden Vale plantation, Bessie?" Carlane McIntyre inquired, picking her way carefully along the winding path, her sable-colored gaze casting a quick glance around her. The valley was rising sharply, the arid ground giving way to more fertile soil on the higher level she could see loom up against her. To the left was a deep gorge cut into the side of the tropical hills, and Carlane couldn't help but appreciate its grandeur as she followed the elderly woman toward a cluster of coconut trees she could see further ahead.

She hadn't visited Jamaica before, but the unexpected invitation to head the marketing and advertising campaign for one of its leading coffeemakers was simply an opportunity she couldn't resist. As the clouds of red arid dust, caused by the movements of her sandaled feet lessened, and the noon heat became unbearable against her bare back and shoulders, covered only by the simple white vest she was wearing, Carlane couldn't help but conceal her excitement at taking on her first major international advertising contract, even though the one man who was expected to meet her had failed to keep their scheduled appointment.

"He's been here seven weeks," Bessie responded with irritation in her voice. "And things have been turbulent ever since."

"Oh?" Carla exclaimed curiously, as the ground became more bumpy, strewn as it was with heavy clumps of earth and debris. The Cockpit Country was much further afield where the maroons lived, if her knowledge of the island served her well. But they had just come off the road from Falmouth, heading south to where she'd been told the Linden Vale coffee plantation was situated.

"This isn't the first time he's missed a meeting," Bessie continued, her Caribbean accent deepening suddenly. "You must have been wondering what was going on, sitting alone in that hotel waiting. It's just as well you telephoned me. I was secretary and housekeeper to young Mr. Richmond's grandfather, you know."

Carlane offered a courteous smile as they suddenly came out of the coconut trees and into a clearing where an imposing whitewashed Georgian house with a terra-cotta tile roof confronted her startled gaze. Allowing her sable eyes to travel the length and breadth of the house, she took in its wooden balcony and the tall stairway at the side of the house which led there, the dozen or so windows all with red louvered shutters, and the several number of pillars, each adding a characteristic strength to the face of the house on her approach. An abandoned jeep was outside with its motor still running, but no one was around, and the air was still and quiet with only the sound of the engine humming.

"Will Mr. Richmond be seeing me here?" Carlane asked, pulling her small bag over her shoulders and struggling with the small folder she'd carried, consisting of the few rough ideas made at her London desk which she'd intended on showing him.

"I do not know," Bessie admitted forlornly, taking brisk steps up to the front door of the house, fighting the fireflies in the air as she proceeded to enter. "I managed to find Mr. Morgan, and he said he would see you here."

"Is he a working member of the plantation?" Carlane continued as she, too, fanned away the fireflies before following the old lady into the house.

"Good lord, no," Bessie gasped. "He's young Mr. Richmond's first cousin, twice removed. His mama's cousin's boy."

Carlane made a mental note to figure that one out as her feet connected with the hardened wooden floor of the entrance hallway and her gaze quickly swept the area in open and blatant curiosity while Bessie was making her departure. "Wait here," she said quietly. "I'll go find him."

Carlane nodded as she left. Looking around her, she could almost feel the intrigue and mystery of days gone by. There were wooden carvings, crafted from Jamaican cedar into a wide selection of animals and birds on top of an antique table where two Queen Anne chairs were positioned at either side. Contemporary pictures of maritime history littered the wood-clad walls where two old flintlock blunderbusses and an ivory trumpet also hung, and a grinding board for mashing peanuts, again from carved wood with an eighteenth-century look about it, stood diligently on the floor as though waiting to be taken elsewhere.

She was looking at all this silently when a door across from her suddenly swept open and a young woman appeared angrily from the room within. "Leave me alone," she yelled over her shoulder, sucking her teeth murderously. On seeing Carlane, she stopped dead in her tracks, her braided canerow hair glistening like polished onyx, her youthful features a perfect foil for an unsmiling, dark satanic manner. "You waitin' for somebody?" the elongated, cinnamon-stick woman breathed, her voice filled with ill-conceited curiosity.

Carlane raised her dark brows. "I'm Miss Carlane McIntyre," she said, introducing herself to the young woman in her early twenties. "I did have a scheduled appointment with young Mr. Richmond, but . . ."

"Oh, you are the girl him bring in from London to put us all in line," the woman drawled with caustic irony, rich in her native lingo. "So, wha' happen? Mr. Richmond no meet you?"

"He didn't arrive," Carlane admitted quietly, feeling slightly nauseous as she felt her body begin to fight against the warm air surrounding her.

"His grandfather never missed a meeting, you know." The woman adjusted the straps on her yellow dress, before taking long leggy strides toward her. As she did so, a man came running out of the same room, pulling up the zipper of his trousers, and his face adopting a sheepish grin as his surprised gaze met Carlane's.

Carlane swallowed, her throat dry from the sweltering heat. She was tired from having already wasted a half day, waiting around at the Trelawny Beach Hotel where she'd checked in the night before. As she found herself listening to further complaints about the elusive Mr. Richmond, who it appeared took great care in overlooking his appointments, she wiped her forehead and asked, "You are . . . ?"

"Tata, his cousin," the woman quipped, her cool hazel gaze flicking slowly over Carlane's petite frame. "So you are Darnell Farrell's ex-mistress. Who end it, really? Him or you?"

Carlane closed her eyes as the sizzling heat caused droplets of sweat to run slowly from her forehead down to her tawny-brown cheeks. The thought that this woman knew who her ex-partner was didn't surprise her one little bit. Darnell Farrell was internationally known for claiming the WBC title. He was also the British heavyweight champion and a future contender to Mike Tyson. What did surprise her was the fear that she might lose her temper at the sheer mention of his name because that could still evoke bitterness on her part, and she had long since decided that she was on the road to healing.

It had taken skill and practice learning to dress the broken emotional wounds, her first lesson beginning the day she'd started to coach her way through a multi-million-pound separation of assets, the sins of cohabiting her mother might say. Iona McIntyre, a stoical Christian woman and being of the firm opinion that boxers were not for marrying, triumphed in what she considered to be the outcome of such shameful, modern living arrangements.

But she'd found a way to vent her tearful, hopeless frustration. She'd taken charge: juggling money and transferring her property and all with the brave, stolid face one would expect from a Bank of England clerk that even her uncle, Quayle Wagnall, had been weak with admiration. She'd learned to lose a lover without losing herself, finding power in walking differently, dressing differently, even thinking in deep complicated patterns on how she was going to improve her life.

The mental sorting-out process had also taught her to let go of her anger, even when confronted with someone who threw Darnell's name into her face. And so twitching her mouth in a motion which could subtly pass for a slight smile, she told Tata stiffly, "Darnell ended it."

Tata laughed. "Me thought so. You can never trust a man."

"Babee." The sheepish man who'd appeared from the room smiled apologetically and came up behind Tata. "Me love yuh style, honey. Me want to talk to yuh."

"I said leave me alone," Tata yelled at him, wedging herself free from the male arms which had clung possessively around her waist. "I want to tell Miss Carlane McIntyre a few t'ings about the young Mr. Richmond."

"I really don't wish to hear them," Carlane rebuffed, suddenly irritated at being kept waiting. This would not have happened had she insisted that the meeting be held in London, but her uncle had confirmed the arrangements, booking her room and the conference suite in the hotel where she was staying. Not wishing to lose her first international advertising contract, she'd accepted the arrangements willingly. Now as her gaze caught the two people smiling luridly at her, Carlane wondered exactly what sort of coffee plantation she'd walked into. "Someone named Bessie went to get a Mr. Morgan to discuss the Linden Vale advertising contract with me. Is he here?"

"Mr. Morgan!" Tata giggled as though some point had not been made plain. "That natty-head brother of mine can't see you. He's—"

"Tata!" A male voice rang out, moments before Carlane's gaze strayed mercifully to a set of long lean hairy legs wearing brown leather sandals. The man who emerged from the main entrance door towered over Tata's friend in an imposing manner, an easy six foot four, Carlane guessed, of rugged hard power. "What's *he* doing here?" he asked of Tata, referring to her sheepish friend, whom he regarded with distaste.

"He's here to see me," Tata challenged instantly.

"Really," the man said curtly, turning to Tata's friend. His lips tightened and his cool gaze, shielded by sunglasses, appraised the man's dirty, unkempt clothes. "Get out of here," he barked at the man.

"I hate you," Tata spouted on a high note. "Ever since Papa Peter die, you think you can come here and control us all. Well, not me."

Tata's friend scurried quickly, and the newcomer's gaze shifted coolly to where Carlane stood. Taking a firm hold on Tata's wrist, he asked, "What's she doing here?"

"She is your appointment," Tata returned scathingly before wrenching her wrist free and running after her friend as she heard the jeep's engine fire up.

The newcomer grimaced as he glanced at his watch, observing the dial face which read 1:35 P.M. Pulling a frown to his heavy-set brows, his gaze settled inquiringly on Carlane. She was instantly aware that behind the high-priced, smoke-colored Ray Bans he was wearing, he was committing to memory every detail of her tawny-brown body concealed by the white vest which amply covered her large breasts and the white complementing shorts that hugged an equally endowed hipline. Carlane was aware that he also saw Carlane McIntyre—the world-traveled, delicate-boned ex-mistress to Darnell Farrell, whose shimmering short curtain of black relaxed hair, framing a face of simple but prominent features and sable-colored eyes, often held a breathtaking vulnerability that were at times too revealing.

The British publicity machine were the first to latch on to that flair of vulnerability and innocence, making a field day out of it by outlining her personal life in such precise detail that she had decided to seek refuge in her work. Then began her mission to build an empire, seeking restitution in the hidden talents she'd found within herself. McIntyre & Wagnall, her advertising agency of less than one year and which she'd partnered with her uncle, was now close to billing its first quarter of a million pounds sterling and she'd since felt confident that she could take on anyone whatever their background or circumstance. Yet as Carlane met the gaze transfixed on her small frame, her senses felt a little alarmed at the way this man's cool gaze met hers.

"Miss Carlane McIntyre?" he acknowledged, rolling her name on his tongue more in statement than in query, his sensual lips twisting as he took a step forward, towering over her like a dangerous shadow waiting to envelop her in eternal darkness. "Aren't I to meet you at the Trelawny Beach Hotel?"

"Yes," Carlane said, peeved and annoyed that he hadn't instantly offered an apology. "I sat in the conference suite my agency hired for the best part of the morning before finally calling your office. Someone named Bessie met me on the road to Good Hope, but of course I let the taxi go before she decided to tell me that there would be a fair distance walk the rest of the way here."

"My diary has you listed for two o'clock," the newcomer insisted bluntly, seemingly oblivious to how put-out she felt. "What in the devil are you doing here?"

"I had you down for ten o'clock this morning," Carlane instantly responded, again wiping her perspiring forehead.

"Then there's been an oversight," he responded flatly.

Carlane chose to ignore him in an attempt to force her mind to remain calm. "I take it you're the young Mr. Richmond?" she began, observing the big, strong brown hands pressed against a pair of faded jeans which were cut off at the knees. They were such a contrast to her own small, slender fingers, she realized he could crush her without an effort. His sinewy flesh was covered with a simple blue T-shirt, sporting the amber brown of his arms and chest where muscles rippled against the heat that the late August sun had caused, indicating that he pumped iron daily. "Do you mind—"

"Colebert," he interrupted her midstream.

Carlane looked at him hard then got cheeky, spurred on by the interruption. "Bert," she downgraded.

"Cole," he one-upped, a smile playing with his lips.

"Cole," Carlane approved, forcing down the weak smile tugging at her own lips. "Do you mind if I have a glass of water. The heat in here is so intense."

"Of course." Cole snapped himself into action. "Follow me." As he led the way through the house, his sandals, like Carlane's, made slapping squeaking noises against the expanse of wooden flooring. Carlane felt the heat on her face intensify. The house obviously lacked air-conditioning, she thought, allowing her gaze to travel upward to the ceiling in search of a fan, only to find it rendered and painted in buttermilk tones showing little wear and tear. Despite its age, the house had held up very well over the years and, as she followed silently behind Cole Richmond, her gaze studying further colonial artifacts in her wake, it became evident to her that everything within the house spoke of a bygone age, the remnants that had obviously been collected and left by Papa Peter's untimely departure, she decided.

They approached a kitchen that had not yet caught up with modern times, where the oven appeared more like a furnace and all the cooking pots seemed like objects from the Georgian century gone by, adding an intriguing air to the room. There were all manner of fruits spread across a worn wooden table: cassavas and plantains, mangos and pawpaws, each providing their individual pleasant aroma against the smell of bread-fruit and yams roasting in the oven. Carlane's knees trembled as she found herself leaning against the door frame, the aromatic fragrances making her nauseous and giddy and something akin to nostalgia triggering at her senses.

"My grandfather never missed a meeting," she heard Cole Richmond say as the sound of running water filling a glass bounced against her ears. "This is the fourth time in near as many weeks that I've missed one. I think it's time I had a word with Bessie." He came over with the water. "Are you all right?"

"Yes. No." Carlane's fingers shook as she tried to take the glass.

"I think you'd better sit down," Cole advised, taking hold of her arm and positioning her on a low stool he sought from nearby. Kneeling on one knee and taking the folder from beneath her arm, he placed the glass against her trembling lips. "Is this your first trip here?"

Carlane nodded as she began to sip the water he offered.

"Your body needs to adjust. You're suffering a little sunstroke," Cole explained.

"I feel so embarrassed," Carlane stammered, now able to hold the glass herself from which she drank another measure of water. "It just came on suddenly." She paused for air, then took another sip. "I'm sorry."

"No need to apologize Miss McIntyre." Cole smiled, removing his Ray Bans so that Carlane was able to capture the deep depths of his cocoa-colored eyes. Even in her heightened state of disturbed emotions caused by the attacking heat, she felt awed at the way those eyes suddenly ensnared hers.

"Please, call me Carla," she insisted shakily. "Carla McIntyre." That was something else she'd decided to do differently, shorten her name. It had brought to mind a new image of herself, made her conjure up new changes at a time when she'd buried into the deepest corners of her soul to find the strength to move on and redefine herself. It had also brought to mind other positive *C* words to which she could aspire: *chic . . . charismatic . . . charming . . . carefree . . . calm.* Yes, she needed that last one right now. "Carlane's a little long winded." She smiled. "And Miss McIntyre is certainly too formal."

Cole smiled, accepting her invitation. "Carla sounds nice," he agreed. "I saw you at a booth at the Jamaica Expo when I was visiting a friend in London and took a leaflet about your agency from there."

"That would have been three weeks ago," Carla acknowledged, pleasantly amazed that such business interest should swiftly come her way. "It was the first time we've ever exhibited. My uncle's idea, of course, but I'm glad his marketing tactic has paid off. I'm really surprised it's gotten us noticed abroad. I don't remember you though."

"I took one of your leaflets while you were busy," Cole began, "and then from time to time, watched you from afar."

"And?" Carla's brows rose in professional speculation.

"I put you down for future reference," Cole finished on a more personal level, a man none too afraid to get right to the point, Carla realized warily. "You're a very pretty woman. Are you dating?" His inquiring gaze, blatant in its interest, settled on hers.

Carla felt something akin to fear surge and propel

inside her. After all the pain she'd suffered at the hands of Darnell Farrell, she couldn't forgive this man for asking such an impertinent question, especially when she had expected him to be making ready to launch into their meeting.

Though it had been just over a year since she and Darnell had parted, the media machine had kept the news on a treadmill like it was still a current item. Then when Darnell had spilled out the reasons for their troubled relationship throughout the pages of *People* magazine, she'd rebuffed by telling hers to the *National Enquirer.* And so had begun the media bidding for each version, their accounts becoming punctuated with fiction, adding to fantasy, adding to nonsensical rubbish that it wasn't long before her mother had decided upon bringing her spiritual beliefs and God into it.

It had been difficult just finding a way to hold on, but she had been rewarded when the worst was over. If she could now measure herself beyond the financial, she could be quantified with words like *survivor, unbeaten, invincible,* and evaluated on her self-preservation.

But there was one area Carla did not care to gauge and for which she could devise no slide rule, and that was the adversity she had developed toward men. The distance, degree, and pitch were beyond computation, the lengths to which she would go to prove the point incalculable. And ever intent on proving the point, she often manifested her dislike for them even in the simplest of conversation. "I will never love again," she quavered.

Cole's curious, watchful expression deepened. "I didn't ask you whether you will love again," he ventured quietly. "I want to know if you're dating someone."

"Why?" Carla instantly recounted, knowingly aware that she was in danger of betraying how low her self-esteem had become where men were concerned. "Are you about to make me some kind of proposition that doesn't involve what I am here to discuss?"

"I'm sure you've been propositioned before." Cole smiled knowingly.

Carla breathed uneasily, then took another sip from the glass. She didn't like this kind of questioning, however friendly. It was one of the disadvantages of being attractive, she thought without pretense or vanity. Since her split with Darnell, many suitors had attempted to try to get to know her, but she'd decided that her heart was best kept hidden in an invisible cage where it would be safe—where she would need never worry to offer it to anyone. Yet as the giddy side effects of the sun began to sedate and the water cooled her from within, some feisty compulsion and bravado dared her to ask, "What exactly are you offering?"

"What do you want?" Cole returned just as quickly, now raising himself back to his feet and toting the folder he'd taken from her.

Carla allowed her gaze to stray upward, eyeing Cole Richmond with avid interest. His head was shaven, the "R" Kelly look, she noted wryly, realizing that his beard covered only the upper part of his lips and traveled a square line around his mouth and chin. He was quite fetching, an acutely handsome man in his late thirties, she decided, and she was aware that she could easily develop a deep attraction toward him, if she allowed it. But she'd already made one bad decision in her thirty-one years. She wasn't hell-bent on making another one. "I want more than the woman in your life now gets," she told him sternly.

Cole stiffened, and his eyes narrowed as he looked down and searched her emotionless face. Rubbing the

Ray Bans against his jean-clad thighs, he contemplated her smoothly. "What gives you the idea that there *is* a woman?"

"You strike me as being the type who likes to have one, constantly," Carla relented. "So how much am I worth?"

Cole licked his lips in arrogance, his eyes flashing with intrigue as though the question seemed somewhat unreal. "I'd say a condo maybe—as a second home—top-quality car, some more financial security," he taunted in reply.

"In return for . . . ?"

"My time with you."

"Your time with me," Carla repeated, nodding a pretense that she was actually considering his outrageous proposition. "Which is . . . ?"

"Two, maybe three times a week."

"And afterward?"

Cole frowned his puzzlement. "Afterward?"

"You know, when you've considered that I've depreciated in value and you're about to trade me in for a younger version. How much would my residual worth be then? Do I get dumped in the used-and-abused junkyard, or am I allowed to keep anything for my toil?"

"We can come to some arrangement," Cole said evenly.

"I see." Carla's mouth pursed into a hard line. The last thing she wanted was a romantic entanglement, and she imagined that Cole didn't want that, either. He was obviously of the opinion though that she liked to work and play, that she was of that caliber of advertising executive who enjoyed blending the two extremes to bind a contract before sealing the clauses with a romp in the hay. And she'd known contracts to be won that way, where sexual favors were as much an intricate part of the details as planning the budget. Though such practices appalled her, she didn't want to appear a prude. So tipping her head back, and offering one of her most compelling smiles, she said, "Well, Mr. Colebert Richmond." Her tone was formal, a reminder to herself that they were expected to be conducting a meeting. "There's a problem."

"What's that?" he inquired.

"It's the amount of time you would be spending with me," she informed him blithely, her mind admitting that she had to admire his barefaced nerve. "You see, even once a week would be too much. Now, are you interested in hearing my ideas for Linden Vale coffee?"

Cole's eyes flashed deeply brown, unperturbed by the put-down. "You will get over the pain, you know," he offered, his tone sympathetic and softly spoken as though he knew some deep secret about her. "British news travels here, too."

Carla glared at him, a mixture of confusion and anger suddenly welling up inside her. The simple reassurance came so unexpectedly, she hardly knew how to deal with the wisdom of it. There was a tense silence as the words sank in, as his cocoa-brown gaze, shrewd as it was, took in the confused state he'd plummeted her into. Carla noted the sincerity in his strong bold face, remembered the way he'd spoken with calm serenity, and was suddenly aware of the neurotic child-woman she'd become.

He saw too much, she thought nervously. He could see the harsh lessons of life lurking somewhere in the troubled background of her eyes, and she didn't like it. She'd thought herself a good businesswoman, a person who could achieve immaculate control when things were at their worst, yet this man could see through her so clearly.

And what he'd said wasn't new to her, either. So many people had attempted to boost her confidence in that way, and she'd been fortunate enough to have had a strong network of friends to hold on to. Her only self-doubt had been through the eyes of her mother. Iona McIntyre never held her tongue once through the ugly months of her daughter's awful ordeal, but instead chose to remind her that she had brought a mark of shame and ridicule upon their family name. An unpleasantry that had even surmounted the truth on how Uncle Quayle had become the black sheep of the family. Perhaps that was why Carla gravitated toward him so. He was her mother's younger brother, and he knew what it was like to become an outcast in Iona McIntyre's eyes.

"You're probably right," Carla conceded, her eyes flashing with pain as she recalled the last time she and her mother had spoken. Quickly dispelling it from her memory, and her business acumen propelling her onward, she rose from the stool and placed her empty glass on the nearby table. "Are we having the meeting here, in the kitchen?"

"Wait a minute." Cole took hold of her wrist, gently restraining her as his eyes carefully measured the length of her against him. "Are you sure you're all right?"

A sense of unease instantly shot through Carla's loins, but what was more disturbing was the way her pulses had skipped with delicious delight by the simple feel of Cole's strong fingers against her delicate wrist. Cautioning herself by removing it quickly, she composed her expression to one of formality and allowed her gaze to skirt across the room. "I'm feeling much better," she insisted. "And I really don't think this is the place for a meeting."

Cole smiled. "No, it isn't." Returning her folder he

offered, "Would you like to see the plantation before we begin? I think you might appreciate some background knowledge."

Carla searched his face, detecting a telling sign there. "That's a good place to start if you can stay on the subject of our meeting." She smiled, a little nervous at her candor.

Cole Richmond's gaze was steady. "Until we've exhausted the subject," he promised her. "Then I expect to learn a little about you."

Carla didn't like the sound of that one little bit.

The flat expanse of grassland sloped up ahead at the rear of the house, enveloping everything as far as the eye could see. What little clouds were in the sky seemed to settle on the estate's horizon, becoming almost part of the plantation and its abundant plant life. Carla did not know the geography of the place, nor how much acreage of land her calculating gaze had settled on. All she knew was that from the vantage point where she stood, thousands on thousands of coffee trees beckoned her with their welcoming blossoms the way nature dictated they should greet a fascinated onlooker.

"These are all coffee trees?" she asked, craning her neck from left to right, her expression a betrayal that she'd never seen anything so wondrous before.

"Yes," Cole answered lightly. "And it all begins with the coffee seeds. I'll explain it all to you as we go along."

He invited her to join him as he made his way upward, his running dialogue full of knowledge and explanatory detail. The coffee tree had a basic life cycle that determined the real activity of the plantation. Careful selection of seeds was vital. They had to be chosen from the heartiest, best-flavored, biggest-yielding, and most disease-resistant trees, and stripped of their cherrylike skins and pulps, but not of their parchment wrappings, before they were planted in special nursery beds.

She observed the nursery beds closely on her approach, listening intently as Cole explained how carefully they needed to be watered, shaded, and watched. After a few months, when they would be several inches high, the trees would be transferred to individual pots in which they would live until their first birthday when their growth would have reached two to three feet tall.

That would be when the real work began, Cole continued, taking her further along her route of discovery. Each tree would be planted in rows about ten feet apart, and in between each row would be planted fast-growing shade trees to shelter the young coffee plants and filter Jamaica's intense sunlight to maintain humidity.

As that same sunlight caused her to worry whether she might have another heat attack, Cole began to explain that it took two to three years for a tree to reach maturity. Only then would it become a real citizen of the plantation. Though the trees were capable of reaching growth exceeding twenty feet, Cole informed her that the Linden Vale trees were kept pruned to about six feet, a way of preserving energy and aid in the harvesting, he added.

When she inquired on how he came by all this knowledge, she hadn't expected his answer to be so academic. "I graduated in agricultural and environmental sciences from McGill University in Canada," he stated crisply, lowering himself to the ground between the row of coffee trees they were standing in presently. Carla followed him down, watching as he took a handful of soil into his hand and worked it diligently between his fingers. "It's funny how things work out," Cole added absently. "I would never have thought my love for agriculture and wildlife could've somehow been a preemptive decision that would one day map my future. Certainly not to find myself inheriting this coffee plantation."

"I was trying to work that one out," Carla admitted, her mouth forming a clear untroubled smile that made Cole's eyes widen in appreciation. "I expected someone much older than myself. Even when Bessie called you the young Mr. Richmond, I imagined some fuddy-duddy in his forties, married and set in his ways."

"Married?" Cole registered that one word quickly. "Why that?"

Carla suddenly found herself struggling for an answer, wondering why on earth she'd pulled up something so intimately personal. "I understood your grandfather, Peter Richmond, was a very old man when he died. Naturally I assumed his beneficiary to be someone more mature in his years."

Cole digested her answer then let it go. "My grandfather was eighty-six when he died. He inherited this estate from my great-grandfather, who was an Englishman. But before that, he fought in World War Two for England against the Nazis. Papa Peter was a bombardier in the Royal Air Force and was in the famous Mysore Fighter Squadron, too."

"Really?" Carla gasped.

"Yeah." Suddenly Cole's smile was all for her, and Carla felt the full force of his personality causing a shivery awareness of him that knocked hard against her trembling nerves. It was a feeling she had no intention of encouraging, so she willed it down by quickly reaching to the ground, taking a pile of earth into her own hand. But as she began to work her fingers into the soil in her palm, Cole took her hand into his massive empty one and poured his handful of earth into hers. "We have to till the soil regularly," he told her smoothly, "and pull up intruding weeds."

Surprised at her pulses pulsating by the simple contact, Carla managed to answer in a modulated voice. "Do you have to watch for diseased trees, too?" It seemed a silly question, given that she knew all plants, particularly on a plantation, had to survive bugs and insects. But because she was working on keeping her concentration, her mind was in a quandary to think up something more sensible.

But Cole answered nonetheless. "All the time." He rose to his feet and Carla followed him up. His shoulders seemed weighted with the task, she thought, as his teaching dialogue continued. "Wood borers and scale insects mostly. They can engulf large parts of a tree quite easily. We use pesticides, they combat most afflictions, but it's never a complete remedy."

"So when do you harvest the beans?" Carla asked, following his footsteps as they moved along, even absurdly thinking to herself that Cole Richmond was nothing like the man she had promised herself she would get over. Even in Cole's mild Jamaican accent, she found an attractive pleasantness that pleased her ears and yet his English was so well spoken, a dead give-away that he'd been educated abroad.

"It's impractical to have harvesting equipment," Cole explained. "All the trees bear blossoms, red berries, or green berries at the same time. Six plantation workers man this estate, and they harvest the crop every day, going to each tree to make sure that every bean is picked at its peak."

"What happens then?" Carla's interest sustained.

"Well, this estate prepares coffee the old way. We dry them in the sun."

She was taken along to another section of the plantation where there was an air of muted activity. An old man dressed in worn dungarees got out of a Toyota Land Cruiser and disappeared out of her line of vision and, as Carla craned her head to see where he'd gone, she could see a little distance away from the house, several more buildings she'd never expected to be there. Most of them looked like shacks and there was one, almost like the Georgian house itself, but it was much smaller and in keeping with the countryside round about. As her gaze took in the three men raking the ground, her first thought was a simple one. Whoever said things stood still in the country?

"Is this how you dry the beans?" She suspected that was what was going on.

"This is how it's done," Cole confirmed lightly, taking her closer. "The coffee cherries are spread out in the open sunshine, then they are raked and then respread several times a day. After that, they are gathered into piles and covered at night for protection from moisture. In two or three weeks, they will have dried thoroughly, and that's when these cherries will be ready for a milling machine."

"What does that do?" Carla wondered exactly when the whole process would end.

"It removes the husk, parchment, inner covering, and skin from the bean inside," Cole answered.

"It's all so complicated," she admitted. "Is that the end?"

"It is here," Cole told her astutely. "Linden Vale has no grading plant, so once our cherries are dried and sorted, they're transported to our nearest exporter. But normally, coffee has to be graded before it can go to market. The criteria include altitude at which they were grown, size and weight of the beans, whether dry or wet preparation had been done, and whether the beans had been hand sorted. But ultimate grading is given by cup tasters."

"Like tasting wine in France?" Carla was surprised.

Cole laughed. "They roast the beans fresh and brew it before they sample," he informed.

"And they spit it out, too?" Carla asked, disbelieving, enjoying Cole's pleasant burst of laughter which made her feel unusually safe in his company, even though her first impression of him had been one of general uneasiness.

"Absolutely." Cole began to steer her further along. "Once they grade the coffee, only then is it classified ready to be sold. Jamaican coffee tends to be mellow and sweet. I'm sure you'd like to taste a cup."

Carla welcomed the invitation. "I'd love to."

Cole's smile widened. "Then let's go to my house, and I'll make you a brew."

Carla accepted willingly, telling herself that this meeting was going better than she'd expected. She felt she'd learned so much in such a short space of time and realized that not only had she enjoyed the education but that she wanted to learn more. It was almost extraordinary to her, knowing that her mother was born on this beautiful island in the tropics, but that she'd never told her much about it. Up until Uncle Quayle had mentioned the coffee contract, she hadn't even realized that Jamaica grew coffee. That was one of the disadvantages of being born and raised in England, not knowing one's true origin, she thought.

Cole Richmond was changing all that. As she kept pace beside him, rubbing absently at the earth still present in the palm of her hand, she braced herself ready for the new influx of knowledge. But as her sable gaze traveled curiously along the route Cole was taking her and they began approaching the small house she'd seen earlier, Carla found her senses jumping involuntarily. Until that minute, it hadn't occurred to her that Cole didn't live in the Georgian house she'd entered on her arrival. She kept her pace, reminding herself that they were still conducting a meeting, that she was just on her way to taste some coffee.

A movement of someone close to the house suddenly caught their attention and a young woman, fair-skinned with long dark curly hair, came toward them at Cole's loud call. "Robyn, come and meet Carla McIntyre." He urged the woman over with a firm wave of his hand, and she approached coolly, her expression guarded, her gaze firmly set. "This is Robyn Morrison, our right-hand girl and the greenest fingers Papa Peter could find for miles," Cole introduced.

Robyn didn't smile, though the compliment was meant for her. Instead she held out her hand dutifully, merely touching Carla's fingers gently and accepting her quiet apology for them being covered in earth. Carla noted instantly that Robyn wasn't pleased to make the acquaintance. The woman, younger by some four years, she guessed, turned immediately to Cole and offered him a beaming smile before whispering something in his ear about a coffee order having gone astray. She noticed, too, the covetous glance Robyn threw in his direction as Cole listened attentively, suspecting that women looked at Colebert Richmond like that all the time.

His strong, hard body held a menacing sexuality, an implicit threat of sexual magnetism which probably attracted women to him like crocodiles to water. And she had to admit, he was pleasantly magnetic. But she would fare better to keep him at arm's length, she reminded, even as she felt abandoned watching the two of them huddled together, talking covertly.

When Robyn finally went on her way, Cole returned

his attention. "She's a pretty girl, isn't she?" he prompted, almost absently.

"I'm sure she is," Carla responded, a woman's instinct warning her of the meaning to Robyn's barely concealed resentment. Either Cole and Robyn were having an affair, or Robyn wished that they were having one.

"I'm afraid I'm going to have to cut this meeting short," Cole said evenly, taking Carla by surprise. "A problem has arisen with a shipment of some coffee, and I'm going to have to go and deal with it."

"Oh." Carla felt instant disappointment. She suddenly realized she had rather been looking forward to that cup of coffee.

"There's another part of the estate I would like to show you anyway," Cole explained. "It's a private beach on the coast about 16 kilometers away. We call it Bay Rock, and I'd like to take you there tomorrow morning, if that's all right."

Carla was annoyed. She knew she was the moment she felt her lips tighten, but she kept an even smile. "In that case, what time would you—"

"If you could be at Eden Lea at nine o'clock, then I'll drive us both up there," Cole cut in.

"Eden Lea?" Carla queried. "What's that?"

"The name of the big house," Cole confirmed turning on his heels and indicating that she follow his great strides back toward there. "It's the original plantation house, and it's about two hundred years old. In the basement, you can still find the slave quarters. We use them for storage now."

Bessie rushed out to meet them the moment they approached the kitchen door from where they'd embarked. "Miss McIntyre, I wondered what happened to you." On detecting Cole's presence, she added, "Oh, Mr. Richmond. You found Miss McIntyre."

"Yes, I did," Cole quipped. "I'd like you to ask Masa Joe to drive her back to her hotel and then remind me to have a word with you later."

"Yes, Mr. Richmond." Bessie took her orders.

Cole turned his gaze to Carla. "I'll see you tomorrow." He reached over and tentatively took her hand, intending on ending with a formal handshake. But on finding the pile of soil still present in Carla's palm, Cole instead curled her fingers around the earth as though it would find protection there. "The heart of Linden Vale is in your hand," he told her wistfully, concluding their meeting by making his departure.

Carla felt annoyed by the conflicting emotions within her as she watched him leave. Such frenzied feelings shouldn't be chasing around inside her like this, and her heart shouldn't be thumping so erratically against her rib cage. But as her gaze caught the palm of her hand where the handful of fertile soil was still present, Carla couldn't fathom why she felt a twinge of pain. Was it a sense of loss, Cole leaving her so suddenly? Or was it guilt that she was going against the grain? Against her promise that she would never allow a man to get near her again.

TWO

The Toyota Land Cruiser veered round a sudden steep curve in the road, and Carla clung to the side of the seat, the jolt reminding her that Cole was taking her toward Falmouth where he'd told her the Linden Vale estate owned a private stretch of beach.

She'd dressed quickly on awaking, having left her bed later than her usual 7.30 A.M. that morning. She'd spent her second night at the Trelawny Beach Hotel checking out the local television stations, only this time it was in a futile attempt to take her mind off Cole Richmond. She'd slept badly, too, thinking about her ex-partner and then about Cole, and it wasn't long before the truth dawned on her that she wasn't a happy woman.

She thought she loved being on her own, that she didn't want the stress of having someone take up any part of her life. Hadn't this been one of the lessons she'd learned after living in Darnell's shadow for so long? She had been the pretty young thing he paraded at clubs and parties, the woman he loved to control and manipulate to pander to his every whim. And she'd been stupid enough to allow him to do that, wondering how on earth she could make a man destroy the one precious thing she had inside of her: a love for herself.

A man could easily squash that, she'd thought, tossing and turning in her sleep. But Cole Richmond didn't appear to be that sort of man. To her discomfort, she'd found that being in his very presence excited her. Yet it frightened her, too. She'd worked so hard on rebuilding her self-confidence, trying to become that young woman she once knew—the one she'd been before Darnell had entered her life: happy, independent, full of expectant dreams for her future. Starting her own advertising agency had helped her to achieve that aim in returning to part of her childlike self. But she had matured, and she couldn't afford to jeopardize her progress now. She'd found skill within herself to forge a lucrative, thriving business, a skill that did not extend to a knowledge of how to deal with men.

The image of Cole Richmond seemed to soothe her tension on that matter. He didn't seem the type who would criticize her or attempt to make her feel inadequate or undeserving in some way. And she couldn't imagine being dominated by him, either. She decided that he was a person who would be generous with his feelings, who would share them in a way that would coax a reciprocating response.

When she'd awoken that morning, that one thought was still on her mind, making her full of confusion and yearning emotions. There was apprehension, excitement, and a much deeper throbbing feeling she couldn't quite analyze as she thought of meeting Cole Richmond again. She decided that unknown feeling was admiration, but it felt akin to homesickness, and so she began to think that maybe she was lovesick. Carla didn't want that to be true. She just wished she could train her thoughts on their meeting that morning.

A quick glance through the hotel window had revealed that she would be spending another August day under the hot glare of the Jamaican sun, and so she'd dressed in white linen slacks, sandals, and a pale pink T-shirt, fishing out her straw hat from her suitcase, deciding it would protect her against the sun causing another heat attack.

It was 7:55 A.M. when she'd showered, combed her hair, applied a touch of lipstick and the lightest hint of eye makeup before settling down to a hot cup of coffee and jelly covered toast. The coffee wasn't from the Linden Vale estate—she had yet to taste that—but it served in revitalizing her mood, making her ready to embark on the dawn of a new day.

She'd called down to the reception desk and ordered a taxi, then the telephone had intruded while she was briskly thumbing her way through the contents of her folder, making sure she had her ideas ready to show Cole. Uncle Quayle was on the line, inviting comment on her meeting the day before, and she'd explained the formality of having been shown the plantation first.

"So does he appeal to you?" Uncle Quayle asked, a tactless prompt she'd grown to expect from him whenever he wanted to take her into a discussion about her life and men. Her uncle took no shame in raising such idle gestures, and Carla could just imagine in her mind's eye his boyish expression and the slant of his smile, features which had at times made her find it hard to believe he was her mother's brother, only eleven years her senior.

"Uncle, I've told you already," she objected profusely. "I don't need a man."

"I thought all women needed a man," her uncle's voice drawled in disbelief. He always knew how to sound incredulous, a real illusionist in his old age, Carla thought.

"No, we don't," she argued sternly. "I don't think things have changed with men during the last three years of my relationship with Darnell. I'm sure their ultimate goal is still the same."

"Isn't that the fun part?" Uncle Quayle debated, amused.

"Until you fall in love with them," Carla concluded, her voice quavering as a recollection flashed through her mind. "That's when they walk all over you."

"Carla, baby." Her uncle's voice sounded disturbed. "I've told you before. We all act on the lessons we learn and continue to grow from them, generally much stronger from the experience. Don't give up on love."

"I have a jaded view about men right now, Uncle," Carla admitted ruefully. "It's making me feel self-protective. I just need some time to work my way into the best part of myself."

"Well, I hope you get there soon." Quayle sounded serious. "These mood swings of yours are making me concerned about how you're seeing your meetings through. Most of our clients are men. I hope you're not infringing any of your male prejudices on this prospective client in Jamaica."

"Uncle, that's an insult." Carla reeled, knowing full well he'd hit a chord of truth.

"Okay, then I'll say no more about it." Quayle backed down. "Call me soon and let me know how things are going."

As the phone clicked dead, she couldn't help but panic. Perhaps she was being too cold. Perhaps she was being too cynical. Perhaps she should just relax and enjoy her meeting with Cole this morning. The flurry of debate was still pondering heavily in Carla's mind as the four-wheel drive took her steadily through the tropical countryside, past mango trees and native town folk riding donkeys or traveling by foot.

Although her mind was in turmoil, she felt comfortable against the leather seat with her arm laid casually against the open window of the passenger door with the breeze sweeping against her short, dark hair as her hat rested unworn on her lap. But as her troubled thoughts persisted, she allowed her gaze to study Cole, charting the way he coolly handled the steering wheel, his gaze firmly fixed on the road.

He was easily more attractive than Darnell, she thought, the harsh lines on his jaw put there by life's experiences rather than by cruelty. He was also a man given to smiling freely, she sensed, noting the fainter lines embedded in the skin around his mouth that bespoke of that one simple fact. She liked the way he looked, liked the way his soft features—rounded nose and full lips, amber-colored complexion, and thick dark lashes—disguised his English heritage but made him appear masculine and sweet. As her sable gaze intensified, he turned and caught her unawares, those cocoa-colored eyes ensnaring hers as they'd done before.

"It's lonely in here," Cole intoned warmly, returning his gaze to the road.

Carla instantly steeled herself against the rush of beguiled feelings which flooded her system and forced out a steady tone. "What would make an interesting conversation?" she wavered.

"You," Cole told her frankly.

Carla tensed and scolded herself for it. "I'm not interesting, but your plantation is." Turning the conversation around to settle her nerves, she said, "I wanted to ask you whether any other crops were grown on Linden Vale."

"Cassavas," Cole announced, "and coconuts."

It was the opening Carla needed to keep her mind ticking over and away from heady thoughts to a more professional manner. In subdued tones that disguised the control she was fighting to regain within, she quickly launched into a discussion about the other crops, paying attention to Cole's every word as her interest grew on the subject. Again she couldn't deny the attractive sound of his voice. It was one of the first things she'd noticed about him and which she liked, she told herself with self-loathing. Cole's voice was full of all the richness of coffee, laced with a hint of his Jamaican accent that was none too broad or heavy with the local dialect. And he didn't wear any jewelry, either. She liked that also. Darnell wore rings and a medallion, and she'd never let herself admit that he overdid it to the extent of looking heavy laden and slightly effeminate.

As the Toyota cruised onward, she relaxed and took particular note of her surroundings, the tall spire of a church catching her attention and which Cole was quick to tell her had been dedicated to one of the abolitionists of the early nineteenth century. He seemed to have some knowledge about everything and Carla liked that, too, even though she knew the danger in telling herself so.

"There's so much about this island that's a reminder of when slavery existed." She continued the momentum from when they'd passed the church. "Don't you ever wonder about it?"

"We're approaching a new century," Cole returned an answer that Carla knew had been given some thought. "I think slavery is something we should consign to history. We should put it in its rightful place in the museums where all mankind can learn from its injustice." His gaze briefly left the road to catch Carla's watchful expression. "If we all dwelled on the past and let it affect us in a personal way, then we'd be in danger of allowing ourselves to self-destruct."

Carla nodded in awe, understanding something of what he meant, even thinking that he might be implying some deeper meaning as she thought of her own dismal past. "I made my long journey of inward discovery years ago," she told him with honesty. "And I've reconciled myself about what the days of slavery now means to me."

"But you're lonely," Cole surmised with an accuracy that shook Carla profoundly.

She hadn't expected that and even knowing it to be true, she offered Cole a prevaricating answer. "I've gotten used to solitude, being an only child."

"I'm an only child, too," Cole declared instantly. "But I don't believe in solitude."

"Neither do I." Carla felt protective and in denial both at one and the same time. "I'm not a recluse or some frightened little hermit, you know. I have my work."

"You can have more than that if you really want it," Cole challenged.

"I'm sure I could," Carla answered, a little anxious.

"Then what's stopping you?" It was a direct question, demanding an answer.

Carla shrugged carelessly as a cool breeze feathered her cheeks. "It's hard when you have good in your heart and you're trying to find that same goodness in someone," she declared with sincerity. She hadn't spoken like that before. The honesty took her by surprise. It seemed to capture Cole in some endearing, heartfelt way, too.

"I owe you an apology," he intoned lightly, self-mockery evident in his tone. "I was a little loose lipped in trying to make you a proposition yesterday."

"Loose lips sink ships." Carla chuckled, helping him

to clear his conscience. "I have to admit, you had a nerve."

"I've never done that before," he told her truthfully, remembering how he'd felt like a teenage kid, clumsily attempting to get a date. It was a foolish thing to do, adolescent by all accounts, but from the moment he'd seen the vulnerable suspicion of him in Carla McIntyre's eyes, Cole was lost. Plain and simple. "I'd like to think I'm still afloat where you're concerned, if you can forgive me."

Carla glanced over at him, appreciating the handsome, dynamic personality that she didn't find at all boring. "I'll let you know when I'm ready to throw you a lifeline," she joked pretentiously.

"I can wait." Humor colored Cole's voice as he drove the Land Cruiser further north toward the coast. He liked this woman with her small face and vulnerable features and the big sable eyes that he found irresistibly provocative. He loved talking to her, finding her natural, sensual grace in the way she tilted her head forward, hanging on to his every word, an attraction that had kept his pulses racing from the moment they'd met.

She had a soft sing-along voice which he loved hearing, and she reminded him so much of himself. A loner. Sure he was no backwoodsman living a monk's life. In fact he considered himself quite sociable and a good mixer with people. But there was something missing in his life. It'd been missing from when he started telling himself that he'd reached a point where he knew what he wanted.

He wanted to feel a woman snuggle up against his chest where he could circle his strong, safe arms around her. And he'd found many women willing to give him that. But now Cole realized he wanted a special woman, someone who could be a friend as well as a lover: someone he could share a home with and build a family. He wasn't quite sure what he was looking for, but he'd always told himself that he would know it when he found it.

And Carla McIntyre was suddenly starting to parade around in his mind making those heady thoughts taste even sweeter. There was only one problem. She'd been hurt and badly it seemed. He recalled the sound of her voice whenever she'd spoken. Even in its singalong fashion, it'd throbbed with sadness, holding an aching kind of pain that made him want to understand and know exactly what had happened to her. He could make her forget that pain, he told himself. But did he want to try? And more precisely, would she even allow him?

Falmouth seemed a pleasant town as the Land Cruiser slowed, making Carla aware of the number of Georgian buildings, many of which seemed to have been carefully restored for the visiting tourists and sightseers. Signposts indicated that there was a bus station and a market, a church named St. Paul and another named William Knibb Memorial. As the Toyota made an easterly turn, local restaurants met her leisurely gaze. Many advertized seafood, mostly lobster, and exotic fruit punches with a variety of cultural dishes. The ride through the town was a short one, it seemed, for suddenly the coastline was looming up ahead and when the stretch of beach appeared, Cole parked the car and began to disembark, explaining the area in a deep, calm baritone.

"This beach runs between Falmouth and St. Ann's," he began, closing the driver's door of the Land Cruiser before walking around to the passenger side. "There are a lot of tour operators who run day trips here from

Ocho Rios and Montego Bay. Your hotel is a little down the coast, that way." He pointed east with his index finger.

"It's beautiful," Carla said easily, hopping from the car and closing the passenger door behind her. Observing the golden, sun-baked sand, she added, "This private beach could be a good investment if you don't mind working with the tour operators."

"That's one of the things I wanted to talk to you about," Cole answered quickly. "Papa Peter concentrated more on the plantation when he was alive and kept the beach for family visits and the locals. It's not a large beach, but it could pay its way and so could the plantation."

"I have some ideas in mind about that," Carla said eagerly. "When my uncle told me that you wanted to hire us to help develop the plantation into a tourist attraction, I began thinking about all the potential it could offer. When we exhibited at the Jamaica Expo, I learned that over the past twenty years, tourism to the Caribbean had tripled to more than fifteen million visitors annually. That's amazing, don't you think?"

"It is," Cole agreed, indicating that she should follow him down to the beach. "When I was a boy Negril, which is on the southwest coast, used to be a quiet fishing village hardly noticed except by the residents. Now it's practically a mecca for single travelers, and many luxury hotels are now built there. So the potential is there."

"Which is all the more reason for you to start looking at the Linden Vale plantation with a keen profitable eye," Carla concluded.

As they made their way toward the beach, she began to feel confident. Her businesslike bravado was returning by the minute and, as she placed the straw hat over her bangs of short black hair and swung her small bag over her left shoulder, Carla felt certain she could convince Cole with her ideas and win him over to accept her agency's contract.

She eyed him coolly as his large strides advanced before hers. He was dressed casually as he was the day before, only this time he wore a pressed white shirt with the sleeves rolled up, and camel-colored shorts that embraced his athletically shaped thighs. Again his feet were sandaled, but they were not bare. Cole wore gray ankle socks, and she wondered whether that meant he didn't like sand between his toes.

"Tell me your ideas," he urged, as they began to walk leisurely along the beach.

Carla welcomed his invitation launching, full steam ahead into their discussion. She told him how Eden Lea could be used as a museum and that it could take guests at two hundred dollars per night, U.S. currency. The spectacular scenery could be visited by jeep or horseback. It would mean hiring a second group of staff that could concentrate solely on the guests who were visiting. She also mentioned that there should be a plantation shop where visitors could buy keepsakes of the place such as postcards and bookmarks, or pick up leaflets about its history. Perhaps there should even be specially prepared coffee beans, packaged fresh for resident guests only. Her ideas engulfed her quickly as she realized that the other produce of the plantation, such as the coconuts and cassavas, could also be delicately and commercially packaged. In fact there was no harm in devoting part of the acreage to growing cacao beans and breadfruit and other tropical delicacies that could be sold in the Linden Vale shop.

"I formulated some ideas on how Linden Vale could be marketed," she continued smoothly, blinking against the glare of the intense sun. "I think full-color visitor information leaflets should be made available at all the Jamaican Tourist Boards. We should also look at advertising in the tourist magazines, as well as the historical and naturalist ones. I'm sure the plantation would attract a hoard of cultural experts." Suddenly she realized she'd left her folder of ideas in the car. "My folder," she gasped, her concentration broken. "I threw it in the backseat of your car."

"I can look at it when we get back," Cole answered warmly, completely absorbed by Carla's bursting enthusiasm about the work she could do. He wondered whether she would speak to him intimately that way, to any man, with such passion and excitement.

"I had some ideas about using the Internet as another information point"—Carla sighed heavily—"and working with the major airlines and cruise liners that bring their passengers into Jamaica."

"I think we should discuss it over lunch," Cole instantly invited.

Carla tensed the instant she caught the smoky overtures in Cole's eyes. "I think a business lunch would be fine," she underlined hesitantly.

They worked their way back across the sand to the car. "How did you find Bay Rock?" Cole inquired, curious.

Carla recalled the blueness of the sea and the fine dry white sand, the many palm trees which had offered some shade, and the seclusion which had lent an air of serenity. "It's a wonderful place to clear one's thoughts," she declared, wondering exactly where the boundaries were laid.

"Maybe I should bring you here again," Cole prompted smoothly. "For a picnic perhaps?"

Carla refused to answer. The last thing she wanted was to take her mind back to brooding over Cole Richmond, especially when their meeting was going so well. Instead she allowed Cole's words to sink into a pool of silence as they seated themselves in the car and headed back toward Falmouth.

The Glistening Waters restaurant was understood to be one of the best in town. Carla wanted a light lunch, so she ordered the crab salad, but Cole opted for something more filling and took his pick of banana bread and fish chowder, a popular barbecued fish, he explained. It was only as the waiter left to deal with their order that Cole's gaze became more alert, assessing Carla closely.

"Have you been out with anyone since your relationship ended with Darnell Farrell?" he asked bluntly, his question hitting Carla point-blank and unexpectedly.

He knew her ex-partner's name, too, she gasped, feeling hot with indignation at the sheer mention of it. She disliked the question immensely and loathed even more having to answer. "Darnell Farrell is a painful experience I would much rather forget," she answered coolly, trying to sound unperturbed.

"You can't change the past," Cole sympathized warmly. "You can only accept it."

Carla glared at him, stunned, feeling as though she'd been stripped of her every defense. She'd always known that she had no choice but to accept the past. Looking back, she now realized that she should have done things differently, but such were the lessons in life—she could only learn by her mistakes. The fact that Cole Richmond seemed to understand it all bothered her as did his aptitude for putting things into perspective. "What are you, a shrink?" she gasped.

"I'm just someone who's trying to get to know you," Cole answered, ignoring her angry reply.

"Well, I like to keep my life simple," Carla lied unhappily. "I don't need a man to define my role as a woman."

"I'm not suggesting that you do," Cole rationalized in response.

"Then why are we on the subject?" Carla blazed. "Why aren't we continuing our discussion about your plantation?"

"If we are going to be working together," Cole suggested slowly, measuring his words as he went along, "it would help if we knew a little about each other. Could make working together more pleasant."

"Okay," Carla fumed, her tone sardonic, disliking how calm Cole appeared. "I was born in England at a very early age. I had to cut cards with the teacher to see if I would make it through school. When I grew up, I tossed a coin. It threw up heads which told me I should work in media and publicity. Then my work—"

"Threw you into the arms of a boxer named Darnell Farrell," Cole finished, his eyes gleaming in amusement. "And he wasted . . . how many years of your life?"

Carla swallowed and dipped her head in consternation. Describing her life like it was a friendly joke didn't fool Cole Richmond one little bit. She could feel the penetration of his glare on her tawny-brown cheeks, forcing the vulnerability within her to surface through her unblemished profile, until it took hold as it had done the day before when she'd considered that he saw too much. It was akin to the experience of drifting inexorably further and further away from a safe shore, yet unable to get back to dry land.

"So you are a shrink." She didn't know why she felt so defensive. Perhaps it was because of the tears which were stinging at her eyes, making her forcibly aware that some insecurity was presently attacking her system.

"Well, I don't need a lecture from you, Mr. Richmond. My mother did enough of that."

There had also been her own lame attempts at playing lay psychiatrist, none of which worked to take her out of her black hole. The masseurs and chiropractors, acupuncturists and aromatherapists all came and went as quickly as the faith healers. Shiatsu treatments and yoga were as easily discarded when t'ai chi ch'uan had caught her avid attention. And even then, she'd dropped that in favor of reflexology, the latest craze in foot massage. In the end she'd decided that good inward self-debate had been more therapeutic and a better healer than any mystique invention had to offer.

Now as another *C* word sprang to her nervous mind, and her senses became alarmingly aware of how closely Cole was watching her, Carla hastily reinforced the word *control* with a positive reminder to herself that her body traversed its energy meridans with the yin on the front flowing upward and the yang on the back flowing downward. That had to mean her "tsubo points" were in complete alignment and balanced. Or had she got that wrong? She couldn't think.

"You're being careful with me," Cole conceded, when he realized he'd plummeted Carla into complete silence. "If you're lost for words—"

"What do you want from me?" Carla interrupted him quickly, slanting Cole a suspicious, withering glance.

Cole's eyes danced warmly. "I thought I'd made that obvious."

"I don't play games like that, Mr. Richmond," Carla warned. "I earn my contracts the good old-fashioned way. With honesty and fair play."

"You're jumping to conclusions." Cole grinned. "I told you—"

"I don't want to jump into a debate about my conclusions," Carla growled weakly, the words popping out unsuitably matched as her quiet voice, belied with nervous tension, rattled her silly.

"Now you're sounding confused," Cole said dryly. "As I told you before, I just want to get to know you. If I'm making you feel uncomfortable, then I'm sorry."

Carla regained her composure with difficulty "No, I'm sorry." Somehow his apology made her feel stupid. She was a grown woman, capable of handling herself, so why was she behaving like an idiot? She knew it was because she was scared. She was fearful of getting into another disastrous relationship. "I don't know what you must think of me," she sighed heavily. "Some little kitten frightened of water."

"Frightened of not knowing how deep the water is," Cole clarified.

The lunch arrived mercifully before she could respond. When the waiter departed, Cole's eyes narrowed slightly. "Do you mind if I tell you about me?" he offered, detecting that Carla seemed unrelaxed and fidgety.

She tried to smile. "That would be nice."

"Well," Cole began as he cut into his portion of banana bread. "I was born in a part of Jamaica called Mandeville—in my mother's cousin's house I'm told. I never knew my father, and my mother never spoke of him. We went to live in Canada when I was nine years old, and I spent much of my life there until I returned to Jamaica eight months ago when my grandfather died. I discovered that he left Linden Vale to me. It took me a while to sort things out, and then I moved back here about seven weeks ago."

"What sort of work did you do before coming to Jamaica?" Carla grew curious as she bit into her crab, feeling a little more settled now that the topic was not about her.

"I worked in Africa," Cole responded easily. "I did a lot of photography with animals and plant life and managed to land a job with Dr. Henry Klooner, a lecturer in zoology at the University of the West Indies. He was doing a study on elephant behavior, and I was hired to work with him. I also did some photography in the Pacific where I lived in the Solomon Islands doing research on flora and fauna with an ecology professor. I then returned to Canada and did some teaching at a school in Toronto. My geography class were children aged eleven to sixteen."

Carla nearly choked on her crab. She hadn't expected this of Cole Richmond. "What was it like in Africa?"

"A great life experience," Cole began warmly. "We used to sit in the top of a tree in the middle of a herd a quarter of a mile from a native village in Uganda and watch two hundred and fifty elephants chevy themselves around. There were times when we would spend a night in the Budongo Forest learning about their feeding grounds, their paths, watching them in herds. African elephants are very fascinating, not quite as domesticated as their Indian cousins."

"So there's a difference?" Carla inquired, surprised.

"Many differences," Cole explained. "The low point of an African elephant's back line is the highest point of that of the Indian elephant. And the African's ears and tusks are larger and usually the tusks are spread wider at the points instead of coming together. The African elephant also has a wilder habitat."

"What was the research study in aid of?"

"The Bronx Zoological Park in America wanted a conclusive study done on the African elephant in captivity for comparison to the African elephant in its natural habitat. Dr. Henry Klooner is one of the best in his field of study. It was a honor to work with him."

"Then you went to work in the Solomon Islands?"

"Another great life experience," Cole began. "The warming experience and ozone problems and the unexplained climate conditions that we're having, like El Niño which hit last year, are affecting much of our plant and animal life. The *Jamaica Naturalist* magazine was happy to take on my suggestion to chronicle some of the changes and commissioned me to write up a study. So I chose the Solomon Islands to study some of the harvest failures in relation to climatic changes."

"Then you moved back to Canada to teach?" Carla finished. "Were you sorry to leave and come back to Jamaica?"

"Not really." Cole's tone was truthful. "Canada is a lovely place and its geography is pretty diverse. It has fertile plains for agriculture, vast mountain ranges, lakes and rivers. And the climatic variation is huge with icecaps in the north to luxuriant vegetation on the west coast in British Columbia. But Jamaica is where I was born, and I always felt that I would come back here."

"Which part did you live in?" Carla felt intrigued.

"Montreal, in Québec."

"That's the French part of Canada, I think."

"Yes, it is," Cole confirmed. "There are people there who are interested in preserving and protecting the French language and culture. The promotion of Québecois has been at the forefront of the Canadian political agenda for decades, but for me, it was simply a place where I lived. After Papa Peter died, I sold my apartment because it seemed pointless holding on to it when I'd inherited the plantation and releasing my equity now means I have the investment required to put into the plantation."

"And your mother?"

"She died four years ago."

"I'm sorry," Carla muttered. "She never told you who your father was?"

"No," Cole answered lightly. Too lightly, Carla thought. She heard the artifice of it in his voice.

"Am I allowed to ask you how the plantation is doing financially?" she inquired, diverting the conversation. She didn't mind giving him a little slack, but since she was vying to win an advertising contract, she decided not to take her hands off the reins, either. "It's just that when you mentioned investment, I got to thinking that it could be substantial."

"The books seem to indicate that Papa Peter had a few lean years," Cole admitted forlornly. "Nothing that's detrimental. Linden Vale is worth around six million U.S. dollars, so I've been quite fortunate to have inherited it. I am worried though about a lot of coffee that seems to have gone unaccounted for."

"Is it serious?" Carla noted the concern in his eyes.

"Could be," Cole responded.

Suddenly Carla realized that she wanted to understand something about the stamina beneath the cool, steely exterior of Cole Richmond. "How have you coped with it all, moving from Canada back to Jamaica?"

"Hmm," Cole pondered. "Responsibly. Maybe a little addictive. I like to work and I like to learn, too. Jamaica's rich environment and its cultivation are areas that interest me a great deal. In fact"—he paused—"how long are you here for?"

"Ten days altogether," Carla answered, swallowing her food. "This is my third day here."

"Then I must show you Jamaica," Cole coaxed warmly. "You don't mind mixing a little business with pleasure?"

Carla raised a nervous brow. "No."

"Then eat up," Cole urged, biting into his fish chowder. "Today I'm going to take you on your first exploration."

THREE

The next few hours flew by in a whirl of activity. After eating lunch, Cole had taken the car westward out of Falmouth to one of Jamaica's most famous sites: the Rose Hall Great House further along the northern coastline. Before they'd reached it, he came off the main highway and allowed Carla to see some of the island's rural housing. She'd been surprised at how poor the conditions were and that street trading seemed to be just as meager.

She bought shrimps from a woman and gave her a U.S. five-dollar bill, hardly believing the woman's delight as she took the money eagerly. Cole explained that United States currency was like green gold because the island's debt crisis and repeated devaluations of the Jamaican dollar had meant that many banks strictly limited the availability of American currency. This was something she'd known when she'd ordered traveling money at her local bank in England, but Carla hadn't expected the situation to be so bad.

She saw a man and his son taking two zebu cows to pasture and street urchins playing along the road as they drove by. Then they were back on the A1 highway which took them into Rose Hall and to a rectangular stone and timber framed house that Cole informed her had been built in 1770, and was not that much older than Eden Lea.

Carla noted the admission fee on their entrance and made mental notes on the basic staff uniform as they were taken on a tour of the Great House's fascinating history. It was rumored to be haunted from the days of old. The duppy, a native word for what was commonly known as a ghost, had been the wife of the grand-nephew of John Palmer, who'd built the house. Now in death Annee Palmer was known as the White Witch of Rose Hall because she'd loved and then stabbed all her male victims until she herself had been killed by a poor slave believing that his days were numbered. For a fleeting moment, Carla secretly admired the White Witch of Rose Hall. *She* knew how to deal with promiscuous cheating men, she thought ludicrously. Carla also felt that this woman was someone who had endeavored to save herself from suffering the pieces of a broken heart.

The two hours they'd spent there had hardly flown by before Cole's mobile telephone buzzed into action, summoning him to return to the plantation. He was expected back urgently, and now the Land Cruiser was pulling up against the gravel of its makeshift drive, the Georgian house grabbing their attention as Cole gestured that Carla disembark from the car.

"What's wrong?" Carla realized that Cole had seemed on edge all the way there.

But before Cole could answer, Bessie came running from the house, complaining and whimpering in her Caribbean tongue, though she tried to offer a cordial smile as she had done when Carla had met her for the first time. "Oh, Mr. Richmond," she breathed, relief etched in her voice. "It's Mr. Morgan. He's not himself again."

Cole's eyes hardened the instant Bessie spoke.

"Where is he?" he demanded harshly, taking long strides into the house.

Carla and Bessie hurried behind until they'd followed Cole directly into the main dining room. A man with short black ringlets of hair was moving erratically around the antique furniture. He stumbled twice over a handwoven rug then ejected a cough before his gaze met his intruders. He seemed her uncle's age, Carla hazarded curiously. And it was evident from the way his body swayed from chair to chair, fumbling against their Spanish elm backs, that he was intoxicated from what he'd taken.

"The prodigal grandson," he slurred on eyeing Cole. "Pass me de rum bokkle." He pointed to a bottle of rum that was among several housed in an elaborate period mahogany wine cabinet.

"Still cockeyed with booze?" Cole accused hotly. "Bessie, go and get some black coffee and close the door."

When she left, Carla realized that Cole was fighting to control himself. She deduced that Mr. Morgan got drunk like this often and that trying to calm him was obviously a regular household occurrence. As she stood embarrassed, watching the man move clumsily around the room, where the interior was much too elegant for a person of his character, she began to wonder how much a problem Mr. Morgan was to the plantation. More importantly how much was he a problem to Cole?

"You have plenty money now, man." Mr. Morgan cleared his throat loudly. "Not a t'ing did Papa Peter leave for me, his great-nephew. Not a t'ing." He was shaking his head, clearly in disbelief. "Your grandfather was a mean man. Mean." Mr. Morgan belched on a hiccup and refrained from apologizing for it.

"Lucas," Cole sighed heavily. "I've told you before.

You and your sister, Tata, have a place here for as long as you both want it."

"You is an illegitimate boy." Lucas ignored Cole purposefully. Cole's expression was mortified as Lucas ranted on. "You did be born in my mama's house, and your grandfather banish your mama and send her to Canada. Then when him nearly dead, he decide to claim you back to take his money when him feel shame. He was wicked and him die wicked. It was me and Masa Joe who look after this plantation when him did sick, and him leave me and Tata nothin'. Not even to say give Masa Joe something."

"I cannot do anything about that," Cole admitted sternly, his voice holding steel. "I only remember Papa Peter vaguely. I was only nine years old when I saw him last, so I never knew him just like . . ." Cole hesitated. "I never knew my father."

Carla's heart went out to Cole the moment she heard the emotion in his voice. Exactly who did Lucas Morgan think he was, upsetting his cousin in this way? She was angered by it and felt like objecting strongly. But it was not her place. In fact, she wondered whether she should be present at all. "Maybe I should wait outside," she said, suspecting Cole hadn't realized she was still there.

When he turned to her, Carla almost died when she saw the troubled expression in his eyes. "No." His voice sounded odd. "My cousin doesn't care where or when he has these contemptible outbursts or when he chooses to get drunk."

"She from England?" Lucas diverted his attention quickly. "Rhass! You really invite she to change up the plantation?"

"What changes I have in mind are my plans," Cole chimed, knowing Lucas resented them immensely. He'd stood in resentment from the day Cole had arrived there, and he was past feeling guilty for what Lucas and his sister had felt they had been cheated out of.

"That's what you t'ink," Lucas snarled, his face crestfallen. "You treat me and Tata like we peasants instead of like we kinsfolk. You t'ink because you educated and your grandfather was a mulatto that you better than we. Man, I don't need no white blood to inherit nothin'. This plantation is part of me, and me and Tata entitled."

"Entitled to what?" Carla could sense that Cole was losing his temper.

"We entitled," Lucas repeated without clarification. His feet were unsteady and his eyes were bulging red and sleepy. Carla watched as he swayed ungracefully from the room.

She heard Cole spit out a profanity as Lucas left, amazed that such a nest of jealousy and prejudice existed. It was like something out of a melodrama, she thought, her head still reeling. Lucas and Tata were obviously poor shirttail relatives who felt that they were at the mercy of Cole, the richer one. But Cole could hardly be blamed for what he'd inherited. It wasn't his fault that his grandfather had left the rest of the family nothing. And Cole had made some recompense, she recalled, daring to look at him. It wasn't as if they were being thrown out by their ears. As his gaze caught hers, they looked at each other in silence.

Bessie entered the room before either could speak. Muttering under her breath and sucking her teeth, she carried a cup of coffee carefully. "Him ina him waters again," she broached, her gaze surveying the room.

Carla shook her head confused, taking her eyes off Cole. "What's that? Ina him waters?"

"He's drunk," Bessie explained. "Your parents never speak Jamaican?"

"No," Carla proclaimed, remembering how well her mother liked the Queen's English. Iona McIntyre never divulged once that she possessed a native Caribbean lingo. Creole, a mixture of the colonial tongue and the African dialect, and patois, a mixture of broken English and Spanish, were both Jamaican languages that had never passed her mother's lips. Iona always spoke well and ensured that Carla did, too, and the few words that she did learn had been captured from her uncle.

"Mr. Morgan gone upstairs?" Bessie addressed Cole warily. When he nodded, she said something about taking his coffee there then left the room quietly.

"I'd better take you back to your hotel," Cole volunteered after a while. He walked over toward the Spanish elm table and rested his hands against it, closing his eyes and taking a deep breath as though he were attempting to clear his thoughts. "Maybe you can leave your folder here for me to look over."

"Don't bother about me." Carla felt apologetic. "Perhaps Masa Joe, the old man who drove me back yesterday can—"

"It's the least I can do," Cole interrupted, his voice harsh. Suddenly he banged one fist against the table, hard enough for the sound to echo around them. Carla was immediately startled by it. She felt frightened that Cole appeared so angry. "I'm sorry." Regret etched his voice, but he did not look at her. "As you've noticed, as well as inheriting this plantation I've also inherited the family politics. It's one of those things in life that are meant to test us."

Carla thought on that as she stared at him. Cole always seemed to rationalize things. It was obviously an inbred habit he had, a kind of strengthening mechanism that he used at will to cope. He'd tried to pass some of that on to her, she now realized. Was that why he'd told her that she couldn't change the past but only accept it?

"You don't owe them anything." She tried to lessen the blow he'd received from Lucas's confrontation, knowing that there was no way she could really offer any comfort. "It's obvious that your cousin is hurt, but—"

"Oh, he's hurt all right," Cole seethed furiously, clenching his teeth and his fists together. "I've done him a misdeed by being born. I swear, if he calls me the prodigal grandson one more time, I'll—"

Carla strode up to Cole and placed her hand on his shoulder. "Don't antagonize yourself," she cautioned softly. "Your cousin didn't mean it. He was drunk. He'll probably forget it all in the morning when he's sober."

"Will he?" Cole knew that Lucas wouldn't, but he didn't tell Carla that. He was more interested in the soft sable color of her eyes and the way her endearing face, full of warm sincerity, was meant solely for him in the most heartfelt way.

Cole took her hand and Carla tensed instantly. She did not feel frightened because she felt much empathy for Cole. He had his troubles and she had hers. They were two loners in need of something, who'd built up a communion through having spent a day together. Now she sensed Cole expected to take from her whatever affection she had to offer. But she had nothing to give and she suspected he hadn't, either.

And if there was one thing her mental sorting-out process had taught her, it was that men did not take a brief fancy seriously, whereas women expected an encounter to lead somewhere promising. She didn't expect Colebert Richmond to be any different. His cocoa-colored gaze traveled along her shaking tawny-brown limbs in the same way that other men had clamored to gain her interest. And there was a telltale flicker of amorous hope spread wildly across his face, all of which scared her to death. Instantly her defenses came up to protect herself from being plummeted into further despair.

"Cole." Her voice sounded weak, aroused by the gentle stroking of his fingers against hers. "I don't handle rejection very well."

"We all get rejected at one point or another," Cole temporized warmly. "When you start taking chances on people, you have to prepare yourself to get hurt. It doesn't mean that you have to stop taking chances. It can't always go the way you want."

He was doing it again, Carla thought frustrated. Balancing everything like the yin and the yang she'd learned about. His inner wisdom made her feel vulnerable, evoking a response that was as fierce as it was reluctant. "I don't like men who take what they want and give back nothing."

"I'm not like that," Cole whispered, running his hand up Carla's bare arm to her neck.

Carla felt the onus on her as having been a jilted partner to be a little more frank than usual with her thoughts. "Tell me that you're different from the rest." She wavered with anxiety. She couldn't fight the pleasure the brush strokes his fingers were causing against her nape, but she stood guard, anticipating an honest answer.

"Let me show you how different I am," Cole drawled huskily, moments before he dipped his head and impelled Carla into his arms. He claimed her lips within seconds, rubbing across them in slow motion with a coaxing intensity that made Carla wild with yearning. She felt immediately flooded with warmth as her senses reciprocated, the seduction feeling as fresh and new as tasting a sweet mango. He sapped all energy from her, stunning her completely, evaporating any fear that may have flashed through her head. She'd never been kissed like this before. It was amazing. It was awful. She felt eager. She felt appalled. She strained and tried to pull back, but his web of passion stretched its long silky threads and engulfed her until she was yielding against him, breathless and panting.

When Cole finally released her and rubbed his forehead against hers, Carla felt powerless, frightened and totally overpowered. "You're still being careful with me." His breath was ragged and his hands were shaking against her arms, knowingly aware that Carla had tried to resist him. "What am I going to do about you?"

"I don't know." Carla was at a loss. "What are you going to do about me?"

"You're so full of . . ."

"Self-pity," Carla confessed unashamedly.

"Yes," Cole intoned darkly, his gaze meeting her sable eyes. "So Darnell Farrell hurt you, and now you think every man is going to treat you the same way he did. Well, Carlane, take a good look. I'm Cole Richmond, not Darnell Farrell. If you think you're going to confuse the two of us in your troubled little mind, then maybe it's time you made me kiss you again."

Kiss me again. Carla ached to say the words, but Cole's blatant scrutiny and impatience caused her nothing but sheer panic. This man was too disciplined for his own good. He'd turned his own troubled emotions into one of seduction and was giving her counseling at both one and the same time. She needed a *C* word and she needed it fast: *composure.* That's the one. That'll do. Where was her damned businesslike composure? Wanting to scream, she searched erratically for words—anything that would put her back in charge.

Taking her mind to their meeting that morning, she quickly threw out the first thing that sprang to her mind. "That kiss, was it a positive yes or a qualified no?"

"About what?" Cole was somewhat bemused.

"About whether I have the Linden Vale marketing contract."

"It'll be interesting to see if you can earn it," Cole said coolly, disliking that he'd not received the response he craved. Putting some distance between him and Carla by deciding to walk over to the window, he added, "I'll look over your folder and let you know as soon as possible. As you seem to like Masa Joe, I'll arrange to have him drive you back to your hotel."

Carla dragged in a deep, trembling breath as Cole left the room. She could still feel his mouth on hers, still feel the telling sign of the hard strength of his arousal against her thighs. Leaning weakly against the back of a chair, she wondered whether she could handle Cole Richmond or whether she should take the first plane back to London and send Uncle Quayle over instead.

But Carla's befuddled heart sank at the sudden thought of denying herself the unexpected adrenaline rush that had followed Cole's kiss. Beyond the fact that it was still playing across her mind and that in many ways it was still knocking her senseless, there was the silent admission to herself that Cole Richmond appealed to her. He appealed to her in the most visceral way possible.

FOUR

Carla tossed and turned but could find no restful sleep. Images flooded through her head with provoking, inimical discourtesy and she bounced and shivered, disturbed in her slumber. The past was haunting her, and she was feverish and hot and the night's sweltering tropical heat made her ever more resentful of the estranged images that paraded in her perilous dream.

All she wanted to do was sleep and think of pleasant things, but Darnell Farrell's sneering face, with his brows drawn like daggers and his quarrelsome expression braced ready for conflict, caused her nothing but panic as her limbs shook with dread. When the figment of her imagination suddenly laughed aloud, her hands moved erratically, unrelaxed and panicked, reaching for something that wasn't there within her grasp.

She was in a deep dormancy, unable to awake yet there was pain in her heart and tears in her eyes. Her languid state grew more active when her mind took decisive turns into her troublesome past where she'd been at her most heartfelt despair. She didn't want to think about this bodiless image. What they had was over and done with, and she was now free to live her life. With no more men, she told herself in the recesses of her fatigued mind. They weren't worth the effort—and that included Cole Richmond with his warm, heartening smile and his ensnaring cocoa-colored eyes.

Impatiently she tossed again as Cole's image intensified, as though a battle between good and evil had ensued in her listless dream. She remembered the way he'd kissed her, how he'd amorously claimed her lips, and her heart quickened as the mere thought of it caused the creases in her forehead to soften. A deeper yearning accelerated her pulses, and she felt the throbbing urge triple her body heat until her limbs quaked with the tension and her mouth dried in wanting. The eagerness caused sweat to caress every part of her, and her breath became deep and heavy, panting in her reckless struggle to awaken from such desire.

It was a disturbing combination to feel so frightened and yet so aroused. The humid air was rich with the terrifying but heady sense of it. Then suddenly she felt terrified. She was in a struggle with water which seemed to appear from nowhere. Her body arched desirous and fearful as an image flashed, hazily passing as quickly as it came. Her body tossed again, her eyebrows twitched, her lashes fluttered, and this time Carla felt herself surfacing, gasping for every measure of breath for her lungs. The jitters were disappearing, the apprehension becoming faint. And when at last her eyes opened, the agitation had gone almost entirely.

Carla instantly sat up and thrust herself forward, throwing aside the clean white sheet which had covered her. It was damp with the fresh evidence of her turbulent sleep, and her limbs were wet and still shaking from the shock of it. As she looked around her, fighting the fatigue, she realized that it was day. Bolting instantly from the bed, she rubbed her perspiring hands through her limp hair and shook herself anew.

Lying there another minute was dangerous, she thought, heading straight for the shower where she quickly allowed the lukewarm water to bathe her naked skin. Just as quickly Carla searched for a new *C* word, desperate to brush aside her crazy dream. *Cranial osteopathy* emerged to the forefront of her mind. That's two words, she told herself helplessly but realized it might be just what she needed to forget the past. She'd read about it only three weeks ago in a health magazine. A physical treatment involving manipulation of the bones which make up the skull could be just the therapy to prevent her brain from having such lustful nightmares.

When she put on a comfortable terry robe and went barefoot from the shower cubicle to the window, she almost sighed with relief that the day was fine. Her spirits rose immediately on seeing the sun. She was going to enjoy today, she decided with a faint smile. She would dress, eat, and then discover this island that was synonymous with four *S* words: *sun, sea, sand,* and *sex,* though only the first three of those were what she wanted.

The day was full of reality at its most potent the moment Carla ventured into her discovery of Jamaica. She traveled by taxi, having instructed the cabby to just drive so she could relax and see the sights. She was amazed to find that he'd picked up several other passengers along the way, but soon realized that this was the custom of the island to profit along a certain route that was laid down as his jurisdiction. They'd cruised along the magnificent north coast where she could scarcely imagine the extremities of life she saw. Along the coast there were chic tourists hotels like the one she'd checked in, and there were extravagant country houses and modern housing complexes with weekend cottages for the rich and more middle class.

But only a small distance inland, where the driver had also taken her, she was to see small ramshackle villages and rural slum settlements: the pockets of poverty and living conditions at their most appalling. Instantly she was made aware of the economic malaise, that unemployment existed in Jamaica as it did the world over.

When the driver told her that it would be more than a two-hour drive to Kingston, the nation's capital, and that she would have to take another taxi or two if she wanted to get there, she decided instead to revisit Falmouth before heading back to her hotel for something to eat. When she'd paid the taxi and he went on his way, she began her leisurely stroll along a public beach within a short distance of Bay Rock. Her watch told her it was midday, and she savored the tranquility evident around her though the beach was not quiet. Native children played at the water's edge and villagers swung in their hammocks, and further along she could see women cooking, their pots above makeshift fires with the steam and smoke rising to greet the intense sunlight.

She'd forgotten her hat and felt the burning heat on her forehead. She considered seeking some shade and perhaps a little peacefulness, so she took herself into the palm trees and sat down to appreciate the ebb of the cool breeze. There was something revitalizing and energizing about enjoying her own company under a cloudless sky, having walked on a soft carpet of sand and dazedly gazing at a clear blue sea. There wouldn't be too many more days like this, for she would soon be departing for England, back to a hectic schedule of clients, contracts, and deadlines.

Her mind adrift, she tilted her head and her eyes

caught a movement in the trees. She noticed a solitary figure resting his back against the upturned hull of an old abandoned boat. Carla peered concentrated, recognizing that the person was Cole. She knew he had to see her, too. Sitting in the soft sand, her hair ruffling slightly in the wind, her feet crossed at her ankles with her body resting on her elbows, he had to see her silhouetted against the palm trees, looking at him in beguiled amazement.

Carla saw him push his body to his feet and dig his sandaled shoes in the sand to take leisurely steps toward her. Her heart began to cavort excitedly as his every step brought him closer. Soon Cole was within distance to see the ardor in her sable gaze, and she was not slow to miss the keen fancy in his own. She sat there, hardly breathing, watching him come closer, and then he stopped within polite distance at the bottom of her feet, looking down at her, his expression surprised.

"This island is full of people and yet you're alone." He smiled. "Are you enjoying Jamaica?"

Carla tipped back her head, sporting one of her most friendly smiles. "It's been lovely," she admitted. "I didn't expect to see you here."

"I didn't expect to see you, either," Cole confessed. "I was on my way back to the plantation and thought I'd stop to smell the beach."

Carla nodded with understanding. The air was clean and fresh here. On the plantation it was more humid and rife with bees and bugs. "How is your cousin today?" She watched as Cole sat down beside her.

"Unforgiving," Cole bristled, crossing his ankles like Carla but twisting to rest on one elbow. "I'm just coming from Kingston which is where I've taken him. He says he's meeting someone about a job, so maybe he's planning to leave."

"And what about his sister?" Carla inquired.

"Tata?" Cole pondered and then raised his brows. "Maybe she can get into some of those ideas of yours. I was very impressed by some of the work your folder presented."

Carla had almost forgotten entirely that she'd left it with Cole. "You liked them?" she gasped.

"Very much." Cole's eyes brightened at Carla's wide smile. "As much as I'd like you to have dinner with me tonight."

Carla's lips trembled. She didn't know why she felt so nervous, but she kept her business thoughts intact. "Are we celebrating something?" she said, anticipating Cole's answer on her agency's contract.

"Me getting to know you," Cole stated tersely, his eyes twinkling with suggestion. "Now that we'll definitely be working together," he added.

Carla nodded in approval. "In that case I'd like that," she told him as she bit her lower lip to stop the tremble.

Cole placed his fingers there immediately and rubbed her lips gently. "Don't do that," he cajoled, sensing Carla's complete surprise. "You'll spoil them and they're much too perfect to be ruined."

She'd expected her nerves to tighten and for her limbs to tense, but Carla felt nothing but heated blood melting every part of her. And the brooding way in which Cole gazed at her propelled her to a restlessness that made her hands warm and clammy. She liked the way he looked in his navy shorts and pale blue string vest. It easily complemented the long flowery blue dress she was wearing, and together their attire seemed perfectly suited. She shouldn't be feeling so comfortable, she told herself, swallowing yearningly. And he had no right to be subjecting her to such pining new feelings when her emotions were still raw from the bruising caused by one Darnell Farrell.

"You like that, don't you?" Cole whispered sweetly, holding her gaze as he caressed her lips with his fingers.

Carla gently moved his hand away but held her gaze. "I don't make physical contractual arrangements," she responded sternly.

A muscle moved convulsively in Cole's jaw. "It seems nothing short of a crisis is going to force you to open up to me. Carlane, why can't you just live your life? Let people get to know you."

Carla sought for words. "I do when—"

"When you're not trying to extinguish your life by overdosing on barbiturates," Cole finished, frustrated. "Tata took great delight in telling me that yesterday."

"It's a lie." Carla felt ridiculously sick and green with embarrassment. Pulling herself into a sitting position, she hugged her knees defensively. "I suffered an allergic reaction to antibiotics nearly a year ago. The media machine labeled it an overdose to add scandal to the news. I cannot believe you could be suggesting—"

"I'm not suggesting anything," Cole declared smoothly.

Carla glared at him mutinously. She could hardly imagine that Cole believed her given the standoffish way she'd been behaving since they'd met. A tremulous fear worked its way into the vanguard of her chest at his blatant scrutiny of her. He seemed to be reading her like a book, turning pages as every piece of her unfolded. Perhaps she had a title that only he could see. And maybe he could see where she began and where she ended, too. It unnerved her somewhat, forcing her to become angry. "Is there anything else you think you have or haven't heard that you want me to correct you on?"

"I haven't heard if you're dating again," Cole's voice said perceptively.

Carla hesitated, her momentary anger dissipating beneath other anxieties. "There's been no one since Darnell," she admitted finally, gazing into the sun. "And I don't intend there to be."

Cole's lips twisted beneath the mock sincerity in his gaze. "Isn't that an absolute refusal on your part to face yourself?"

Carla's mouth drooped. "What?"

"What do you do when the lovebug bites, Carla? When there's that part of you that needs a man badly and that lovebug is biting real hard, what do you do? It seems you want something that you have neither the patience nor the inclination to accept."

"And what would that be?" Carla was peeved, annoyed at Cole's analysis.

"To be loved," he said flatly.

Carla's mouth twitched, disturbed. "I may not have the patience or the inclination," she gasped, "but you certainly seem to have the desire."

"The desire?" Cole's gaze smoked over, and something in his expression relished the two words. "You do have a desperate need for something. Reassurance. Love. Whatever you want to call it. You *need* me."

"I don't want you to give me anything," Carla protested weakly, pulling herself to her feet, alarmed that Cole just as quickly followed her there. "I don't need anything."

"Not even this?"

The moment Cole pulled her into his arms, Carla's body reacted with speed and haste. Every muscle she possessed jumped in delight, except her heart which skipped in beats that tripled at a stroke. The swirling emotions inside her were as fierce as they were exhilarating, made more furious by the intense heat. It enveloped them both like a tornado's approach, reminding Carla that the tropics could produce such an effect, that the swift intoxicating feelings of this man's kiss were accentuated by a touch of foreign madness.

Her throat felt parched as his tongue met hers, as the warm feel of it alighted her molten body. And the way he coaxed her with it, licking and pulsing at her lips served only to scald her fervent passion for more. This time she did not feel appalled or awful. She felt thermal and aglow, even incandescent, with the tempting invitation of such a delicate, *bonne bouche* kiss. And when Cole finally released her, having dragged out the first flurry of ardent fumes within her, she felt weak with longing and wished to be ignited again. "I'm going to take my time with you," he promised her seductively, lazily rubbing his fingers against her arms.

Carla was at a lost for words, thoroughly swept away by Cole's endearing promise. And when she looked into his eyes, she felt heated again at seeing his sincerity reflected there. "I'm not sure if I should like that," she returned, still dazed by the power of Cole's kiss.

"Why not?" Cole whispered against her lips.

"It's not going to go anywhere," Carla answered flatly.

"Stop thinking like a woman," Cole demanded. "A woman who is afraid of love is a woman who's afraid of life."

"Don't say that." Carla felt a moment of panic. She was overreacting and she knew it. Why should her encounter with Cole lead anywhere? Why couldn't she just accept his friendship as he'd offered and oblige his wish in trying to get to know her? It seemed simple enough. It also made perfect sense, too. And if she got kissed every now and then, shouldn't she be thankful that she could still attract the opposite sex? "I'm a little out of sorts when it comes to men," she admitted after thought.

"I know," Cole whispered, brushing a kiss against her forehead. "I'm going to take care of that."

Carla's limbs shook as Cole kissed her again. It was pure, flawless, pièce de résistance and absurdly, she felt purified by it. Cole's lips moved against hers with such orderly seduction, she felt as though he was attempting to brush away every imperfection that Darnell had left there. By the time he released her again, she felt corrected in some way, her body feeling wholesome, strengthened, and intensely female. She was aware of it by the way Cole's hands had cupped the fullness of her hipline, the way he'd worked his fingers to her rounded, blossoming breasts. And if there had been any doubt at all that she was afraid of life, Cole's kiss had scrubbed away its every imprint of fear from her timorous mind.

"You make me feel . . . needy," she gasped, resting her forehead on Cole's chest.

Cole chuckled quietly. "You make me feel hot," Cole admitted huskily.

"How hot is it going to get?" Carla wasn't sure she was making any sense, such were the whirling sensations fluttering around in her stomach. But she knew Cole was aware she wasn't talking about the weather.

"It can get real hot," he told her with a teasing smile to his lips.

Carla smiled, too. "If you know already how hot it can get, how are you going to know when it's . . . different?"

Cole moved Carla slightly so that he could look down into her face, his gaze penetrating as he searched deeply into the sable color of her eyes. "I'll know when the temperature gets almost beyond endurance. And right now, you're pretty close to burning me."

Carla felt the heat, too. It was most definitely sizzling. "You promised me some coffee," she said to break the trance.

"So I did." Cole's smile widened at the reminder. "I'm heading back to the plantation now. Like to come?"

"Sure."

Carla had half expected some dated, antique interior to match Eden Lea when she entered the smaller white, sun-bleached house which stood in a grove of coconut trees and shrubbery. She was pleasantly surprised to find something different, and it had all the indications that Cole lived there. It echoed the country scene with deep comfortable rattan armchairs, soft rugs against the wooden floor, a few good pieces of cedarwood furniture, and a flight of wooden stairs that led upward out of one corner, twisting stylishly.

It was in direct contrast to Darnell's ultrasmart interior. He lived the life of a boxing legend with his thousand-gallon shark-filled aquarium, combination safe for his heavy jewelry, and his Japanese Koi carp-filled pond with its thirty-foot fountain and gazebo guesthouse. And as well as the ten-bedroom, six-bathroom, two-conference-room mansion, there was the Olympic-size swimming pool, racket court and indoor shooting range, all of which he may have used but once. She still couldn't understand why he'd installed the heated driveway, the artificial waterfall, and the hundred and one telephone extensions. It all made no sense, considering he had no built-in boxing ring, a prerequisite she would have thought, to practice his profession.

Everything had been furnished with an eye for understated elegance, and she'd always felt like she'd entered a grand tour rather than the home that they had both once shared. The whole shebang in the Buckinghamshire region of south England had sold for four million pounds sterling when they'd begun their separation of assets. She still recalled her surprise at the newspaper description of the sale to a native Arab sheikh. *The love nest of WBC heavyweight champion Darnell Farrell and his ex-mistress Miss Carlane McIntyre is definitely a main contender for the record books. It's one of the largest private residences under one roof in Britain to have sold this century . . .*

Now as she looked past the plants hung in little wicker baskets and the shelves of disarranged books, Carla felt a measure of relief that Cole was more mellow. "You have a lovely home," she told him, feeling relaxed by the sensitive, country atmosphere.

"I'm glad you like it." He smiled, gesturing with his hands that she sit down. "I've christened it 'The Grove' and thought I'd stay here for the moment rather than at Eden Lea. That way, I'm giving us all time to adjust to my being here and taking over."

"That seems a sensible idea," Carla agreed.

"It is," Cole affirmed, before he left to brew the coffee.

As she watched him go, Carla allowed her gaze to wander with much interest. She could see her folder on an old desk by a computer, where there was a telephone and fax machine nearby. There was also paper littered all over the desk which looked like inventory records and stock notes. The whole thing was one disheveled mess.

A woman's instinct forced her over to the table, and she began to place the things into an orderly fashion. She was used to organizing her own desk, so putting some order to Cole's seemed to take no time at all.

By the time he'd arrived back into the room with a tray carrying two demitasses of steaming coffee, she'd put to order practically everything that had been scattered, with the exception of the contents of her folder. She wanted to sustain his keen interest in those.

"You didn't need to do that." Cole grimaced mildly, as he placed the tray on a coffee table near the rattan armchairs.

Carla saw the furrow of his brows and immediately sensed she'd overstepped her bounds. "I'm sorry." She felt panicked again. "I just thought you could use a little help."

Cole didn't miss the way she'd tensed and quickly softened his tone. "Don't worry about it. Come and sit here." He patted the vacant seat in the rattan armchair where he'd seated himself.

Carla swallowed and nervously accepted his invitation. She could smell the sweet aroma of the coffee beans as she closed the distance between them. It was strong and fresh, and the air was pungent with it as an open window, protected by stylish iron security grills caused a slight breeze to send the rich flavor adrift. "This is Linden Vale coffee?" she asked, as she sat down diligently beside him.

"It certainly is," Cole confirmed. "Taste it slowly. You'll appreciate the flavor more." He offered her a demitasse that Carla suspected had been removed from Eden Lea. Cole deliberately added no sugar or milk, but allowed her to sip the coffee in its raw, brewed state. It was a pleasant taste, quite sweet and yet mild and chicory. The rich smell invigorated her nostrils, and she closed her eyes to fully welcome the invasion to her senses. Then she felt the back of Cole's hand against her cheek, brushing her cheekbones lightly as she savored the brew and its steamy aroma.

She opened her eyes and smiled, trying to keep her

mind on the coffee instead of Cole's deep, lustful gaze. "This tastes wonderful," she purred, relishing Cole's pining interest and her satisfaction in the coffee both at one and the same time. "Something to die for, isn't it?"

"Is it?" Cole traced his hand down to Carla's lips. She instantly bridged her demitasse there and he removed his hand slightly.

Carla could feel herself sinking into the unique, astonishing serenity surrounding them. Could fresh-ground coffee do this? Could it enhance one's feelings and tempt a person into thoughts of recklessness? Because that's how she felt. She felt as rash, impulsive, and as heedless as a fool braving a heroic task. And she was no heroine. She lacked pluck and audacity. She'd never been daring or had the gallantry to take what she wanted. The nearest she'd come to amassing some mettle was when she'd coached herself through the long financial journey of leaving Darnell.

But as Carla met Cole's gaze and enjoyed the breath of coffee that formed a misty line between them, a strong *C* word flew into her fleeting mind: *courage.* Cole had given her that. In his company, she felt fearless and hopeful. She felt suddenly filled with all those expectations she'd possessed as a child. "Do you think I'm being careful with you now?"

Those cocoa-brown eyes ensnared hers. "No. I think you're attempting to be tough."

Carla laughed. "You make me sound like a pair of old boots." She placed her demitasse on the table and rose from the armchair. Walking over to where Cole's desk was situated, she leaned herself against it. "I'm hardly a picture of someone in boots."

Cole allowed his gaze to wander to where she stood. No, Carlane McIntyre was the perfect picture of an angel who'd flown into his life by pure chance. He still remembered his first impression of her when he'd visited the Jamaica Expo in London. Being in England at that time was also purely chance. He'd never expected to be flying over there to see one of his closest friends get married.

All the controversial details of how she'd been hurt didn't for one moment spring into his alert mind when he'd thought about using her to market his plantation. He was still hearing about it all courtesy of his cousin Tata and her cartel of dubious feisty admirers who seemed to frequent Eden Lea on occasion. He would have to do something about that cousin of his and the sheepish men that vied for her attention. But for now his attention was riveted elsewhere. He wanted to know for himself what lay beneath the vulnerable exterior of Carla McIntyre.

He rose from the armchair and followed her over to his desk, coming up behind her so that he could circle his arms around her waist. "I think you're the image of a beautiful woman, and I wish I had my camera," he told her easily. "The only time you'll be someone in boots is when the rainy season starts."

Spasms of electricity shot through Carla's system as she felt Cole's throbbing manhood pressed up against the small of her back, but she kept her thoughts in focus as she leaned into the warmth of his chest, reminding herself that she wanted to keep herself in control. "Has the rainy season been detrimental to the plantation?" she asked.

"Not that I'm aware of." Cole's arms tightened, and his nose nuzzled against Carla's neck where he inhaled the fresh scent of her. "But hurricanes sweep through the Caribbean every year."

"Hurricanes?" Carla gasped uncomfortably as his lips began to nibble her nape. "I didn't know they came round that often."

"Linden Vale seems to have survived them." Cole's head lifted, and he looked down at the papers Carla had tidied on his desk. "From what I can gather, only Hurricane Gilbert was unkind to them. Masa Joe told me that he almost lost the entire harvest that year. The wind velocity left an almost complete trail of devastation."

"Oh, no," Carla sighed.

"A lot of the plantations suffered in 1988. Sugarcane, banana, cacao beans. Only half of Papa Peter's yield was uprooted. But Masa Joe told me that other plantations lost everything."

Carla stroked the back of Cole's hand, aware that he would take the necessary precautionary measures should another hurricane visit again. Not ignorant of the fact that tropical cyclones traveled to Jamaica, she wondered whether the burden of responsibility was suited for his shoulders or whether in fact they were meant for a much bigger person. But Cole was over six foot, and she felt dwarfed against him, and that alone made her certain he could handle just about anything, especially if he was up against something like Hurricane Gilbert.

She'd just entered her twenties when its approach hit the British news. A satellite photograph had warned of the tropical storm, the seventh that season, traveling from southeast Puerto Rico. Her mother had kept a silent vigil by the television set because Uncle Quayle had taken a holiday to Jamaica at that time. He was there when the hurricane's strike was predicted to happen, and everyone in her family was worried senseless.

Every day the news reported that the atmospheric pressure in the hurricane's center had decreased, and by early September it had passed over the Dominican Republic and Haiti. Gilbert's velocity was between one hundred and fifty and two hundred kilometers before it changed course and made straight for Jamaica. There it reached its climax, the eye of the storm following the island's longitude axis until it'd reached almost three hundred kilometers.

The trail of devastation had been enormous. Thousands of cattle drowned in the rivers, entire crop-plants were dragged with the force. Telephone and telegraph lines went down, and almost everywhere had been hampered by material and structural damage. Not until just before Christmas did they hear the news that her uncle was well and that mercifully, in view of the damage, only forty-five fatalities had been reported. Gilbert had struck in September and that month was only two weeks away. The rainy season would be Cole's first test of whether he could handle the plantation, she thought. Even though she felt he would be equipped to do so, as an advertising consultant aware of the avenues where he wished to invest, she thought perhaps that was an area they should discuss.

"Have you made any contingency plans for the hurricanes?" she asked, still brushing her fingers lightly against his.

"Masa Joe knows the procedures," Cole advised. "He's still teaching me a thing or two. He's been working on this plantation for forty-one years. He started when he was just eighteen years old and knows it like the back of his hand."

"He's a very quiet old man," Carla mused. "He drove me back to my hotel in complete silence both times. I wasn't sure if I should say anything to him."

"He's okay." Cole planted a kiss against Carla's neck. "He and Robyn are the only two who seem to have adjusted to me with some ease. The other workers seem to regard me suspiciously and as for Bessie, she's past her sell-by date. She should be retired, sitting on a verandah somewhere telling grandchildren stories, not messing up my appointments and disrupting my schedules."

"You're being a chauvinist." Carla chuckled, turning in Cole's arms to face him. "If Bessie should be retired then so should Masa Joe. He looks as old as she is, and you're not confining him to a bunker."

Cole smiled wryly, though Carla did not miss the piercing look in his arresting eyes. "Old women . . . people can be as hard and stubborn as their arteries," he remarked.

"Well, Robyn isn't old," Carla reminded, suddenly bringing the younger woman's delectable features into her mind. "I'm sure if she messed up a little or proved a little incompetent, you wouldn't be confining her anywhere."

"Robyn's a good worker," Cole said with a level of admiration that Carla didn't miss. "And I like her," he added.

Carla felt uncomfortable with that simple answer and tried to twist herself out of Cole's arms. The crushing realization that she wasn't the only woman in Darnell's life had already given her enough heartache for a lifetime. Knowing that Cole could be just as susceptible was a thought she didn't really want to relish. "Cole." Her voice sounded slightly pained. "I don't want you to compromise what you want because of me."

"What are you talking about?" He seemed confused as he tightened his arms, preventing her from escaping.

"Robyn," Carla said flatly. "You may want—"

"What the devil does Robyn have to do with anything?" Cole muttered seconds before his mouth pressed on hers. Cole's lips were familiar and unexpected, and Carla knew he was trying to erase any uncertainty that had cropped up in her vulnerable mind.

They'd been having fun, and she'd been calm and relaxed—yet for some reason, she had to present a problem that didn't exist.

It was the suspicion she had of Cole. Of all men. Another thing her mental sorting-out process had taught her was that a woman can have one set of expectations and a man another. And if neither made it clear to the other what they wanted, then that would be when problems occurred. But Cole was kissing her with sincerity, and unknowingly she found her fingers softly caressing the smooth skin of his shaven head. Could she really be doing this after all the promises she'd made herself? Delving her tongue into a man's mouth, rubbing her body treacherously against his, accepting the exquisite sensations his hands were creating as they moved sensually against her thighs, raising the hem of her dress in their progress.

And as the palms of Cole's hands rested against the smooth tawny-brown flesh of her thighs, daring in their motion upward until he stroked her buttocks, she began to wonder whether she'd been that cynical woman; the one who'd devised no slide rule for the adversity she'd developed toward men.

Cole held her so tightly she was pinned to the desk behind her, and through the wild unbidden thrill his amorous onslaught gave her was the absurd thought that she hadn't tidied his desk to have the papers scattered again in one lustful moment. The prosaic thought caused her to move her legs upward and circle them around Cole's hardened thighs. He groaned the instant he felt her grip him, and Carla closed her eyes, her body awakened with the glorious renewal that a man could be so intimately pressed against her body again.

Neither heard the sudden opening of the house door or the footsteps of a person walking in. It was one harsh gasp from the throat of a third person which brought reality back in one fell swoop. Carla's eyes flew open to see the intruder, and her heart gave an embarrassing leap at the blaze of fury reflected in Robyn Morrison's dark eyes.

"I just wanted to remind you that we have to deliver that load of coffee to the Mandeville coffee factory tomorrow," she snapped, casting Carla a murderous glare. "But I can see you're extremely busy bothering with something pretty ordinary instead of important things like work."

She turned and marched out of the house, slamming the door behind her. Carla's legs dropped weakly, glad of the desk's support behind her as she stood on hard ground. But she almost crumbled completely when she heard Cole eject a smothered oath and tear after Robyn.

"Robyn, wait a minute. Let me explain—" He threw a backward glance at Carla. "I'll be right back."

Carla almost missed him saying it. It didn't matter if she had. The only thing that mattered was that she'd let down her guard. She had forgotten that her heart was in an invisible cage and that she'd thrown the key as far away as possible. It mattered that she'd been stupid, and it was that same stupidity that blurred her eyes with tears. The last few moments had been unbearably sweet, and now they seemed so ugly. She despised herself. Now Robyn was feeling heartache, too. She didn't care for the girl, but she wouldn't have wished any despair on her, either. Instinct had told her that Robyn wanted Cole. Now he'd rushed after her and that told her more. It told her that the two of them were having an affair, and she was the one left standing completely bereft. She was just the way Darnell Farrell had left her. Alone.

FIVE

Carla watched from the window as Cole covered the distance between him and Robyn. He put his arm about her shoulders, bent his head downward, and consoled her tenderly with words of appeasement. The little scene filled Carla with the most acute jealousy and misery she had ever known.

Minutes later she watched as he strode back toward the house. Whatever had transpired between him and Robyn hadn't taken very long. The younger woman was presumably very easy to pacify. She herself had been so neutral once. So noncombatant, a conciliatory peacemaker. It was such natural accord that made fools out of women, she thought. An absence of hostilities makes a man believe he can get away with just about anything. And that was another lesson she'd learned.

As if Cole had thought her to be upset about Robyn witnessing their little scene, he marched instantly toward her on reentering the house, taking hold of both her hands as he caught the glisten of her tear-shiny eyes. Her heart almost leapt at the caring look in his gaze, but she stunned herself cold, telling her mind not to be fooled by it. It was too easily switched from one woman to another.

"I didn't think you would be back so soon," she snapped abruptly.

Cole's brows narrowed. "I told you I would."

"In what capacity, may I ask?" Carla chimed.

"To find out if you're all right," Cole answered, surprised. "I'm sorry about what happened. Robyn's just . . . overwrought. I'd hate to lose her."

My goodness, this man had almost the same gall as Darnell Farrell, she thought. Carla's first reaction was to slap him and hard, but her second was to weep uncontrollably. She'd reached out to this man because he'd touched something inside her. He'd made her feel like she was definitely on the mend. Yet Carla could read the desire still evident in Cole's gaze, knowing that it reflected her own. They were both the kind of people who needed stimulating partners. Darnell had always been brutish and insensitive, and she would not have thought Robyn to be vivacious enough for Cole.

But he was doing exactly what she despised in Darnell. He was thinking he could keep two women dangling on a string. "I think it's time I left," she said, trying to avoid looking at him. "If I can just have the contents of my folder, then I'll be on my way."

"Wait a minute." Cole's hold on her hands grew firmer. "What'd I do?"

"Look," Carla bristled, feeling herself get angry. "When I was with . . ." She paused. "In my last relationship, he got all of my attention and I didn't get the same back. He gave only a fraction of himself. In fact, every female over the age of consent got a fraction, a piece. I'm a person who like things in whole parts. So maybe it'd be a good idea if you dealt with my uncle."

"You're wrong about me if you think I like to give out pieces of myself," Cole said softly. "You're just going to have to learn to trust me."

"Trust you?" Carla nearly choked as she spat the

two words out. "You're going to have to work damned hard to earn my trust."

Cole shook his head as though disbelieving her outburst. "Carlane. Mistakes are made only when people let you down and misuse your trust. You've been let down, so you don't have to account for your behavior in being hurt."

Carla felt murderously sick at how Cole was rationalizing things again. He did it so innately, she wanted to wring his fingers and vent her frustration on them. "I'm going to leave right now, and then neither of us have to account for my behavior."

"What do I have to do to convince you?" Cole chortled.

"Nothing." Carla snapped.

"Nothing?"

"What? Is there an echo in here?" she cajoled.

"I swear I don't know what's going on in your head," Cole declared, his mouth hard and his gaze intensely fiery. "So you've been bruised by a lovebug's bite. Why can't you just lick your wounds and move on?"

Carla breathed, releasing her fingers from his hand. She swallowed convulsively, wondering why this man could disturb her equilibrium just by looking at her. "Once bitten, twice as shy."

"Or twice as keen?" Cole relented. "Less than ten minutes ago, we were kindred spirits. I pulled something out of you, Carla, and you were willing to let me do it. I want to get to know you, and I wanted to see you again. I gave you the Linden Vale contract—"

"Without telling me that *I* would be the deal," Carla returned. "Is that what you meant when you said you'd be interested to see how I'd earn it?"

Cole's eyes glazed over cold. "I think it is probably best that I do handle things with your uncle."

They both looked at each other silently, each hating

the things that had been said. Awkward and embarrassed, Carla took a step backward, feeling unaccountably nervous, even silly. Cole was so tall and broad, his gaze overpowering, and she wished more than ever to be right back in his arms where all fear of rejection had evaporated in his kiss.

But somewhere lurking in the hidden corners of her consciousness lived a nightmare that intruded in her sleep and tormented her days. How could she trust any man when such provocation reminded her that she could so easily be hurt again? Men knew how to say secure things to win their way into a woman's heart, so that she would ultimately acquire a false sense of security, and she was frightened to be played like that again.

"I think that would be for the best," she agreed, her heart heavy, her mind filled with doubts. "I'm sorry." She walked over to where his desk was situated and began to place her ideas into her folder. Carla sensed that Cole was still rooted where he stood with his eyes watching her every movement as she collated the sheets of paper and finally zipped her folder shut. When she turned on her heels and demurely faced his sullen expression, she felt somewhat guilty that her inability to trust him could cause her to react in such a way.

It was no longer in her nature to be persuaded or take a person's word for what it was. Men seldom mean what they say or say what they mean, she told herself astutely. So why was some inner sixth sense telling her that she should give some credence to Cole's tenable offer to trust him? The moment the thought sprang to her mind, she wanted to abandon it instantly. She couldn't trust anyone, not anymore.

His mouth twitched. "What are you going to do, Carla? Run from men forever?" There was no smugness in his voice. It was just calm and yet he was firmly spoken.

"No," Carla mouthed weakly, taken aback by the suggestion.

"If that's true," Cole urged slightly, "then stay with me for dinner tonight. You did say you would join me."

That was before she'd seen Robyn, Carla thought. Before she'd made a complete fool of herself. But she knew that by declining now after having accepted his invitation for dinner would make her seem even more childlike and less mature. And she didn't want to leave Jamaica with any immature imprint on her accomplished, proficient, yet vulnerable character.

"Yes, I did." She tried to smile, pulling up one simple *C* word as Cole urged her to replace the folder on his desk: *cheerful.* If only she could remain lighthearted and genial, then maybe she could get through dinner unscathed. But as Carla met the bright, accepting glow in Cole Richmond's eyes, knowing that she liked the way his gaze ensnared hers, she felt weary, dejected, and scared to death.

Carla didn't feel that her thoughts were jelling as sharply as they should, such was the effect the tropics had created in tuning her body to the slower pace of life in the country. Her watch had read 4:33 P.M. when Masa Joe had returned her to her hotel to change, and she'd showered and dressed in a plain cotton violet frock with a deep neckline in which she wore a favorite gold chain necklace. Matching plain gold clip-on earrings around which her short hair fell and a touch of makeup and slender-heeled sandals gave her the dusky evening mood she'd hoped for. A few spots of French perfume in strategic, sensitive areas and she was ready to see Cole Richmond again.

Her tawny-brown complexion seemed transformed against the sunset as she made her way up the short steps at the entrance of Eden Lea after paying the cabman's fare. Bessie immediately greeted her on her arrival and dutifully took her to the dining room she'd visited when Lucas had been there. "Young Mr. Richmond will be here shortly," she was told moments before Bessie planted a glass of punch in her hand. "Have you met Tata and Robyn?"

Carla almost froze when Bessie left the room and she found herself facing the two onlookers. She hadn't expected either woman to be there, and she looked at them both uncertainly. She earned a look of derision from Robyn and one of clear speculation from Tata as they mentally dissected her like a scientist would a frog: snipping, judging, scrutinizing every part of her attire. Then the door swept open and Lucas breezed in, his brows raised curiously, his expression scowling.

"Where's the prodigal grandson?" he announced. He hadn't seen Carla and his tone was unpleasant.

"Cole isn't here," Tata returned, tipping her head in a cautionary direction.

Lucas turned and caught sight of Carla's bemusement. "So English gal." His tone became rude, his mouth sneering. "You change up anything on the plantation yet?"

"I don't think I should discuss Mr. Richmond's plans with you," Carla replied formally, trying to relax and keep her stomach from twisting into a knot. "It's beyond my professional conduct to do so."

"Your what?" Lucas appeared not to understand her.

"It's not my practice to outline any of my client's ideas to anyone without his knowledge."

"Boy, you know a lot of English words," Lucas jeered. "Did you know me and my sister, Tata, were raised on this plantation?"

"No," Carla admitted, aware that she'd attracted both Tata's and Robyn's full thoughtful attention.

"Cole never raised here," Lucas continued hotly. "When his mama fall from her social graces to the standards that we all have to live by when Cole did born, her daddy, Papa Peter, banish her from this house. Yes, she come down from the gentry with a bump because she refused to tell Papa Peter the name of Cole's daddy." His eyes were blazing. "And now that she dead and Papa Peter's dead, I cannot believe that it's her son who come claim the family fortunes. What is me and Tata to get? We not even in Papa Peter's will."

"I'm sorry." Carla gulped, disliking the conversation. "I'm sure Cole—"

"Mr. Richmond," Robyn corrected.

Carla eyed her coolly. "I'm sure Mr. Richmond will do what's best for you and your sister."

"Will he?" Lucas spat out.

"Lucas," Robyn implored. "Don't talk about him like that. He hasn't done anything to you."

Carla flushed as she heard the protective tones in Robyn's voice. She took a fortifying drink and then another, wondering whether she could withstand this woman's appraising, murderous glare.

"You think he's generous?" Lucas accused Carla in envy. "He's as mean as his granddaddy. Don't ever trust him."

"I'm here only to help Mr. Richmond organize the marketing of this plantation," Carla proclaimed. "I cannot comment—"

"I've seen how you English women do your business," Robyn intruded grudgingly, her native accent filled with blatant accusation. "Maybe next time it might be an idea to use a bedroom."

"What?" Tata chuckled, and Lucas raised a feisty curious brow.

Carla grimaced, neither offering nor returning any hint of friendship. Robyn could be really pretty if she didn't scowl so much, she thought, but it was evident by the look in her eyes, in the way her brows furrowed and her cheeks sagged, that she resented her immensely and simply didn't want her there. "I thought Mr. Richmond explained," she defended carefully, her stiff English tone adding a deliberate offhand note, though Carla was aware that her anxiety had peaked.

"Explained what?" Cole asked as he entered the room. He looked suave and elegant in black pants and a white short-sleeved shirt, and Carla couldn't help but inhale a deep breath as his expectant gaze swept the room. Within inches of her, his body tall and imposing, she could smell the clean scent of soap and the musk of aftershave, both heightening her senses as an evening Caribbean breeze through an open window wafted the fresh odor in her direction.

"It seems like we have a little situation right here between you and this English gal," Lucas bristled luridly. "Me just hear that the ink on the signature that you sign her contract with not even dry before all your business objectives fly out of the window."

"I'd be very careful what you say next," Cole cautioned with a deadly tone, his gaze traveling to Robyn as though offering her a warning.

Carla didn't miss Robyn's equally steadfast glare at Cole before she watched the younger woman stalk out of the room in a huff. She didn't know what was going on or what to make of their relationship. She felt like she was watching a little play and that she had unknowingly been cast as one of the characters. Staring blindly at the door which Robyn had disappeared through, she wondered suddenly whether she should leave, too.

The last thing she wanted was to play a cameo role in this family drama, especially when she hadn't auditioned for the part. But as Carla took a step forward intent on making her own departure, Cole took hold of her wrist and restrained her from leaving.

"My cousin owes you an apology," he demanded hotly, his gaze determined that she was going to get one.

"It doesn't matter," Carla pleaded as anxiety rippled her nerves.

"It damned well does," Cole returned angrily. "And if you don't get one, then he's banned from this house."

"Banned!" Lucas choked on the word. "You're going to ban your own kin over a woman?"

"Since when have you allowed me to be a blood kinsman to you?" Cole shot back. "Ever since I've been here, you've been against me and I've done my level best—"

"You must t'ink because it's you who hold the pursestrings that you have the right to ban me like your granddaddy did your mama," Lucas exploded. "Well, you're not going to get away with this. Come hell or high water. You wait," he threatened, marching from the room, his face filled with resentment and contempt.

"Lucas!" Tata glared at Cole, her expression shocked and panicked. "Look what you've done. Lucas is your brethren, you can't do that to him."

"No?" Cole ejected coldly. "How long do you suggest I put up with his behavior before I draw the line?"

Carla glanced nervously at Tata and watched as her expression drooped into silence. "What about me?" she asked finally.

"Haven't I looked after you?" Cole rebutted.

"For how long now that she's here?" Tata concluded, pointing a stern finger at Carla. Her gaze chilled to a frosty hue, telling Carla that she, too, considered her presence a threat.

"Carla has nothing to do with my obligations to you as my cousin." Cole's voice sounded confused.

"So it's Carla now and not Carlane?" Tata noted with suspicion. Her eyes locked with Carla's, and she didn't mince her words. "I hope you are not after my cousin for his money," she accused, "because a little bird tell me that you wiped out Darnell Farrell and left him clean broke when him leave you."

Carla's eyes widened. Did she hear this woman correctly? "I took what was mine," she jabbed weakly, wondering exactly where Tata had come by such a story.

"That's not what his family is saying in Kingston," Tata rebuked. "His grandmother live there, and she is telling everybody the truth."

"We all have our own cross to bear when it comes to what is true," Carla responded quietly, disliking immensely the turn of conversation. "As long as I know my truth, that is all that matters to me." Without a backward glance, she placed her punch glass down on the Spanish elm table and left the room. She was on her way through the main door when Cole caught up with her.

"Carla, wait," he implored firmly. But she continued walking until she felt his stiff hand on her right shoulder. "Miss McIntyre?" His formality caused her to stop. She turned and faced him, her expression blank, and she refused to mellow as the bright early moon, its head over the sunset, reflected on the remorse in his cocoa-colored eyes. "I can't apologize enough for my family."

"I think you owe me more of an apology than that," she related, unmoved by his sincerity. "I can't imagine what you told Robyn so that she should single me out for target practice, and it's very unsettling to know that she's now got Lucas and Tata believing that I'm conspiring against them."

Cole's hands rested on her shoulders, and Carla saw his gaze intensify as he looked down into her face. "I told Robyn that you're someone I really want to get to know. I didn't want to hurt her, but I made her realize that she's a very young, sweet girl with plenty of suitable admirers. As for my cousins, they're my problem, not yours. I don't want to put you in another compromising position with them. As soon as we sort out the details for marketing Linden Vale, then I'll explain to them exactly what changes I'm going to make. Maybe then, they'd feel less threatened by me."

Carla nodded. "Or me."

"In the meantime," Cole reminded, "I promised you a quiet dinner."

Carla glanced at Eden Lea. "I thought we were having it here?"

"I've heard enough bickering for one night." Cole grimaced. "I think I can rustle up something at The Grove."

Cole led the way around the Georgian house to the rear, urging Carla to pick her way carefully as they made their way down to his home. The moon still peered at them through sparse clouds, and the sunset could just be seen on the estate's horizon, streaking the sky in its colorful splendor.

She still wasn't quite acclimatized to the southern temperatures, and the humid heat on her skin made her feel uncomfortable against the present anxiety which suffused her face. It was hard to resume a pensive pose when her attempts at control were failing. Trying to forget Darnell while her senses were attracted to Cole, being embroiled in Cole's family affairs at a time when she was still trying to handle her own, and coming to grips in trying to conduct some form of business were all building tension that added a new mask to her features.

By the time they'd entered Cole's house and he'd switched on a light, she felt weary and saddened by the whole sorry ordeal. "I don't think I'm going to be good company tonight," she admitted quietly.

Cole's gaze looked troubled. "Is it because of Lucas? What did he say to you?"

Carla quickly spoke in the collective while she deposited her trembling limbs into one of the rattan armchairs. "They wanted to know your business plans, as you've figured out for yourself," she began. "And they told me the reason why your mother had to leave."

"So you've learned about that, too," Cole commented a shade ironically, taking large paces to a small table where he proceeded to turn on a lamp. "I wonder who volunteered that information so easily."

"It wasn't like that," Carla denied, sensing Cole's unspoken criticism of Lucas.

"Hmm." He seemed to appreciate that she was trying to rationalize the situation, something he himself was so good at, his way of lessening the blow. He would shrug the matter from his mind altogether, he told himself sensibly. He didn't want to talk about his own troubled past, and he was aware that Carla was still feeling some discomfort from the situation. "I'll go and get us something to eat," he invited with ease. "I won't be long."

Carla heard the pleasant tone Cole had tried to inject into his voice before he made to leave the room. As she looked around, trying to calm her nerves, she found everything to be a touch neater than when she'd last been there. Her folder was still on Cole's desk where he'd asked her to leave it after she'd agreed to come to dinner, its content of ideas again spread in all directions, suggesting that he'd returned his attention to them. The room was deathly quiet with the exception of a wall clock with its pendulum providing a ticking sound, its face displaying the correct march of time. There was no television, and that disappointed her. She'd thought it might be nice to catch another talk show or soap that would enlighten her further about Jamaica.

It wasn't long before Cole returned and seated himself beside her. The tray in his hand was placed on the nearby coffee table. "There's breadfruit, shrimp creole, some plain rice, and salad if you like a side dish," he commented.

"It looks nice," Carla approved, reaching for a utensil to spoon small amounts into the plate Cole had offered her. A while later, she was forking her way through the food, not really taking any interest in it. She managed to swallow a bite and felt the taste turn her stomach over.

"What's wrong?" Cole prompted, minutes later. "You and the food not getting along?"

"I don't feel like eating," Carla admitted forlornly.

"This isn't a good idea," Cole voiced, unsure. "You're upset about today and you have every reason to be."

"You're right," Carla agreed, placing her plate on the table. "This isn't a good idea."

Cole held her wrist and Carla tensed at the contact. "Do you like me?" he asked.

The question came so unexpectedly, Carla recognized immediately the insecurity which lay behind it. Since her debacle with Darnell, she herself had lodged this question to unsuspecting admirers. "You have your attributes," she replied carefully, not wishing Cole to know exactly how fond of him she'd grown.

"I have my attributes," he repeated, chuckling over

the words. Then his cocoa-brown gaze caught hers and held. "I said, do you like me?"

"Yes." Carla loathed hearing herself say the one simple word.

Cole's gaze warmed, and Carla felt her pulses racing again, the way it had done when Cole had kissed her so tenderly on the beach and when he had ravished her right there in that very room so that she'd been in complete abandon of her mind and her sanity. "You know," Cole assayed, his voice calm, his mood quite serene and serious. "You'd make a good challenge for some man who would like to be sorely tested."

Carla smiled, finding what he had said to be somewhat comical. "I should imagine I would," she answered just as placid. "If he had enough tolerance and patience."

"Hmm," Cole mouthed in earnest, placing an unsteady hand on Carla's knee. "I like a good challenge."

"And I'm unavailable material." Carla removed his hand, determined not to repeat another humiliating situation.

Cole's brows furrowed as he searched Carla's face. "What did Darnell Farrell do to you to make you so frightened to give in to me? You've been like this from the first moment I met you."

Carla gasped. "I'm not frightened. I'm just—"

"Some little kitten frightened of water." Cole finished.

Carla swallowed, remembering the apt description she'd given of herself. Yes, she was frightened. In fact, she was rattled silly. She wanted nothing more than to surrender to Cole and though the thought brought pleasure with heady excitement anew, she knew she would be unwilling to face the bitterness that would then follow. Her innermost beliefs had always been of permanency and commitment, one day she'd hoped even marriage. But she'd learned the hard way that men didn't want that. Their aspirations went no further once they left a woman's bed. And she'd never been the stuff of which casual playmates were made.

Cole, like Darnell, would have no qualms of conscience about how brokenhearted she would be when the affair was over. She wouldn't be able to handle it, something her present experiences were teaching her. She'd been dumped in the used-and-abused junkyard already, something she'd remembered telling Cole in an uncomprehending way. He'd said she was worth a condo and a top-quality car and some more financial security for her time and attention—things she'd extracted from Darnell during their time together. It was small recompense, hardly compensation enough for being cheated on and lied to. So if she was resisting, then why not? Why not save herself the trouble of being thrown into yet another power-and-control game where she would be continually struggling for her identity.

"I want to know how deep the water is," she reminded him. "Will I sink or swim when I find out what lurks down there in its sunken depth?"

"Don't be afraid to take the plunge," Cole whispered. "There's no deep-seated, ugly self-satisfying character buried there."

"That's what I thought about Darnell," Carla revealed, unable to prevent herself from divulging something personal about herself. "In the beginning, he was a wonderful person, then he turned into something really nasty."

She sensed Cole pull his shoulders back. "What do you mean?" His voice was deadly serious.

Carla immediately felt herself withdraw from the conversation. "I don't want to talk about it."

Cole took her left hand and rolled it between both

his palms. The warmth spread up Carla's arm, even though she tried to reject it. "I want you to talk about it," he urged softly. "I want to force it out of you so you can move on."

"What do you mean, force it out of me?" Carla tensed, making her own misinterpretation. "You like to play power-and-control games just like him, don't you? God, you men are all the same."

"Carla!" Cole brushed his fingers across her face. "What—"

"Don't." Carla pulled away to the other side of the rattan armchair. The move was so exaggerated that Cole chose to stay exactly where he was. "I know how you men operate," she told him fiercely. "Once a man has a woman gasping for more or seduces her into believing that there's a future to hope for, then he believes he can force her into anything. That's what Darnell did to me. I thought we had a future."

Carla knew Cole was amazed at her sudden outburst, of the quick flurry of heated, cynical accusations she'd leveled his way. Yet she couldn't stop herself. In her mind, she had the male character sorted, and that meant they could never hurt her again. But if she'd thought that she'd made Cole angry, she was in for a turbulent surprise.

"How long have you felt like this?" His voice was even calmer than she'd last heard it.

"From . . . from the moment I started to recognize the game moves," Carla conceded, refusing to allow the tears that threatened to reach her eyes. "I have met men since leaving Darnell, and they say the same things he used to. It . . . it starts when a man offers a woman the moon and the stars, knowing full well that he can't reach them. That's when I know that the intimidation and isolation will start to kick, like when he says he's going to phone or come over and then he doesn't. That generally means that some cheating and lying is going on, and the woman is left feeling guilty and alone. I'm sick of—"

"Darnell emotionally used you," Cole concluded, his eyes sympathetic, his voice filled with empathy, feeling her pain.

Carla's teary sable gaze appealed to him. "I don't want to talk about this now. Please don't force me to." She was shaken at how accurately Cole had zoned in on her problem. But to continue the discussion now would only jeopardize the progress she'd made in rebuilding her character. It would endanger the self-esteem she'd surmounted in herself and render her liable to the yearning, desirous urge she had to throw herself into Cole's arms and have him kiss the hurt away. She couldn't risk being so exposed. Her condition was too delicate, too critical to be unsheltered in this way. And explaining anything more to Cole when she wasn't ready would only make her feel as unstable and unsafe as a wobbly bridge.

"I won't force you." Cole backed down instantly, seeming to understand what was going on in her mind. "When you're ready to throw me that lifeline you told me about, I'll be here waiting to catch it."

He offered her a contagious smile and Carla nodded, returning a shaky one. "Thank you." She was truly grateful that he was not going to pressure her.

"You know something?" Cole stood up and opened his mouth with a suggestion. "Why don't you stay in one of the guest rooms at Eden Lea tonight. Just as a little marketing exercise," he added to reassure her. "Maybe some more ideas might spring to your mind on how Linden Vale can attract the tourists."

Carla pondered the suggestion for a cautionary moment. It seemed a good idea, considering her circumstances for being there in the first place. To behave like a guest for one night may also revive her and put her back in control of her faculties. "That's the best thing I've heard all day." She smiled.

"Good." Cole enjoyed seeing the smile on her face. "Come on, I'll take you over to Bessie. She'll show you to one of the guest rooms."

"Thank you." She nodded in agreement.

When Cole left her in the care of Bessie, having reassured Carla that she would feel much better in the morning, he felt an overpowering urge within him that this woman needed protecting and that he was the man to do it. She *needed* him, and he'd told her that before, but in truth he realized he needed her more. His whole body ached to feel this woman against him, knowing that they were perfectly matched like a hand in a glove. That was how it felt the times he'd held her and the times he'd pulled her sweet lips into his mouth. She'd offered resistance then, and he feared she was even more guarded now. The suspicion he'd seen in her eyes when they'd first met had become more revealing and visible, a clear sign that she didn't care to trust him.

How was he to break down that barrier of uncertainty and doubt she'd shielded herself with and make this woman believe that he wanted her badly? And did he even want to try? He asked himself that question again, unsure of the answer. But as his own skeptical thoughts came into focus and he reasoned with and reflected on the issue at length, he began to have a hunch that Carla McIntyre owned his soul. And if he was lucky, he could own hers, too.

SIX

Carla awoke with a start and looked around her anxiously. The dim light of early morning revealed the familiar room at Eden Lea. Of course, she remembered now. She had decided to stay the night as a guest, and Bessie had offered her this pleasant bedroom.

Slowly she sat up in the old, period-designed bed and looked around her with growing curiosity. The events of last night began to flood her mind as she took delight in the room's dusky interior. The bed was covered in white embroidered sheets, the floor was wooden and in keeping with the rest of the house. Two imposing wardrobes that she knew predated the nineteen thirties stood at attention across from her. Slatted French doors were to her left, which she suspected led out onto the balcony.

Her warm feet touched the coolness of the wooden floor when she slid from between the sheets, though she could hardly see her legs for the oversized ankle-length, long-sleeved cotton nightgown Bessie had presented her with the night before. Its high-necked frilly lace collar tickled her nape as she walked over to the French doors and drew back the long creamy net curtains, surprised to find that the doors were already open, allowing the early morning cool breeze to invade the room.

She'd wondered why she slept well. There had been no tossing and turning, no nightmarish images of Darnell Farrell. The room had remained cool throughout the entire night, and when her eyes caught the sunrise expectantly and she took in a fresh breath of morning air, she began to wonder whether Jamaica's intense humidity had in some way contributed to her past troublesome dreams. Now she felt like some of the lead weight had been lifted from her shoulders. Perhaps talking to Cole Richmond was the healing mechanism she needed. Carla couldn't be sure, nor did she wish to ponder on it. Relieved that she felt better and that there was plenty of time to marshal her defenses before she would have to face seeing Cole again that morning, she ventured out onto the balcony and took another intake of air.

The sky was a crystalline turquoise with a hint of yellow, and she watched as the sunrise danced across a beam of light where the microscopic dust particles glinted like gold in its rays. She felt a new energy surface within as she looked around her. Her guest room was situated at the side of the house from where she could see a hibiscus- and orchid-dotted lawn. And she could hear the twittering of tropical birds: an oriole, a tody, or perhaps Jamaica's famous Doctor bird.

The tranquility was so undisturbed, she could stand there all day and just enjoy the bliss. Eden Lea was nestled amid lush vegetation and royal palms, coffee trees and towering coconut trees, its terra-cotta tiled roof overseeing everything. The whole place conjured up an existence as soft and laid back as an American southern drawl.

But she was aware of its imperfections. The rooms were not air-conditioned, there was no private television or telephone, and she had yet to wonder about the bathroom. The antique furniture provided a refined atmosphere, the tone of an old plantation it seemed. She couldn't imagine changing that, but she felt that some contemporary decor—tiled floors and pastel fabrics, bright colors to enhance tropical floral prints and maybe a few modern oil paintings—would serve to attract a combination of class for the more discerning historical sightseer.

She was thinking all this when she had the sudden feeling that someone was watching her from close by. As Carla made to draw back into the guest room, aware that she was wearing only a nightgown though it was not revealing in any way, blood rushed into her face all the same as she saw Lucas Morgan gazing at her from his room. Hastily pulling the ties around the chest of her nightgown closer together, a movement which earned her a lurid smile from Lucas's craggy face, she kept her body rigid and cast him a steadfast glare.

"Are you coming out to play?" Lucas called out to her from behind the French doors of his room before his sandaled feet made heavy strides toward her, the leather soles slapping loudly against the wooden planks that made up the balcony.

"What do you want?" she admonished blandly, staring hard into his face, warning him not to come any closer. His height reminded her instantly of Darnell and though his face seemed no longer to be holding any resentment, Carla was aware of the leering look in his gaze.

"I thought me would take you to the washroom," Lucas suggested in a mocking Jamaican tone. "To scrub your back and oil you up with cocoa butter and give you a sweet time," he added.

"I don't need a sweet time with you," she told him carefully.

Lucas looked at her with glinting eyes. "Me not stupid, you know," he jeered. "You t'ink Cole give you a sweet time already? I can make you feel like honey."

Carla bit her lip worriedly as he ventured closer, telling herself that she should not hurt Lucas's feelings because he was already bitterly envious of Cole. "I think you should leave now," she advised on a cautionary note. "I'd like to get dressed."

"You have no right to throw me off my property," Lucas barked. His hand reached out and grabbed Carla's wrist. "And Cole have no right to ban me neither."

"Lucas!" Carla pleaded, alarmed. She moved backward, unknowing that she'd given him an advantage to pin her against the wall, inches away from the French doors where she'd hoped to retreat. "Don't hurt me," she implored.

Lucas's lips curled into a sneer. "Poor little English gal," he chided, his finger wagging lecherously at Carla. "You make love to Cole yet?"

Carla closed her eyes so she need not look at him, ignoring the question as she felt Lucas rub his body against hers. She tried to push him away, but Lucas was strong and pushed her back harshly. "I like a gal rough and ready," he said, his face hardening as one hand began to press against her breast.

"Stop this," Carla screamed at him.

Lucas ignored her. Instead, he pressed his wet lips against her neck in a disgusting mockery at attempting to coax her. Carla squirmed in distaste, her hand beating at his shoulder while he continued to touch her. It was only when she managed to push his face away with angry contempt, releasing a slap that connected with his unshaven cheek, did Lucas look at her, his face filled with rage.

"Who do you t'ink you mess with?" His voice was dangerous.

Carla was breathing hard and ragged. "If you don't leave me alone," she warned murderously, tears welling in her eyes, "I'll make sure Cole learns of this."

It was the wrong thing to say. Jealous rage flew into Lucas's eyes, and he lurched for her in blind anger. She screamed, fretful of what he was going to do, when suddenly she felt Lucas's being bodily removed from her.

Cole was holding Lucas by the shoulders, shaking him like an old rag. "I might have known you would be planning to cause more trouble," Cole barked savagely. "Weren't you supposed to be packing your things?"

"So you really going to do it?" Lucas bawled, shrugging his shoulders free from Cole's steely hands. "You're ordering me, your cousin, to leave Eden Lea because of she?" He pointed an accusing finger at Carla.

Cole's tone was indignant. "I'm banning you because of the disrespect you've shown toward me," he corrected. "And if you want to walk out of here on your feet, you'd better give Miss McIntyre an apology."

Lucas sucked his teeth. "I'm not going to apologize to no English gal." He eyed Cole, his gaze challenging.

Cole reached for Lucas's shoulders again, but Carla's heart began to gallop as she implored him: "Don't, please." Cole eyed her warily, his face pent up with anger as he released Lucas like a bag of old rubbish.

"Until me get what me entitled," Lucas spat out. "I'm going to see that I get what's mine." Lucas cast Carla an equally defiant look before his feet took him back to his room.

Carla ejected a sigh of relief as her hand clutched the frilly collar of her nightgown. "Thank you," she whimpered softly. "He just came out of nowhere. I didn't know what to do."

"You should have stayed in your room." Cole was obviously irritated that she hadn't. "Bessie would have been up shortly."

"It wouldn't be customary for your guests to stay in their rooms," Carla pointed out just as quickly, her tone annoyed that he should be treating her like some childlike creature. "Have you forgotten the reason why I'm here?"

Cole rubbed his forehead. "It seems I have," he admitted softly. "Did Lucas hurt you?"

"No." Carla shook her head. "I don't think he intended to."

"Don't do that," Cole said sternly.

"Do what?" Carla was confused.

"Explain it away as though he hadn't caused you any harm. That's how men get away with hurting women."

Carla's gaze froze with acute alarm. "You're trying to say that . . . that I'm in denial, aren't you?"

"Well, aren't you?" Cole's calculation of the situation was obvious as he dug his hands into the pockets of his camel-colored shorts and contemplated Carla smoothly.

Carla cast her sable gaze sideways as her mind spun in turmoil. She tried desperately hard to force down the protesting tears which had sprang to her eyes. "This is about Darnell isn't it?" The question popped out the instant she thought it and when Cole stared at her mutinously, his cocoa-brown gaze searching her vulnerable face as though he could see the child-woman she'd become yet again, she took his silence as a plausible answer. The humiliation was more than she could bear. "I shouldn't have told you anything," she blurted, before rushing back into her room.

Cole followed her there and found her stood by the foot of the bed, her arms braced against the bedposts. He came up beside her and touched her shoulder. "I shouldn't have said that. Not after what Lucas has just done."

"You're damned right." Carla could feel her anger surface again. "You weren't there. You don't know what it was like."

"Then tell me," Cole implored, turning her to face him.

Carla shook her head. "Look." She tried to rationalize the situation, just as Cole himself would, she thought. "Darnell made me feel bad about myself, and I felt guilty about it lot of the time. That's it, okay."

"Guilty for what?" Cole was intent on extracting the information.

"For . . . for the verbal abuse," Carla began absently. "For him trashing the house when things weren't going well for him."

"Wait a minute," Cole chimed incredulously. "How in God's name was it your fault that he did those things? Why did he get angry?"

Carla's lips trembled. "When he lost a fight," she murmured, confused. Her mind took her back to the weeks leading up to Darnell's WBA fight, after which five members of the Nevada Athletic Commission had totted up the costs of his savagery in the ring when he'd decidedly ripped off his opponent's nose with his teeth and not with his fists.

His earlier work had proved so impressive that Luciano, his Cuban trainer, had begun to boast on how infinitely sharp Darnell was looking at gym. No one was surprised when he gained his WBC title, dethroning the mentally disturbed Puerto Rican holder. That was one of many triumphant fights in which Darnell had put in a competent, risk-free performance, but his last two fights following were quick defeats. He'd started carrying around too much bulk in the ring which was against his trademark of lean, natural athleticism. And she'd tried to warn him against his huge intake of food, but the hard edge of ambition had become somewhat dissipated by easier living and a growing acquired taste for raw steak.

Then came the inevitable WBA fight. The old Darnell Farrell could've easily disarmed the man without breaking into a sweat, but Darnell couldn't win, not with the weight he'd piled on and so his defeat was almost a predicted outcome. Her troubles with him intensified soon after and she had continually tried to put it right until she could hold out no longer. When the Nevada Athletic Commission took away his license to fight for one year, she knew that it was time she should get out of the relationship. Her only problem was she'd taken too long to make up her mind. Had she decided to leave him earlier, she would have saved herself the further heartache in discovering the truth that Darnell had managed to fit three affairs into his gym practice schedule during his relationship with her.

"Darnell intimidated you whenever he lost a fight?" Cole could hardly believe what he was saying. "Was it some kind of game to him? You talked about power games last night."

Carla sighed in an attempt to calm her nerves, though she was unable to look at Cole. She knew that he was trying to gauge her response and that the whole thing seemed incredible to him. This she knew by the way his gentle hands rubbed at her arms consolingly and by the soft voice of clemency which belied in his tone. She didn't want to talk about this. Not here, not now. Yet Lucas's impropriety made it seem that much more important to warm to Cole's understanding grace and seek comfort from easing the load off her mind.

"It . . . it just felt like I was on a carousel." Carla didn't know how else to explain it. "One minute we'd be like a couple socializing with our friends. Then the next, he'd disappear for days on end and then come back in a mood to start on me. He never took responsibility for his behavior."

"Come here." Cole hugged Carla to his chest, protecting her as he felt compelled to. But he could sense that she did not like that.

"Don't." Carla felt embarrassed and ever more tearful as she gently pushed herself away. "I don't want you to feel sorry for me."

"I don't feel sorry," Cole lied between his teeth. "I feel sorry for him." Cole looked at her sternly. "Was he like this the whole time you were with him?"

Carla shook her head, still fighting the tears. "No. Darnell was a charmer. I was with him for just over three years. We moved into this mansion he chose in England. It was joint ownership and far too extravagant for my tastes, but he always made all the big decisions. When the split came, he set his rottweiler lawyers on to me to try and scare me from claiming my share of the house. But I had some hound dogs of my own, and he was forced to allow the house to go on sale because having lost his license to fight, he couldn't afford to buy me out." Carla looked at Cole in earnest. "Tata's wrong about me. I didn't leave Darnell broke."

"I've learned not to take seriously the things my cousin says where you're concerned," Cole declared, taking Carla's hands into his. "But I do want you to know that not all men are like Darnell."

Carla didn't seem convinced, even though she remembered everything about the way Cole had kissed her. She pushed herself away from the bedpost and began to slowly pace the room, trying hard to distract herself from the warmth which flooded her senses when she recalled the way his mouth had sapped all energy from her. "How can I be sure?" she asked, trying not to allow her feelings to rule her thoughts, trying not to allow the tears to fall, though she lost the battle and they tumbled from her eyes. "A girl doesn't know whether a man wants to play with her or play with her mind."

Cole turned to face her, his gaze charting the slow graceful way Carla moved around the room. But his brows revealed that he was troubled by what she'd said, especially when he saw that she had now begun to cry. "Carla?" He boldly walked toward her. "I'm not a person who reaches for the moon, and I have no interest in promising any woman the stars." He took hold of her hand, halting her pace as his other hand slipped around her waist. "And I've told you before that if you're going to confuse me with Darnell Farrell, then I'm going to kiss you to remind you exactly who you're with."

He dipped his head and took her tears into his mouth, and the sensuality of it took Carla over the edge. She gave a half-smothered moan, amazed to find that her body had instinctively leaned into him and, when Cole pulled her tear-washed lips into his, she felt drugged by the power and force of his kiss. A panicky desire immersed her completely as he smeared her mouth with his tongue, licking her like a playful puppy, inciting desire with every stroke. His mouth moved down to her arched throat, then to its tender hollow and without volition, her body pressed closer, accepting the hard pumped-up muscles that met her tender breasts.

When his mouth returned to hers, she linked her hands behind his head, her feet on tiptoes as she enjoyed the convulsive pleasure that existed between them. Cole kissed her so deeply, she felt frantic by the pressure and was unable to fight the elation and frustration that tripled the monstrous quivering inside her. She was frustrated because she wanted to touch Cole so much, but was afraid to because she didn't trust herself or her judgment. And the last time she'd behaved so recklessly, Robyn had walked in on them. That protruding thought made her even more wary than she had been before. Until that point, she'd begun to accept kissing Cole, even telling herself that she should be thankful that she could still attract the opposite sex and feel herself attracted, too.

Now as his hand cupped one throbbing breast and she went perfectly still, the blood rushing to her face because she knew Cole would realize that she wasn't wearing a bra, she wondered whether she should be submitting to him at all.

Cole's breathing was strong as his forehead rested against hers and his fingers moved into the front opening of her nightgown, teasing one of the brown nipples he found within. The pleasure she felt was so ecstatic that Carla was thoroughly absorbed by the soft flesh against flesh. She was falling fast. She felt vulnerable and afraid. She risked being humiliated again and told herself so, even though the tears were gone and she was taking delight in the way Cole was exciting her. "Cole." Her voice sounded nervous.

His lustful gaze caught the dark sable sparkle of her eyes, his bold black brows, the rounded nose and full lips, intensely concentrated on her aroused features. "Still running from men or do you think you can learn to trust me?" he whispered softly against her lips.

Carla's own lips trembled as she felt Cole's hot

breath feather against them. He was a man to surpass all men: seductive, sensitive, disciplined, intelligent, with an outward appearance that was undeniably, aggressively masculine. She yearned for him. It was so overwhelming. The heat of the day hadn't begun to intensify, yet already she felt like a flaming furnace within, such was her need for this man. He deserved someone better than a woman on the edge. Someone who didn't view men as enemies, she thought.

She moved one hand from the back of his neck and gingerly smoothed the outline of his beard around his mouth and chin. She would make him understand as gently as she could that another woman could best serve his needs. But when Cole turned his head aside and kissed the palm of her hand, Carla was chagrined to find the friction forcing another assurance from her lips. "I trust you," she returned in an audible whisper.

"Good," Cole whispered softly, before taking her lips again in offering of yet another deeply bruising kiss.

Carla trod carefully down the steeply sloping hillside when she'd had her shower in the makeshift washroom situated not far from the house. That would be something else that had to change, she thought wistfully, as she took her fill of the native plant life in the makeshift garden which looked so exotic around her. She could see magnificent palm trees and wild bougainvillaea wherever her gaze took her, the red-petaled flowers glistening among the pink Jamaican periwinkle.

Eden Lea looked solid and comfortable amidst it all with the morning sun on its terra-cotta tiled roof, almost hidden beneath the slant of the hill from where she stood. She could only just pick out Cole's house from the far side with its mellowed stone walls, though it miraculously looked as if it had always been part of the scene, instead of having been built after Papa Peter had arrived there, so Cole had said.

They'd talked about the plantation before she left for the washroom, and between kisses she'd recovered from her torment and was able to pour out a few ideas of her own. He agreed with her suggestion to have ceiling fans installed and not ozone-depleting air-conditioning systems. She was also told that Eden Lea had twelve guest rooms, a few of them already occupied by Lucas, Tata, and Bessie. But there were hamlets situated close by, all along the Martha Brae River, Cole had told her, and Robyn in fact lived in Good Hope, so he couldn't imagine the others having any difficulty relocating to somewhere nearby.

Carla reached Eden Lea, looking ruefully at her sandals. Some of the ground had been soggy around the washroom and she'd stained them with red earth and foliage. It was just her luck that Robyn Morrison should be coming out of the nursery around the corner to take in her appearance with a contemptuous look.

With the hem of her dress damp, her sandals soiled, and her hair slightly windblown, Carla hardly felt that she appeared to be anything to look at. In reality, she looked robust with health, with a radiant color whipped up in her tawny-brown cheeks and her sable eyes sparkling above the rich red lips that still betrayed how passionately they'd been kissed. But she was conscious of her disheveled state and chose to be as cool as the other woman, passing no comment as she made her way indoors and up to her guest room. By the time she emerged for breakfast in the dining room, she managed to dust clean her sandals and towel sponge the wet spots out of the hem of her dress.

An unbidden little rush of pleasure ran through her as her gaze caught Cole sitting at the long Spanish elm table. His cocoa-brown eyes deepened as he followed her strides toward a vacant chair and as she sat opposite him, he threw her a radiant smile above his coffee cup. She was sorely tempted to throw him one back, but Tata was also sitting at the table and seemed intent on watching her.

"So you stay here last night?" Tata asked suspiciously, seizing her chance as Carla reached for a cup to pour herself coffee. "I wonder where Cole sleep?"

"In my own bed," Cole bellowed. "And while we're on the subject, exactly where were you last night?"

"How you mean?" Tata insisted innocently.

"I mean the men you've been inviting here," Cole chided knowingly. "I have plans for Linden Vale, so I want the secret visits to stop."

"You dictate to me now?" Tata cursed harshly. "I wonder which one of you is going to put me in line. You or she?" An accusing finger pointed at Carla.

"Keep Carla out of this," Cole warned, placing down his coffee cup hard on the table, the thud signifying beyond words that he was attempting to discipline her.

Tata rose abruptly from her chair. Staring at them both, her eyes blazing angrily, she threw down her napkin and left the room.

"Cousins. Who'd have them?" Cole breathed wearily.

"I don't know any of mine," Carla answered, succeeding to pour some coffee. Cole was quick to pass her the sugar before eagerly offering her some milk. He was trying to make amends for Tata's outburst she thought, or was it that he still felt aroused as she did. "My mother has one brother, my uncle Quayle and he has no children," she explained quickly, trying to deflect the rush of pining she had developed for Cole. "My father has three brothers and two sisters, but he doesn't know where they are. I know that sounds awful, but he was the only one who emigrated to England, and he sort of lost touch with everyone from St. Kitts."

"He's from one of the small islands?" Cole seemed surprised.

"He was born in St. Kitts," Carla confirmed, now sipping her coffee.

"The name McIntyre. It's Scottish," Cole noted. "Do you know if your ancestry is Scottish?"

"Probably it is." Carla smiled. "I'm not sure if father would even know. Caribbean genealogy is hard to trace."

"What's your father like?" Cole's eyes mirrored his interest as he passed over to Carla the bowl of bammy bread.

"Quiet," Carla admitted. "My mother controls him, literally."

Cole heard the dismay in her tone. "You don't like that?"

"No. I never did," she told him.

"So what's your mother like?" he asked.

"Domineering. Bossy. Proud," she responded, spooning saltfish into her plate.

"Harsh words."

"Harsh mother."

"And what's your relationship like with her now?" Cole queried.

"Difficult," Carla confessed smoothly, ignoring the pain she felt as the memory came back to her of what they'd last said to each other. "I think you could say that I was a letdown to her. She wanted an upstanding pillar of the community, Christian-minded daughter. Instead she got an independent, free-spirited, female-of-the-world."

"She didn't like you like that?"

"She hated me like that." Carla wrestled with her conscience, not wanting to sound too damning about

Iona McIntyre. "She resented me working in the job that I did, and when I met Darnell . . ." She cast her eyes heavenward. "Mother was adamant that I shouldn't live with him. Okay, you could say she was right about that. But to ridicule me to our friends, to the church pastor, to her entire congregation, not to mention the newspapers. In her eyes, I'd caused a great sin by cohabiting and an even bigger one when I left Darnell and the scandal hit the papers."

"She didn't support you?" Cole inquired, slowly chewing on some fish.

"Mother?" Carla scoffed, shaking her head. "She'd rather read her Bible than support me."

"You're against her religion?" Cole seemed curious now.

"No. No," Carla repeated. "I just don't like her using it against me. I'm in touch with my own spirituality. I have a one-on-one relationship with God. I don't think of God as being up in the sky like she does, among the clouds somewhere. I think he's right here in that void that we call time and space, and maybe he walks around us and look into our faces on occasion to see what we want and what we really need. None of us really knows, but some people are hypocritical that way, and my mother happens to be one of them."

"My mother was God-fearing, too," Cole began. "That's why she never married, and there had been plenty of offers. I think she felt guilty over the years for getting pregnant with me. I also think she felt that she'd been justly punished by my grandfather. He wanted to know who my father was, and she wouldn't tell him. She always said it was between her and God."

"Aren't you curious?" Carla probed.

"Not anymore," Cole said, dismissive. "There's no point to it now. He's probably dead, like Mom."

"You always have a clearheaded answer about everything," Carla ventured quietly, knowing it was the one thing that frightened her about Cole. "You reason and rationalize situations. I don't know how to take you sometimes."

Cole's gaze warmed suddenly, and Carla felt the fondness grow between them. "If I let things fester, I might develop some peculiarities like lose my teeth, or come out in warts or lose my hair . . ."

"You have no hair." Carla laughed. "You've shaved it. Do you like it that way?"

"It's very comfortable like this." Cole smoothed his hand over his freshly shaven scalp. "It's cool. Don't you like it?"

"Yes," Carla admitted. "It makes you look . . ."

"Say it," Cole coaxed, his cocoa-brown gaze flirting with her. "You can trust me, remember."

Carla felt warm blood rush into her face. Cole's amorous voice seemed to stroke all over her, and the affection between them seemed almost visible. "Sexy," she whispered, almost embarrassed.

Cole's eyes beamed as he took Carla's hand across the table. "You have to stop being careful with me," he rasped, bringing her hand to his lips. Brushing a kiss across it, he added, "That wasn't difficult, was it?"

"No," Carla said.

"Darling, I want to be with you today," Cole exclaimed, his eyes brooding. "Let me show you some more of Jamaica while I get to know you."

"What about your work here?" Carla was going crazy inside by the smitten look in Cole's fanciful gaze.

"Everyone knows what to do," Cole broached. "And I'm talking about only a few days."

"A few days?" Carla gasped. "I'm here only another five days before I go home."

"Not long enough." Cole kissed her hand again. "But while you have them, spend them with me."

His keen enraptured gaze was so enchanting, so deliriously captivating, that Carla could hardly deny herself the irresistible urge to be charmed by such an attractive, sexually appealing man. Her own ardent expression was so attached to Cole that she knew not who was more devoted to the other or who found the other more adoring. Such tender, enamored feelings just couldn't be ignored, she told herself, especially when they were still fresh and new like she'd never felt before.

She *was* lovesick after all, she admitted finally. This ardor, this passion, this fascination she had for Cole from the first day she'd met him had only intensified and could no longer be put down to a touch of foreign madness. She appreciated his company, she liked everything about him physically, and if she had any sense, she should cherish this moment. "Where shall we go first?" Her acceptance earned her another kiss against her fingers.

"Bay Rock," Cole intoned in a winsome tone. "For that picnic I wanted you to share with me."

A colorful umbrella, spinning like a solar-powered pinwheel as it soaked up the sun against the burning beach, shielded Carla and Cole from the intense rays overhead that showered them like a downpour of rain from a clear blue sky. The briny smell of the sea enveloped them as did the smell of salt and the feel of sand, their tiny grains working into Carla's bare feet. She'd taken off her sandals and placed them at her side so that she could work her toes into the tiny crushed limestones. A salty breeze rippled across Cole's features as he gazed over at her, realizing that she was absorbing the beach and its shore.

"Can we do something?" he suggested, knowing that

they were both seated comfortably on the towels he'd spread on the white sand. Between them laid the white tablecloth he'd brought with him where he had placed a selection of appetizers that were neither heavy nor rich in taste. A red bottle of wine, two glasses, cubed mango, king-sized prawns, a bowl of Florida salad, and sliced bread seemed the perfect combination to constitute a light picnic lunch.

"What?" Carla's voice held all the appreciation of his company and his effort. Her gaze transferred from the sea to the wonderful food laid before her eyes for the taking to Cole's manly frame seated opposite her.

"It's a game," Cole began, projecting a note of confidence into his tone. "I ask you a question and you must give me an honest answer, then you ask me a question and I give you an honest answer. But we can't ask each other the same question."

"And we take it in turn?" Carla queried, the idea growing on her at how revealing such a game could be.

"Yeah, while we eat." Cole nodded. "Do you want me to go first?"

"It's your idea." Carla laughed, relaxing, immediately ready to give him her attention.

"Okay. What was your earliest memory?"

The present faded as Carla took her mind back. "Being in my crib," she recalled hazily. "I remember trying to open my eyes and when I did, someone was there giving me a toy airplane to play with. I never did remember who he was. What was yours?"

"Remember, we can't ask the same question." Cole smiled.

"That's not fair," Carla teased. "Okay. What would you do if you ruled the world?"

"I'd remove all the weapons of war," Cole responded, reaching for the bottle of red wine which he proceeded to pour into the two glasses. Offering one to Carla, he asked, "What's your greatest indulgence?"

"Music," she said, quickly reaching to accept the glass. "I have over one hundred and fifty CDs. My favorite song is 'What a Wonderful World' by Louis Armstrong because that was the song I listened to when I got my first job. What was the last book you read?"

"Fauna and Flora in the Caribbean," Cole said, sipping his wine slowly, his cocoa gaze committing to memory every part of Carla's image with fascination. "It's incredibly boring, but it's a good book. It's about the ozone and climate changes that are going on and how it's affecting the plant and animal life here. What was the strangest idea you had that worked?"

"Having a female singer that I was doing some promotion work for appear in a magazine shoot with a national rugby team. It got her noticed immediately. I think it was the image of a solitary female set against all these heavy-set men that did it." Carla smiled, her heart beating madly as it reacted to Cole's sultry glare. "What was the worst thing that happened to you?"

"That would be when my mother died, and I felt like the world was no place I was meant to be in. I've often wondered whether I should've been here at all, being an accident at conception, but that was when I also decided that only I could make my life how I want it." He looked into Carla's sable eyes with sincerity, and she felt moved by what he'd told her. Equally it made her frightened at how deep the probing elements of this game were going to get, and she thought perhaps it might not be such a good idea. "What constitutes a problem to you?" she heard him ask.

You, her heart yelled out silently. *You're pulling too much emotion out of me.* She sipped her wine quickly to give her time and space to decide how she could inject a nonserious slant into the conversation. A shaky laugh left her lips before she responded lightly, "Something that I can't solve like a mathematical equation." Cole chuckled, and so it was her turn to ask. "Where do you see yourself five years from now if you were to work back to this very point in time?"

"Being married to someone like you," Cole answered. Before Carla could even begin to translate or correlate what that meant in her head, even though she was aware of the flicker of hope in Cole's eyes which sent a heated shaft of fire to run along her loins, he said, "Describe your first sexual feelings for a person."

"Cole!" she gasped, her eyes widening.

"Come on," he coaxed. "The game ain't over."

"At school, when I was nine," she rebutted, disbelieving that she was doing this. "A boy in my class climbed a tree in the playground and picked a flower from it then came down and gave it to me. Then the teacher came over and got hold of his ear and yelled at him never to climb the tree again. But it didn't spoil the feeling he gave me. That day I felt like the most special girl in the school."

"That was sweet." Cole smiled, sipping his wine. "Very sweet."

"What was your favorite romantic gift?" she asked.

"Hmm. A girl gave me three red roses once." Cole thought back to the precise time. "It was on Valentine's Day when I was in my teens, and she gave me three—one for each word, I Love You—but I didn't love her, so I felt guilty and embarrassed to receive them." His gaze suddenly deepened. "What turns you on in a man?"

"His smile." Carla laughed, enjoying the giggle in her answer. "What brings out the beast in you?"

Cole's eyes smoked over. "Feeling my way around fleshy curves and a decent hipline."

"I have a great hipline."

"I know you do," he responded dazedly. "What is your sexiest film?"

"*Sweet Sweetback's Baadasssss Song* by Melvin Van Peebles because it was outspokenly loud about black sensuality and sexuality. And it was racy."

"You're racy?"

"I'm very racy." Carla laughed again. "Have you ever been in love?" she probed, the question popping out before she could stop herself. She hadn't wanted to ask that one. She was at a loss as to why she'd even ventured there. But it was out now, and all she could do was brace herself ready for what he was going to say.

"I have loved and received love." Cole chose his words carefully. "And," he added, "I have many regrets. Have I been *in* love. No. There was always something holding me back. I've always felt like I don't know what I'm looking for but I'll know it when I find it."

"Hmm." That one enthralled Carla. "So you're looking for your inner person?"

Cole's gaze deepened in surprise. "Yeah."

"Me, too."

Cole leaned forward, his hand resting on his knee, his gaze searching Carla more readily. "Do you feel like you've lost yourself?"

Carla hesitated, then prevaricated the truth so that she would still be in keeping of giving an honest answer. "People lose themselves when they're either drunk, drugged, or . . ."

"Making love," Cole finished mildly, his gaze ensnaring and capturing her entirely.

Carla's pulses tripled at a beat. "I think it's time we ate something," she announced, alarmed at how husky her voice sounded.

"Sounds good to me." Cole's smile slanted wickedly. "Then we can talk some more."

This time Carla did not feel so panicked.

SEVEN

Two days later, Carla was comfortably reclined on a green and white chaise longue beneath a parasol strategically sited so she could overlook the azure-blue sea at the Trelawny Beach Hotel. Fixing her sable eyes dazedly on the holiday-makers and their children playing leisurely in the sun-bleached sand, rather than concentrating on the book she'd tried to read, her emotions were a mixture of confusion and fascination when she thought back to the delightful weekend she'd spent in the company of Cole Richmond.

She'd begun to do battle with her emotions the day they'd agreed on a midday picnic at Bay Rock, and such was the conflict parading around in her mind that for a fleeting moment she'd thought to call Paulette, her closest friend, in order to try and gain a different perspective on what she was feeling. She wasn't sure if she had been sensible or plain stupid to have accepted going to a picnic with Cole. All she knew was that she had to give herself the opportunity to know someone who seemed to possess the same goodness in his heart as she herself did. And not only had she enjoyed learning more about Cole, she'd listened to his crazy tales about Africa and made him laugh by telling him of her own antics on how she dealt with starstruck celebrities with egos a little too hard to cope with.

They had many things in common, including the love of travel and history, and the fact that they each had a Caribbean ancestry. There were differences, too. Cole had experienced a reasonably content childhood, while she had thought hers to be isolated and alone. He had been a good boy for his mother. There had been no wild parties, wild girls, or destructive behavior. She, on the other hand, had been quite rebellious, liberating herself from the rigid, often suffocating restrictions her mother had inflicted on her as a child. Skipping school routinely and purposefully smoking, though it had been a habit she disliked immensely, were just two of the tribulations she'd forced her parents to go through. Her father had given up worrying when he discovered how headstrong and determined she'd become. But her mother, on a mission to prove that she was not going to spare the rod and spoil the child, sought nothing other than to have Carla toe the line. And so had begun the conflict that dogged them both into her adulthood.

Sharing it all with Cole had been a relieving experience, and getting to know him had been just as special. It was like unraveling a chocolate delight, plucking it from beneath its wrapping, to discover even greater secrets when bitten and the soft center became revealed. And their knowing each other hadn't ended there. The entire weekend had been spent building blocks of personality on each other. She'd told him that her father had retired and was now a keen amateur ornithologist. Cole in return decided to take her to a bird sanctuary at Rocklands, near Anchovy, where she'd seen over two hundred and fifty bird species endemic to Jamaica. They'd also visited a rum factory and sampled rum at a backstreet bar called Fatty's Hot-spot. There, Cole's knowledge captured her yet again when he explained how the English traders had discovered rum, first using it to pacify their slaves before it'd become the very mascot for pirates and buccaneers.

Sunday had been spent visiting the Arawak Caves just beyond the Rio Bueno. While talking more on topics of interest, ordinary subjects taking on a fascination which surprised her, she learned that the Arawaks were the first natives of Jamaica, who had colonized the island before the Europeans arrived there. The caves, which had originally been used as a form of shelter for the Arawaks, and then as a haunt for pirates to bury their loot, were now in modern times used by smugglers, more interested in drugs than hidden treasure.

It was one of the realities Cole had explained to her on Jamaica's economy exports that transcended agriculture, bauxite, and tourism. But most of the island's foreign currency was still from the extraction and processing of bauxite, the raw material of the aluminum industry known as red gold to the Jamaicans and found in abundance in the limestone plateau in towns like Mandeville, where Cole told her he'd been born. He would take her there one day, he'd said casually, where she could see the open-cast mining of bauxite and experience the high mountains and cooler air and visit the many craft shops to buy souvenirs.

Everything about him appealed to her heart and her sanity. She liked his seducing cocoa-brown eyes, the pumped-up amber-colored muscles of his physique, the way his shaven head looked polished in the sunlight, and how he talked about life so openly. He was quite a philosopher with homespun morals, the kind of man Iona McIntyre would approve of, she'd even thought.

Throughout their time together, he'd kissed her, and

often, telling her how lovely he found her lips, even venturing to express in words that wouldn't frighten her too much, how much he had a yearning to take her to bed. She had that same yearning, too. It was all she'd begun to think about since their parting late into the night, when Cole had finally brought her back to her hotel. He'd wanted her to remain at Eden Lea from the night she'd first stayed there, but ever wary of what his cousins would make of the situation, she'd declined and instead kept returning to her hotel room where her dreams of him had been full of craving and wanting.

Carla sucked in a hoarse breath and touched her lips. The tingle that lingered there was still present, just as the throbbing between her legs refused to leave. She closed her book, knowing there was no point attempting to read it. Her body was aroused and she felt irritated and impatient. She could feel the tip of her nipples rubbing against her bikini top, and her mind began to conjure up images of what it would feel like if Cole's lips were pressed softly against them.

Shaking herself, she closed her eyes. Falling head over heels in love was not what a woman on the edge should be doing, she goaded herself sternly, telling herself that she might even be on the rebound. He'd been friendly and she'd been friendly, and that should be all there was to their relationship. Their professional relationship, she hastened to add. So why then was she feeling so confused? And why was she so afraid at having to see Cole again later that day, as they'd arranged?

She was about to ponder that subject when her dark brows rose suddenly. An intruder's upright body was posed indignant at the side of her chaise lounge casting a menacing shade across her own. "I thought I'd find you here." Robyn's voice was filled with caustic irony. "Soaking up all this luxury. It must be costing you money."

That's all I needed, Carla grimaced sadly. *Another taxing problem on top of my own.* The morning had started off well enough. She had awakened to another beautiful day and was grateful that she could relax under the glare of a hot summer sun on a private beach without enduring avid, lustful glances from men delighting in running their eyes over her curvaceous body. Her only initial disturbance had been the sound of holiday-makers playing nosily in the sea, but the happy buzz of their laughter had acted like a tonic, sedating her against the heated atmosphere on the beach. And as the lazy hum of a distant motorboat had sped by, with a water-skier trying his luck against the still waters, she'd thought herself thoroughly relaxed and engrossed in her heady, amorous thoughts of what it would be like making love to Cole Richmond.

It was almost cruel that Robyn should come and destroy such a desirous daydream, disrupting her need for tranquility when she was so desperate to clear her confusing thoughts. She eyed Robyn suspiciously, her eyes fixing on her medium-sized frame dressed in a simple pink frock, her dark curly hair pulled back into a neat coillike knot. Opening her book and slipping a finger between the pages to reserve the spot from which she hadn't been reading, she railed, "Have you come to see how I look, to see how I'm bearing up, or to discover how rich I am?"

"Neither," Robyn chided, her cool brown gaze flicking slowly over Carla's bikini-clad body in jealous disapproval. "I wanted to see what you were wearing. I would have thought you had more taste."

Carla's sable gaze narrowed, unbelieving that Robyn could be behaving this way. "What do you want?" She refused to be nettled by Robyn's snub.

Robyn moved under the green-striped parasol above them, her gaze darting quickly from the pretty white fringe, which were waving softly in the sea breeze, to Carla's growing expression of deep-seated annoyance. "I suppose I really want to ask you something," she jabbed.

"Ask me what?" Carla inquired.

"If you love him," Robyn said flatly.

Carla gasped. "I don't throw that word *love* around easily. It means different things to different people."

Robyn scowled. "How interesting."

"Anything else bothering you?" Carla said, peeved.

"I suppose you think we country folk are primitive," Robyn jeered. "It's so easy for some rich young girl from England to come take and use then leave a native girl to help pick up all the pieces."

She was speaking in metaphors, but Carla knew the direction Robyn was going. "Is that what you think I'm doing?" she demanded. "Is that why you're so offhand every time I'm around because you think I'm deliberately using Cole, that I'm out to hurt him?"

"Well, aren't you?" Robyn countered.

Carla felt her temper rise, but she was not going to lose it in front of this cool, brown-eyed, fair-skinned girl. It wasn't any of Robyn's business what she did with Cole, but the other girl's sneering condescension got her on the raw. Robyn saw her as a frivolous outsider, unlike Tata and Lucas, who saw her as a threat. And as long as she was not a native to Jamaica, Robyn seemed intent to keep her at arm's length.

"Apparently you don't think very well of me," she snapped. "The fact that I'm English and you're Jamaican doesn't mean I think myself to be any better than you. I'm not any worse, either, just that I choose to accept that a man knows what he wants and that I have better manners. Don't worry about Cole and me."

"I'm not worried about you," Robyn pronounced. "I love him and I've got him"

"The way you say that sounds . . . temporary," Carla chided.

Robyn's body shook at the remark. "I came here to politely ask you to leave Cole alone. Now I think I'll fight for him."

"Well, whatever the rules are," Carla drawled, unfazed. "I don't abide by them. Now run along." She had taken enough and opened her book wide to assert that they were done. "I'm finding this conversation to be bawdy, boring, bad-humored—and I'm busy."

"That's a lot of *B* words for an English girl," Robyn pounced, totally frazzled by Carla's cool exterior. "Here's one you didn't use. You're a—"

"Miss McIntyre?" A hotel attendant arrived in time to plummet Robyn into silence. "There's a telephone call for you from England. We can patch it through to your room."

"Thank you." Carla rose from the chaise longue, tossing Robyn a contemptuous look. "The next time you come to see how I live, make sure Cole knows you're coming. I'm sure he'd like to hear you make a clean breast of it on exactly how you plan to fight for him." With that remark, she tossed down her book into the chaise longue and made swift strides back toward her hotel room.

A calming breath took great effort and fortitude. How dare that young girl think she could come up against her, especially when she was thinking that her mind was in a quandary over the entire situation. She didn't want to hurt Cole. That was the last thing she wanted. And exactly what would happen when she returned to England? Her cheeks burned with jealousy at the thought of Robyn attracting Cole's attention. If she felt like this now, then she would be in for a miserable time of it when she found herself back at her office desk in London.

She was frowning when she picked up the telephone handset in her hotel room and heard the irritation in her uncle's mature voice. "Carla? Where in the world have you been?" Uncle Quayle asked on hearing her greeting. "I've been calling all weekend only to be told you're not there."

"I've been closing the deal," Carla answered a half-truth.

"So you're confident with it?" Uncle Quayle prompted, his tone thoroughly pleased.

"We've formulated some great ideas for the plantation," she responded. "I'm looking quite forward to working on the contract."

"For a while back there, I was worried," her uncle admitted calmly. "But it seems you've landed on your feet with this one."

"Mr. Richmond is very easy to get along with," Carla said easily. Too easily. Her uncle wasn't oblivious to the note of promise in her tone.

"Is something going on that I should know about?" he pressed.

"Like what?" Carla feigned ignorance.

"A little romance perhaps?"

"Uncle!" She failed to inject some firmness in her tone.

"Well, I never." Uncle Quayle decided to make his own interpretation. "So he did appeal to you. Well, that's what you needed. You'll come back feeling like a new woman."

"Uncle, I've got to go." Carla didn't wish to be dragged into a lengthy discussion about Cole. "I'll see you in a couple of days."

"Wait." Her uncle's voice caught her attention. "You'd better go see your mother when you come back. She's not feeling very well, and I think she'd welcome the visit."

Carla grimaced at the thought of being in the same room with Iona McIntyre. The last time they'd looked at each other, an angry confrontation had ensued. She didn't want to repeat the ordeal, not now while she was on the road to healing. But if she felt anything, it was an obligation to the fact that Iona was indeed her mother and as such she would keep to her duty as a daughter should. "I'll go see her," she promised her uncle, before they said their good-byes and the phone clicked dead.

Seating herself on the freshly made bed, she stared vacantly into space. Her body sagged with the release of tension and doubts which flooded her mind again. Robyn was right. She should stay away from Cole. How could she plan a relationship with him, with anybody, when she couldn't even forge a relationship with her own mother.

Perhaps that was where she'd gone wrong with Darnell, knowing that Iona hadn't approved of him in the first place. No. She amended that thought pretty quickly. Darnell had been a bully who liked control and manipulation games. And her childhood—this craving she always had to be loved—had served only to make it easier for him to abuse her. She'd allowed it because she'd wanted someone to love, children to love, and a home of her own. She'd wanted to fill this gaping void in her life. Now, Cole seemed to be filling that hole.

How cruel it was that in two days there would be a great ocean between them. Except for the odd passing visits on business, they might never get to really know each other again. She couldn't imagine that he would write or keep in touch with her, and she could just envision the love scenes between him and a native girl such as Robyn.

A frisson of sorrow ran through her. It was just as well they hadn't gotten any closer, she told herself morosely, the tears stinging the back of her eyes belying the tremors which shook her limbs. And it was just as well they hadn't made love, either. It would make it easier to sew up the last vestiges of their business together. She would not mention Robyn's visit or that she planned not to see him again. In the morning, she would prepare to pack her bags for the journey home.

A heavy silence had fallen over Carla as she waited for Cole in the hotel's lobby. She nodded with a smile at a passing chauffeur and then at the few familiar faces of guests arriving and departing for the evening, dressed to flatter the tropics.

The time on her watch face read 7.34 P.M. Cole was already four minutes late. Absurdly impatient, she toyed with the white handbag resting on her lap against the flowery, low-cleavage dress that accentuated her womanly curves. It was a favorite of hers, the type of attire that always made a lasting impression, and she still remembered the picturesque day when she'd bought it in Paris, closing her eyes disbelieving that she was charging such a large amount onto her flexible American Express.

Her makeup was finely applied, though it was a little heavy around the eyes, a futile attempt to disguise the vulnerability which lurked within them. She looked at her watch again. It read 7.41 P.M. Eleven minutes had now passed. Where could Cole be? She was becoming more impatient and began to look around the lobby, expecting to see him.

She toyed with her handbag again then smoothed the finer strands of hair at the tip of her forehead. The short relaxed style was fashionably brushed back, adding a theatrical compliment to her classic evening look. She'd made an effort tonight, stupidly thinking she would feel better, but in reality it hadn't done the trick. She felt even more miserable and less accepting of the hard blows life had dealt her way.

Why couldn't she have just come to Jamaica, done her business, and gone home? Why instead develop deep feelings for her first international client? It wasn't as if she hadn't already had problems when she arrived there. Now she had compounded them with others more terrifying, and she was terrified of losing Cole—even more terrified of being hurt. It was a no-win situation, and she hated being part of it.

Irritated, she glanced at her watch again. The dial face now read 7.47 P.M. She stood on the white kitten-heel sandals she was wearing and walked nervously over to the stairs which led back to her room. She would call the plantation and check that everything was all right, and maybe it would be a good idea—it seemed the perfect opportunity—to decline the invitation to go there after all.

But back in her room, she did not pick up the telephone. Instead, Carla sat on the edge of her bed and threw her handbag down to gaze listlessly at her feet. After a while, she kicked off her sandals, refusing to fight off the anguish which had come and claimed her. She felt sorry for herself. Sorry for feeling like this and even more sorry when she began to think about how lonely her life was presently. Solitude had patiently followed her from her childhood into adolescence and throughout her time with Darnell. It had decidedly kept in touch, never leaving once, proving to her that no one had ever really been there for her. Even Cole could not be there for her now.

A timely *C* word sprang into her timorous mind: *camouflaged.* Yes, she'd always felt like that. Unseen, like some obscure character cloaked behind the scenes. That's what life with Iona McIntyre had been like. She had to be quiet at home, extremely hush-hush in church, and was often confined to her room when her mother developed one of her moods. It was little wonder that she'd sought adventure—by being difficult—to gain attention.

But Cole had told her that he didn't believe in solitude. *You can have more than that if you really want it,* he'd said. And she wanted more, damnit. She was a woman who'd found her inner strength, who'd survived losing an abusive lover, and who'd taken charge of her financial future. That had to prove to her that she was now someone worthwhile, someone who was worthy to be . . . loved.

Her senses jumped. She'd found the awful truth. The knowledge of having never been loved was what underlined her insecurities. And Cole had known it from the first moment he saw her, correctly analyzing what she needed. Lifting her head, she saw the darkness outside her window grow. The night had come and still no Cole Richmond. She turned on a bedside lamp and blinked against the sudden light, watching as it propelled her solitary shadow against the smooth peach-painted wall.

Her heart contracted as she walked trancelike to the window, gazing for brief seconds through the glass before pulling shut the curtains. She was loath to turn on the television set, deciding instead to allow her misery to seep into every bone and muscle. Pain twisted her face when she sat at the dressing table and began to tissue away her finely applied makeup.

A vulnerable, childlike image was reflected in the mirror, and she tensed at seeing the harsh knocks of life among the glacial tears welling in the troubled background of her eyes. Cole had seen that same expression the day when they'd first met. He had seen through her so clearly and she'd felt like an idiot, so messed up, so pathetic.

And yet within days, he'd given her courage, and her anxiety-ridden persona was sedating. She was healing, the nightmarish dreams had stopped. She was able to kiss a man again. Her mouth went dry and grief made her face look old. That same mouth that had kissed Cole now tasted like bland porridge.

She sneered at her reflection then almost gasped aloud when the shrill of the telephone caught her unawares. "There's a gentleman here for you," the desk clerk told her, his words spoken in a rich Jamaican burr. "Shall I give him your room number?"

"Who is it?" Carla's voice was barely a whisper.

"Hold a minute." The desk clerk paused. "Mr. Colebert Richmond," he told her finally.

"Yes." Carla's mind went into a happy daze. She exerted a breath. "Send him up." She almost threw down the telephone. She rushed back to her reflection and smiled at it weakly before attempting to pinch back some radiance into her tawny-brown cheeks. She hadn't time to reapply any makeup and so quickly brushed some blusher to her prominent cheeks. But although she'd refused to cry, her eyes looked red. A few dabs of cold water from the bathroom sink and she would look fine, she pointedly assured herself.

When the inevitable knock at the door alerted her senses, she was forcing herself to swallow a laugh of hysteria. For the first time in her life, she felt she hadn't been forgotten—and that made her feel alive and superlative. Opening the door, a smile lit up her face when she noted the suppressed gleam of atonement in Cole Richmond's eyes.

Without words they seemed to gravitate into each other's arms, solitude dying slowly in the breathless fascination that enveloped them both. Cole's gaze dropped to her lips in secret longing, and Carla felt them tingle as though he had already touched them. A tiny moan escaped her parched throat, the sound begging a protest that she be kissed. And Cole instinctively understood her silent protest, instantly taking her lips into his eager mouth. Hungrily he pressed his against them, tasting, biting, evoking a response that she gave willingly. With a whimper of need, Carla's lips parted with appetite, welcoming his invasion without question or guilty torment.

He was right. She *needed* him. She needed to heal, needed to love again so that she could be capable of accepting and giving love. Cole could help her do that. He'd told her so. He'd said he would take care of the way she felt out of sorts with men. He was doing it now, inflaming every part of her, and she responded in a way that was as alarming as it was breathtaking. Her arms clung to his neck, fearful to let him go as they each offered fevered caresses that raised body heat to dangerous proportions. Glorying in the arousal of his body grinding against hers, Carla sought to quench this dizzying spiral of need, but she lost all control when his tongue began a discovery of her mouth within, adding to her thirst for more of him.

She groaned. She needed this. She liked the taste of Cole, so supple, wet, and intense. It felt good to forget her present confusion, her past trials, and just submit to her true self: the one with dreams and expectations, who desperately wanted to learn how to value her own feelings, judgment, and needs.

Cole's mouth left hers, his deep gaze meeting her

eyes. It felt to Carla as though he had claimed her very soul in the few short minutes that they'd kissed. "Sweet heaven, Carla, I missed you, too," he growled huskily, gently stroking her neck where her pulse throbbed rapidly.

Her heart tripled a reckless beat. "Where were you?" she breathed.

Cole released her and promptly closed the open door behind him. Carla felt the loss of being in his arms, but Cole's gaze didn't deprive her of how much he found her appealing. He walked back to where he'd been and retook her in his arms. "Lucas presented a problem." His voice was calm but unsteady as he tried to curtail the turbulence she'd aroused in him. "I think he's been stealing coffee from the plantation and selling it on the black market. I needed to check it out, that's why I'm late."

"Oh, Cole, I'm sorry." Carla kissed his chin lightly. It was cruel that they were both dogged with relentless problems about one thing or another. "And is he?"

"What?"

"Stealing the coffee?"

Cole's attention was lost in the deep sable of Carla's eyes. "I'll know when I hear from a man in Kingston. He's offered to sell me some information."

"Sell you information?" Carla repeated, disliking the sound of it. She nervously smoothed the cream polyester fabric of his waistcoat, absorbing how perfectly matched the color of Cole's amber skin easily complemented the white silk short-sleeved shirt beneath it. With his cotton cream pants hugged against his hardened thighs, a gold buckle clasping his virile waistline, and brown patent shoes finishing his choice in evening wear, she eyed him doubtfully, worried that anything should happen to him. "Is this man someone safe to talk to?"

Cole's gaze deepened at the concern he observed in Carla's eyes. "I haven't seen him yet, but don't worry. I'll make sure I look after myself."

"When are you seeing him?"

"Tomorrow."

"Where?"

"In downtown Kingston."

"I heard it's rough there." Carla felt alarmed. Even though she'd never visited the island's capital, good knowledge over the years had made her aware that most capital cities, not so unlike Kingston, harbored an area where it was unspeakable to mobilize without security.

Cole smiled halfheartedly, brushing a kiss against her neck. "I'll be okay." He held her close, smiling into her face. He appreciated the warmth he saw there that began to send his pulses racing. "Have you eaten?"

"No."

"Hungry for some food?"

"A little."

"I'd like to try a cocktail and see what entertainment this hotel has to offer."

Carla smiled. "Okay. I'll just put on my shoes."

She sat down on the bed, locating her kitten-heeled white sandals. As she began to slip into them, Cole's gaze swept the room. It was spacious and airy, perfumed with the smell of fresh fragrant flowers, and modern ivory furniture enlivened it with artwork against pastel-colored walls. The focal point was the double bed, a lace design comforter spread neatly over—and he felt his manhood throb, impatient, when his mind fantasized on them both using it.

He'd promised himself he would take his time with this woman, so he took himself to the window, drawing back the long net curtains to look at the view. It overlooked the private villas below and he could see a lighted pool and much further ahead the darkly azure Caribbean Sea. "You comfortable here?" he asked curiously in an attempt to curb the feeling of his swelling desirous emotions.

"They've looked after me very well," Carla admitted, buckling the straps of her sandals. Aside from the bad dreams, she'd enjoyed it there. But she would not tell Cole about the nightmares. Besides, she hadn't had one since staying at Eden Lea, and that made her certain they'd ebbed entirely.

"You like hotels?"

"I love hotels." Carla retrieved her handbag from the bed. "It's nice to have a little luxury once in a while."

Cole turned from the window and found her standing on her feet. She looked beautiful in the flowery dress she was wearing which hugged at her hipline and presented to him all her female-endowed curves. From her shapely breasts to her rounded behind, the dress style and fabric seemed designed purposefully to create havoc within him. Seeing her in it increased his longing to make love to her, and it was an effort to force down his electric desire of peeling away the fabric from her sensually shaped limbs. His sweaty hands dug into his pockets and he uttered a husky, "Let's go."

On hearing his thick, throaty voice Carla, too, realized what she'd done to him. If only Cole Richmond knew exactly what he'd done for her.

If there was one thing about Jamaica that would leave a lasting impression on Carla, it was its fusion of ethnic traditions that was also present in the country's zesty and varied cuisine. During her stay at the hotel, she'd kept to food that was familiar. But sitting at the table in one of the hotel's two restaurants, Cole encouraged that she sample something new from the many cultural delicacies the chefs had prepared for a tantalizing taste of the island.

She chose an exotic gourmet dish, a local recipe cooked from fresh produce, peppered and hot and thoroughly seasoned. Cole joined in her selection, playfully fanning his mouth whenever the chilies tangy bite took hold. And she took her chance to partake of the Pickapeppa sauce. "It's the king of all pepper sauces," Cole had remarked. She was also to learn that it was the standard by which all others were judged and found wanting. They laughed their way through an appetizing dessert named "matrimony" which was a mixture of purple star apples with oranges and grapefruit in condensed milk.

The unusually chosen name was an appropriate prompt for Cole to steer the subject to a topic more probing. "Did you and Darnell ever plan to marry?"

Carla shook her head and gave a small shrug. "No. He didn't . . ." She paused. She was about to elaborate, but then shook her head, deciding against it.

Cole, feeling that he'd touched on something important, that what she was about to say would have given him a clue to how much more serious he should take her, said persuasively, "Tell me."

Again Carla shook her head. "I don't think I should."

Reaching out, Cole took her hand across the table. "You can trust me, remember?"

Carla looked up into his face. Her beautiful sable eyes became vulnerable, almost childlike. "I don't want to look back." There was a note of pleading in her voice.

Immediately detecting it, Cole smiled, lightening the moment. "I have a suspicion that you're being careful with me again."

Nearby, a guitar player struck a note and the band on the small stage in front of them began to play a tune, a folk song imitative of the musical style of their forefathers. When four performing dancers, both men and women, began to entertain them against the hypnotic and seductive rhythms of reggae by night, her gaze shifted, concentrated, on the long shapely legs that swayed beneath elaborately designed costumes as each dancer became one with the music.

"I haven't seen anything like this before," she prevaricated, noting evidence of how the field slaves' methods of entertainment came through in the vibrant movement, the tropical heat and eroticism. The banjo and shak-shaks combined with modern instruments allowed the dancers to shift their feet cleverly, and when the colored strobe lights flickered across their slim bodies, she could feel the repertoire of strong African links lift her spirit and her consciousness. "It's beautiful." Even her voice was in awe.

Cole moved his gaze with hers, unworried. Her thoughts had turned decisively, but her alertness hadn't. He watched the play of emotions in her face and how she clapped and cheered the dancers on. She was smiling, and he felt fascinated all over again. There was still so much he wanted to learn about her, and he felt lucky that she'd confided so much in him already, but she was a woman lost in past memories that were painful, and there were times he had to remind himself not to push too hard. "It's Etu." His voice was crisp, strong, sure of itself.

"What?" Carla raised a brow.

"The dance. It's an African folk tradition called the Etu."

Carla's gaze fixed curiously on his face where she saw his eyebrows rise in amusement. To her relief, she realized that her evasiveness hadn't disturbed him at all, that Cole's personality was as joyous as ever. "What don't you know?" She smiled into his eyes.

He absorbed her warm, astonished expression, stroking the back of her fingers as his gaze held hers, becoming intent. "I don't know if you'll let me love you tonight."

Carla looked into his brooding face, taking in the implications. The embedded intense fire dancing in his eyes fueled a sudden yearning that burned at the deepest pit of her stomach. "Cole . . . I . . ."

He squeezed her fingers, undaunted. It wasn't his way to force the issue. "Come on."

"Where are we going?"

Cole rose from his chair, pulling her up with him. "I want to take you for a romantic moonlight stroll along the beach."

He took care of the bill and linked her arm through his. Together they made their way toward the sea. It took a while—they had to circle the hotel's pool and walk through the complex of private villas as she herself had done when bathing on the beach that morning. But they'd reached the moon-kissed sand and began a leisurely stroll, enjoying the humid lushness of the tropical morass against the night in the company of each other.

"What's your vision for your company?" he asked seriously.

Carla looked at him, startled, though the question was not imposing. "I'm not planning to become a conglomerate, if that's what you mean." She thought seriously to herself for a second. "I think I'll be happy just serving the local ethnic community businesses, tapping their resources to reach a much wider audience."

"Hmm." Cole digested her answer, then asked, "And international businesses?"

"You mean clients like you?"

"Like me," he nodded.

"They'll make pleasant experiences. I can learn a lot." Her answer seemed too vague. Carla didn't like the emptiness in it. "I mean, it'd be nice to give my agency a more global appeal. Not many African-Caribbean advertising agencies pull in overseas clients."

Cole dug his hands into his pockets, walking steadfast beside her. "You sound like you've achieved a tremendous amount already. Is it what you've always wanted?"

This time Carla really stared at him, frankly assessing Cole's smooth, thoughtful expression. The moon made it easy. It shone on him and lit up his features: his freshly shaven jawline that sported his square-line beard, his rounded nose, and cocoa-colored eyes, all laid-back in a casual sort of way. It was deceptive. She could tell he was purposefully attempting to be cool. Deep down, he was probably feeling as unsure as she was on exactly what, or where, their emotions were trying to take them. "I never planned to have an agency," she told him honestly. "Circumstances—leaving Darnell. It was what I needed at the time."

"And now?"

"What do you mean?"

"Do you need it as much now?"

"I . . . I don't know what you're asking." Suddenly she felt nervous and confused.

"I'm sorry." Cole took stock of the situation. He stopped and pulled her toward him. "I'm asking you too many loaded questions. I don't want you to feel like there's a gun to your head."

Her throat felt dry and Carla felt weak. She leaned into Cole, enjoying the musky scent of him. Their conversation troubled her, as did her instincts. That sixth sense unique to women warned her that she was about to embark into the unknown, into a future that was unseen and uncertain, that could be divulged to no one. There was an almost wary look in her sable eyes as she thought just how scary the unknown could be. She rarely trusted her instinct or her judgment, but impulsively, she did so now, saying slowly, "The barrels are empty. I'm already full of artillery I'm trying to offload." She stroked absently at Cole's chest, hardly aware of the tremor that shook him. "Truth is, I now know what I need. You were right. I do need to be loved."

Cole smiled as he held her eyes, drawing her closer. "I want to love you," he whispered against her trembling lips. He found them with his own and took them eagerly with reassuring nips of delight, one slowly after the other.

Carla's eyes closed and she sank into him. If she'd once thought that he had nothing to give and she had nothing to offer, she knew now that she was wrong—now that they were both in each other's arms. Cole kissed her as though his heart were in his lips, searching, wanting, pulling her own from the safety of the cage she'd locked it in. He had found the key and was feeling his way to the lock, his hands awakening her senses with every caress, every feathery touch.

She felt safe against him, unafraid as to when he would be ready to open her cage. His lips were warm, vital, infinitely deep, evoking passion and longing as he teased with his tongue, licking and playing with her mouth. A tremor bolted right through her, and her emotions surged. She pulled her lips away, her breath erratic. "I don't want to say good night."

His eyes intense ensnared hers like magic. "There's only one way not to say good night."

EIGHT

The idyllic Caribbean paradise with its lush natural beauty and its superb climate were all Carla could think about as Cole's hot sweltering lips met hers again in a heated, drugging kiss. Tantalizing little kisses were being rained on her, engulfing and claiming her in the name of seduction. He nibbled at her lower lip, nuzzled his tongue into the secret warm interior of her mouth, pulled passion from the languid, wet taste he found there, letting every brush of his lips tell her how much he desired to show her what he could do. She breathed his name, groaning softly and moved her lips to his throat, standing on tiptoes to trail kisses along its length, giving herself time to steady her heart rate.

But Cole pulled her back to his lips, exerting a low groan as he lifted her into the air and twirled her around, showing her off to the moonlight. It was the most romantic thing. Wondrous. Stupendous. She was trembling from the experience when he placed her back on her feet in the warm carpet of breeze-swept sand to look at her. "Cole . . . I feel—"

"I know," he gasped. "Come on." He pulled her hand steadily, leading her back toward the hotel. They reached her room far quicker than when they'd left there. Closing the door behind them, Cole leaned his back against it and gently pulled Carla to his hardened chest. Her mouth was open, waiting for him the moment he claimed her lips. She felt wild and hot, almost undressed in his arms and he longed more than ever to lose himself in her.

His lips outlined her mouth, delved in for a sweet arousing taste, then deepened when he got the response he wanted. Carla craved him as much as he craved her. She measured his need in direct equal proportions of relished, crazy unadulterated appetite. They were both hungry for each other, famished to feed their sexual longing, greedy with keen desire to fill their mad lust of pining emotion.

They kissed with all the fondness and attachment they'd developed throughout the days spent together, adoring the fiery spasms that caused their lips to tingle with ardent passion. Carla felt weakened by the overwhelming tenderness within her, like she was melting into liquid with no bone structure to hold on to.

Almost falling, she felt uprooted from her feet yet again, this time swept up in Cole's arms as he carried her over to the bed. His lips never left hers. He continued his amorous claim on them, captivating Carla completely as he lowered her to the bed. He joined her to cuddle her into him, feeling crazy when she lifted her lips to greet him in wanting.

Locked again, Carla snuggled even closer, caressing Cole's cheeks before her fingers dropped to his lips. "I like you so much," she whispered on a hoarse, throaty note.

He kissed her fingertips, each in turn. "I want to undress you." His eyes drew her to him. He could see her so clearly. The moonlight invaded through the window where he'd earlier pulled back net curtains. It shone down on her face of surrender as her loveable gaze consented to his touch. Carla felt him slowly lower the zip at the back of her dress and her breath feathered against his throat when his warm hand tickled her bare spine. He looked down into her face, and the feeling between them intensified as he slowly pulled the fabric from her trembling limbs.

She had been wearing no bra so her breasts became instantly exposed to the enraptured gaze reflected deeply in Cole's eyes. He wasn't slow in brushing the back of his hand against them, gently charting his way to their delicate brown peaks. Carla gasped in delight at the exquisite sensation when his fingertips acquainted with one of her nipples. He twisted it between his fingers gently and she closed her eyes, enjoying the expertise with which he handled her. Instinctively she wanted to kiss his chest, but a fear held her back. She reminded herself that she was unaccustomed to doing so.

"Touch me." Cole coaxed her gently.

Carla sensed that he knew she wanted to feel him. "I can't. I . . . I don't know." She turned her head away. "Darnell—he never encouraged me that way."

Cole raised his head, stunned. "You never touched him?"

"He . . . he never liked me to . . ." She was gasping with embarrassment and with delight because Cole hadn't stopped caressing her breasts.

He pressed his forehead against hers and kissed her cheek until she instinctively turned her face back toward him. "What did you guys do?"

Carla closed her eyes. "He was always quick. I . . . I didn't mind."

Cole growled murderously. As a man, he knew Darnell had used her. It was easy for his sex to do that for quick gratification. He'd never been that insensitive, but he knew pals of his who were, and there had been a time when he himself had been tempted to take a woman so easily. It didn't take skill, just a quick fondle and a few strategic kisses. If a woman wasn't demanding or wasn't awakened to her sexual needs, then it was a safe option to use her that way. He kissed Carla on her lips, intent that he would make her discover her needs. "I mind," he told her, his hand sensing the hot passion he knew lay hidden beneath her skin. "Haven't there been others?"

"In my early twenties . . . I tried, with three. I wasn't good at it." Carla closed her eyes again. "I can't remember what they were like."

"You've been with Darnell too long," Cole sighed, kissing her again, determined that his line of questioning would not sedate her. He wanted to keep her on fire. He was going to show her just how hot it could be. "Tonight I'm going to teach you how to touch me." He kissed her lips. "And I'm going to touch you." He kissed her again. "And together we're going to enjoy this."

Carla melted as he sucked her lips into his, enthralled by her own honesty and his. Then Cole laced his fingers into hers, pulling her hand gently to his chest. "You can help me undress." He placed her hand against his waistcoat, moving to rest on his knees as he did so. Carla sat up, the fabric of her dress dropping to her endowed hipline as she, too, positioned herself on her knees and faced him.

Cole stroked her breast tenderly as she pulled away his waistcoat and took courage to embark on removing his shirt. Her fingers were trembling. She'd never undressed a man before. Darnell had always come to bed eighty percent ready. She would always be the minuscule twenty percent that he needed.

But with Cole it was different. They were both evenly matched. As she undressed him, he caressed her breasts. When she attacked his belt, releasing the catch, he brushed kisses along her neckline to her shoulder. She pulled his cream trousers over his buttocks and found herself marveling in the way he planted kisses wherever his fingers touched.

She was inflamed with desire by the time she pulled his trousers from his legs, and he in kind removed the remnants of her dress down over her thighs, dropping it carelessly to the floor to join her clothes with his. She didn't feel nervous or fearful as she expected she would. Instead, crazy bewilderment had followed her every movement.

Cole pulled her down to lie beside him. "Touch me here." He placed her hand against his chest, and Carla felt his tremor beneath her fingers. Embarrassed, she pulled away, but Cole chuckled softly and replaced her fingers. "You're being shy with me." He reached up and kissed her neck. "Don't. Trust me." His own fingers stroked gently against her breast.

Carla relaxed instantly and worked her fingers softly against the hardened flesh where curls of hair rubbed into her. She felt the wide expanse of his muscles and brushed against them gently, moving downward to the rigid flesh of his flat stomach. Looking down at her handiwork, at Cole's amber-colored limbs in the light of the moon, she could hardly believe that he was allowing her to touch him so easily.

Everything male about him was there for her, ripe and waiting, and she almost shook with anticipated delight in thinking whether she should dare move down any further. To remove Cole's white boxer shorts would be the ultimate task, and she felt uncertain whether she could do that. Yet as her fingers worked in circular motions, and she saw Cole's rigid shaft pulsate with urgency beneath those very boxer shorts, she gingerly risked moving ever downward until she brushed a light stroke against his flank.

Cole moaned. "Baby, you hit the spot."

Carla stiffened, heightened with desire, yet afraid; she moved her hand away. She hadn't made love in such a while, and this was all new to her because Darnell had never allowed her to behave with him in this way. "Cole, I'm nervous—"

She was silenced. Cole dragged her into his arms and kissed her thoroughly. "I'm going to play with you," he said, the very words coaxing her to open up to him. He kissed her behind one ear, in the soft spot behind the lobe. He then moved down to the insides of her wrists and kissed her there, too. Then her toes received the pliable brush of his lips before he deftly attacked the undersole of her heels. And when his lips trailed upward, nibbling at the tawny-brown flesh of her calf, she delighted in the soft feel of his mouth as it rested against her thigh.

Cole touched her in places Darnell never ventured to go, and she was enjoying every minute of this extrasensory discovery. He replaced his lips with his hand and feathered the soft inner skin of her thigh. "Do you like the way I touch you?" he asked huskily.

"Yes," Carla opined in response.

"I want to touch you here." Within seconds he'd removed her lace panties and placed his hand against the thick, damp curls which he was intent on exploring.

"Cole . . . no . . ." Carla couldn't remember the last time when she'd ever been touched there. She was about to shake with involuntary alarm when an exquisite heat of delight took over and rendered her into a complete frenzy. Cole's fingers were working intimately into her folds, caressing so expertly, she felt herself moan and relax at a stroke, greedy for him to go on.

Her eyes closed and she was lost, somewhere pleasurable. Love overflowed under the hand of this man. Her sensitive bud, eager for something much more intense, throbbed violently and a quiet scream erupted from her throat when Cole gave her what she wanted, his fingers applying just enough pressure to have her yearning.

Everything within her begged for him and something intensely female, she couldn't explain from where it came, demanded that her fingers work on him just as intimately. With a vigorous squeal that propelled her body to him and caused her thighs to lift upward, Carla grabbed hold of Cole's wrist, halting his delicate movement. He seemed to understand as she aggressively rolled him on his back and silently began to remove his white boxer shorts from beneath him. Words wore irrelevant. He was ready for her. Ready to feel the kisses she longed to give him.

Carla's senses heightened quickly, knowing she could please this man. She'd gone from terror of rejection to bold lover, learning quickly to concentrate her kisses in small areas of Cole's body, like he had done with hers. Her butterfly strokes massaged his buttocks and thighs and she licked at his navel, reveling in the way his body tensed, his heart thumping for the want of her.

Her tongue played with his nipples, going from one to the other, and she got gutsy by following an invisible trail right up to his right ear. Blood pounded in her temples as she nibbled his lobe before taking manageable bites, giving him pleasure. And it wasn't long before she worked her way down again, losing all her inhibitions in every brush of her lips.

She didn't feel like the same woman, whose sexual impulses and desires had been suppressed over the years. Her mother had always taught her that sex, except from a puritanical marital state, was amoral. God would seek reprisals, she'd said, and there had been a time in her deepest moments of despair when she'd thought he'd done just that, his punishment in giving her Darnell, a man so predictable and lacking in imagination and who'd become violent.

Now a new *C* word urged her on—*confidence* played across her racy mind. She'd certainly attained that with Cole, thankful that he'd also introduced her to *courage.* Tilting her head, her mind adrift, she sought his shaft and applied enough pressure with her lips to have his thoughts running free and wild, as were her own. He pulsed with urgency and she worked his hard, rigid flesh lovingly. He rolled her onto her back and reached his hand to the floor to feel his way to the pocket of his trousers. He grimaced with impatience when he couldn't easily locate what he wanted.

Carla turned and planted kisses along Cole's back, sensing his relief when he returned his attention to her, armed with a packet of condoms. "Let me put it on you." She surprised herself.

Cole smiled, deeply aroused. "Baby, you slay me." He kissed her, handing over the entire packet, his body and mind eager to feel Carla's hands against him.

Carla worked slowly, removing one of the items. She'd never done this before. But she was gentle, her sultry effort concentrated as she applied with ease the protection that they both needed. Cole was instantaneous, putting his weight on top of her. She was so small and petite against his tall frame and built-up muscles, he decided against that position and instead pulled himself to his knees. Burning with need, he wanted to feel himself inside her, felt he could wait no longer.

He took hold of her waist, running feather strokes against it before he pulled Carla to join him on his lap. Her legs straddled him and curled around his hips. Her mind-set was in perfect unison with his. Blood rushed through him like the Martha Brae River when he worked his way into her, gently probing against her tightness until she relaxed to accept him.

Carla closed one arm around Cole's neck, her throat parched and panting as her body filled with him, measure for measure. She kissed the top of his shaven head, brushing her lips against the sides, and her free hand worked into the small of his back, her mind totally abandoned to him. She'd once told him that she would never love again, but that now felt like an age-old proverb. Every sweet movement, every hot thrust, every rise of him within her sent a fierce twist of ecstatic pressure to the deepest part of her womb, making her gloriously aware that she possessed every female facet to love again.

Cole, too, was swept away by the magic between them. Carla was a quick learner. He'd made her relaxed enough to want to please him, and her response had set him on fire. If years of searching for that one woman he longed to find had led him anywhere, it was straight into the arms of this alluring beauty, who possessed the most tender touch he'd ever known. They were two people exchanging hearts as he moved with her, as he kissed her cheek and enjoyed the way she read his thoughts and moved her lips to capture his in the moonlight.

His tongue delved into her mouth and followed the pattern of their body rhythm, riding the crest of a tidal wave that was making to hit the shore. For him, it was the ultimate dream to make this woman a part of him. For Carla, it gave her a deeper understanding of herself. Heat, sweat, torment, and memories climbed the wave with her, provoking at her desire.

All her life she had been dominated, first by her mother and then Darnell, forcing her into a race against herself to prove that they couldn't outdo her. She was a survivor, invincible, unbeaten—and she didn't need anyone anymore. She'd told herself that so often, she hadn't realized she'd come to believe it. Now, she realized she could actually share herself. Not everyone was out to control her because Cole had never been that. He'd shown her that she could be secure with herself, that she could learn to trust someone at last.

She trusted him. She longed for him. Her panting screams and gasps of delight told her she was in total surrender only to him. They rode the wave together until it came crashing down around them, hitting the shore with such gigantic force, she became lightheaded and dizzy, hardly conscious when Cole ground his last thrust of ecstasy into her. She collapsed against his shoulders, totally exhausted, her emotions shaken and rocky. Suddenly tears fell from her eyes. The reason eluded her as to why she was crying.

"Carla?" Cole's fingers ran a snake's trail down her back.

"Hold me." She sobbed.

He held her. He kissed her neck. There was no going back for her now. Cole rocked Carla gently in the light of the moon that broke through the window, knowing he hadn't physically hurt her. She belonged to him and he belonged to her. That's why she was crying. She'd finally come to terms with shedding her past, relinquishing hurtful and heartfelt memories, and her cry of lust and anguished emotional pain was the release he felt so glad he had given her.

"Carla?"

"Don't say anything," she cried.

"Carla." He brushed a kiss against her lips, taking her wet tears into his mouth, as he had done before. "There's something I want you to know."

"Please . . ." Carla looked at him, shaking her head in denial.

Maybe it was too soon to tell her anything, Cole realized. But he could still feel himself pressed so deeply into her, and he knew how much he wanted this woman to be a part of his life, to be a part of his soul. His cocoa-brown eyes ensnared hers with sincerity, tugging at her heartstrings as he whispered into her ear: "I think we're beginning to mean something to one another."

Stiff with exhaustion, Carla held her breath when the bed rocked and she heard Cole make himself comfortable, rubbing her shoulder as she lay silently against his chest. Ears straining in the darkness, she waited for the change in his breathing to tell her that he'd fallen asleep. Only then did she begin to relax, despairing that she would not be able to sleep herself.

What he'd told her troubled her immensely. She didn't want to hurt him, something she'd decided already. She was a woman on the edge, still coming to terms with who she was, and though Cole had done so much in urging her to find herself, she couldn't help but feel he deserved someone who hadn't been hurt. And besides, she would be returning to England the day after tomorrow, giving Robyn ample opportunity to bore her claws into him. He would soon forget her in an instant, she thought.

Men were like that, she reminded herself pathetically. They never made plans once they left a woman's bed. She shouldn't take him seriously, his endearment about their meaning something to one another. They'd just made love and his emotions were high, definitely the wrong time and wrong place to verbally spill out the feelings that were running riot in his gut.

She was being cynical again. Perhaps she should . . . She yawned. Her body took charge, drawing her into an uneasy stupor. Finally she fell into a deep and somewhat troublesome sleep.

Her own scream awoke her, hours later. Carla found herself sitting up in the darkness, her limbs shaking with her hands frantically moving around for something. Beside her, Cole was shaken into immediate wakefulness, hand shooting out to switch on a light by the bed as he, too, sat up. "Carla?" He shook her out of it.

Still trembling, Carla dropped her head into her hands and turned to face him. Cole's arms enclosed her at once, rubbing gently against her perspired body. "What happened?" she gasped.

"You had a nightmare."

She heaved sickly, rubbing her wet tongue around her dry lips, knowing that the past had returned to haunt her. "Oh, God."

"Can you remember any of it?" Cole asked softly.

Dread coursed her body. "He was sneering at me again. He always did that when . . . when . . ."

"When what?" Cole demanded.

Carla shook her head, trying to piece it all together. "When he was . . . angry," she sighed. "But I don't understand about . . . about the water."

Cole stilled for a moment, slowly rationalizing the situation. His hand moved from her shoulder down to her wrist. "What do you see when you see the water?"

"I don't know." Carla felt confused. "I just seem to hear the sound of someone screaming."

"Carla." Cole's voice was firm even though it held all the resonant tones of compassion. "Have you had any victim support for Darnell's behavior toward you?"

Carla's mind spiraled. "What?"

He looked at her sternly. "Any counseling or therapy?"

"I don't need a shrink," Carla bellowed so aggressively that Cole held up both hands in surrender. She'd had her fill of playing lay psychiatrist and balancing her tsubo points with the yin and the yang.

"I'm just asking," Cole reasoned in a helpless, teasing tone. "Don't shoot the lover."

Carla smiled weakly, even attempted at falling into the joke. "If I hear another homespun word of philosophy out of you, I'll be asking you to draw, with a kiss."

Cole lowered his hand to her wrist again, becoming serious. "I was only thinking that maybe you should talk to someone. You've been hurt and—"

"Only from his deception and I'm fine now." She convinced herself. "Besides, I've talked to most of my friends, who've all been more than supportive, and I'm talking to you, aren't I? I haven't talked to any man the way I've talked to you. So I've licked my wounds from a lovebug's bite, and I don't want to be bitten again."

"Not even by me?" Cole asked, his eyes softening with seduction. "I knew it was going to be hot with us."

"It's been hot with you before, you told me," Carla wavered.

"But I've never been scorched." Cole's hand dropped to her waist. "And you've burned me to a bruise."

His deep voice turned her on instantly. "Cole."

He recognized it in her tone. "You're tender."

"I'll be all right."

"I know. In my book, you're one hundred percent all right"

She laughed. "I bet you've said that to every woman you've slept with."

"I haven't." Cole was serious. "Only to you. And when I told you that we're beginning to mean something to one another, I haven't told a woman that before, either."

Carla grew nervous. She was unsure how to react because out of all the *C* words she'd grown accustomed to using, there was one that frightened her immensely and irrevocably: *commitment.* She was petrified of that one. "Cole . . . I . . ."

"Hush." He gently laid her against him. "Let's get some sleep. We can talk in the morning."

For Carla, the minutes seemed to go by like hours as she nestled against Cole's breathing chest, but finally she became aware of Cole's heart beating solidly under her ear, a steady, comforting rhythm that ebbed her slowly into sedation. Her eyelids drooped until they closed completely. She slipped into sleep with a quiet soft moan that reminded the man who held her of a lost, lonely child.

The sky had not yet paled to day when Carla awoke. Cole was not in the bed, and she turned and sat up to find him on the floor, putting all his energy into doing pushups. She had suspected he pumped iron daily to build up his biceps, but working out in the early hours of the morning had never crossed her mind. "What are you doing?" she remonstrated, absently pulling the sheet over her chest, even though she could see quite clearly his actions.

She caught him unawares. Cole paused long enough to glance over at her. "Good morning," he panted heavily. "Just two more, then I'm done."

"You do this every morning?" Carla inquired, watching as he worked. He was dressed in his boxer shorts, and his naked back and chest were perspired with sweat that seemed to glisten in the dusk that spelled the dawn of a new day.

"Most mornings," Cole breathed, finally pushing himself to his knees. "It clears my head." He breathed before he stood on his feet. Walking over to the bed, he sat down at the side of her. "How are you feeling?"

Carla shook her head in denial. She knew Cole was referring to her terrible nightmare, but she deliberately decided to make her own interpretation. Not daring to look at him, she uttered, "I'm fine. You?"

Cole smiled wickedly, running a lazy hand down her arm. "I enjoyed you last night."

Carla allowed herself to smile as she looked at him with relief. "You were good, too."

"I made you feel good?"

"You made me feel great," she told him shyly.

He delved to pull the sheet away from her chest, his eyes intensifying as they caught the bare exposure of her breasts. Cole's strong hands tentatively brushed the soft peaks of first one breast and then the other, absorbing with delight as they swelled and hardened to his touch. He heard Carla moan and looked into her face, detecting that his slow, coaxing movements were causing blood to rush into her cheeks. Her sable eyes locked with his in amorous invitation, and suddenly he felt his manhood rise, ready to take her.

His arms swept around her waist and he pulled her to his muscled frame, kissing her with all the pent-up emotions he had hoped to release in his workout. He'd sensed that Carla wasn't ready to hear what he'd told her last night and it worried him to the point that he blamed himself for her nightmare. He should've known better than to tell a woman something so revealing so soon, especially after only spending such a short time together. But he felt like he'd known her a lifetime. Everything about her seemed to evoke some understanding in him. He understood her. It was time he made her understand him, made her know that he could never be a jackass of a man like Darnell. He would show her with his lips, with his fingers, with his very being, he told himself wholeheartedly as he kissed her ardently, lowering her back down onto the bed.

Carla wrapped her arms around Cole's neck and savored every part of his hot body pressed so close to hers. The heat that projected from him enveloped her so quickly that she felt instantly submissive to the animal passion that possessed them both. She pulled him to her and kissed him passionately, skirting her tongue between his teeth as she felt herself loosen into his embrace.

Cole was ultra-quick in accepting every part of her. He was much more impatient than he had been earlier in the night. In the throes of passion, his urgency impelled him to rip the sheet aside which covered Carla's limbs before he swiftly shifted on top of her, his heart drumming at mad speed, knowing that she wanted him like this.

And Carla welcomed his dashing, impetuous haste. She was in complete abandon the moment he'd exposed her bare breasts to his sensitive gaze, even more so now that he'd exposed her completely. Her heart rate quickened, and their kiss deepened in yearning. The fast-paced love play was just what she needed to take her mind off the disturbance she'd created in the night.

"Baby, I need a condom." Cole was lost to her for brief seconds as he left the bed, though the ache in his voice never left her senses. As she awaited his return, the silent echo washed over her completely, invigorating her nerve endings, touch zones, and amorous emotions.

When he was back, moaning in anticipation as he positioned himself between her thighs, she almost sobbed with pleasure at seeing the contorted expression of pain and ecstasy reflected in his eyes. Raising her hips, she coaxed him into her, her breath panting, taking his thrusts as they became even fiercer. He felt so sweet, her body was thoroughly shaken. "Cole, don't you dare stop," she almost growled as her feelings ran rampant.

"I'm going to take you all the way there, baby," Cole promised in a gasping whisper, his pace becoming more urgent, inspired by how much she was enjoying him. He kissed her again harder, more insistent, and together they rode another crest in the wave until their bodies stiffened and the world vibrated with the force of a crashing tide.

Carla felt like she had the strength of a lioness as she descended from her euphoria, sated and happy. She felt as though she could easily conquer the world, too, just like a lioness when it hunted and caught its prey. And in that instinctive, primitive, dizzying height of jungle awareness where knowledge taught her that a lioness always bit its prey to bespeak that it belonged to her, she reached up and bit her teeth into Cole's neck.

He looked down into her sable-colored eyes in sublime happiness, not understanding why she'd made such a tactual gesture. Yet Carla was amazed when he bent his head and, in kind, bit into the side of her neck. She didn't know whether lions caught their prey in that way, but if they did, she felt certain that Cole was telling her that he belonged to her, too.

As he pulled away from her and they snuggled into the warmth of each other, she slept peacefully and dreamlessly into the early hours of the morning.

NINE

"What time is it?" Carla whispered in a strange languor, as she became fully awake and reached out for Cole only to find the bed empty. In a sudden panic, she sat up and looked around. The midday sun cast its rays through the window to alight upon the ruffled sheets which encased her body and as her eyes focused, Cole strode from the bathroom fully dressed.

He looked adoring, his face washed with hardly a night's stubble evident across his jawline. Without hesitation, he crossed the room and took her in his arms, kissing her long and lingeringly. "Good morning." His voice was full of mirth as he sat down beside her on the bed.

"Good morning to you, too," Carla returned in kind.

"So. This is your last day in Jamaica," he sounded out, the ache rich in his voice.

Carla nodded, though the weight of leaving felt heavy in her heart. She felt as though she'd found something with Cole that she couldn't bear to lose, and yet she was still too protective of her heart to risk disassociating herself with solitude because she'd grown to know it so well. She had learned harsh lessons in life, and somehow Cole had managed to see them in her eyes and in the way she'd behaved since coming there. Yet he'd extracted something from her that had made her submit to her true self, the one with dreams and expectations she'd never hoped to find.

"I will always remember my trip here," she told Cole nervously. "I feel like . . . I've found a part of myself."

"Did I help you do that?" Cole's voice suddenly became serious.

Carla nodded.

He took her hand and held it gently. "We can still see each other, you know."

Carla immediately shook her head, unconvinced. "Will it last long?"

"What?"

"Us?"

"Why do women always worry about the end rather than the beginning?" Cole asked irritated.

"Because I have dreams," Carla admitted shakily, tears welling in her eyes.

"Dreams?"

"You know," Carla bit back harshly, resentful almost in admitting them to Cole, let alone to herself. "Of a life with somebody, of having children with someone."

"You like children?"

"I love children. Don't you?"

"I've never really thought about it." Cole shook his head as though dazed. "Yes, I have thought about it," he admitted quietly after thought, rubbing her hand as though approaching the conversation was leaving him uncomfortable. "My mother did a good job in raising me, so I guess I know what kind of parent I'd like to be. I never felt unbalanced, not having a father, but I didn't like his absence, either. And if I'm really truthful about it, I did resent my mother in some way for it. There was a time in my life when I needed a stronger guiding hand, something much firmer than what she could offer. I think one of the reasons why I was so good for my mother is because I never wanted to hurt her. I never wanted her to cry a tear for me because I always knew somehow that it was because of me why she felt so much pain."

"So you knew she left Jamaica because of you?" Carla asked, herself feeling troubled by Cole's inward search to explain himself.

"She talked to me about it one time, when I was fifteen," Cole began. "I was very eager back then to know about him. And she did begin to explain, but not enough. I also got the impression that he was someone Papa Peter would not have approved of. I was a mistake. I should not have happened, and she did tell me that Papa Peter was making demands on her to disclose to him my father's name."

"But she didn't," Carla interjected.

"No," Cole affirmed. "She chose to leave Jamaica. I don't think she was ever banned from Eden Lea, not really."

"So you think the circumstances of you being born were—"

"I don't want to speculate on it, Carla," Cole said, pained. "My mother obviously didn't like to think about it. In my life, it was just her, me, and God. She never married, she never seemed to really have men around, though I do remember two that discreetly came and went. My idea of a role model came from questioning myself and, yes, listening to Mom. She always told me that if I don't want to be somebody then I'm not going to be somebody, and that if a white boy could so something then I had to learn to do it better."

"My mother said I couldn't have everything," Carla recalled wistfully, appreciating the way Cole was opening up to her so readily.

"Mine said I could," Cole answered slowly. "She may

have lived her life full of pain, but she was focused where I was concerned. That's why I feel I understand what you went through, what you're going through." Cole's voice grew more heartfelt. "And when I think about children, if I do have them, I want to be around—so the mother of my children has to be someone pretty special."

Like Robyn, Carla thought, fully aware that she was leaving in the morning. "So you have an idea what you're looking for?" The words tumbled from her lips uneasily.

Cole's eyes penetrated hers. "There are a lot of men who are not looking for anything more than a pretty young thing who's sexually active and available," he began, rationalizing reality. "And there are plenty of women who spoil themselves by giving in to such shallow morals."

"And those who don't give in are sometimes left with a man who wanted less than they were giving," Carla added.

"That, too," Cole agreed. "But I want something more. I want someone special with an intelligent mind, with a warm and caring nature. I want her to feel that she can trust me and that I can trust her, inexplicably. That goodness in your heart you were talking about that you want to find in someone, I'm looking for that, too. All those things in a woman make a special beauty shine through that attracts a man—and, baby, you have that beauty with a vengeance."

Carla felt shaken. Justifiably so, since she'd never expected to hear such heartfelt feelings. Suddenly she felt unable to handle what Cole was telling her. Sickly feelings were churning in her stomach, and an apprehension gripped her so tightly she almost felt choked by the nauseating, suffocating emotion. She reminded herself that she was still that same woman on the edge, who was childlike and vulnerable, still in need of healing. That little kitten frightened of water. Cole was moving too fast. Since her coming to Jamaica, he had swamped her with emotions, all kinds of feelings that had led them to making love. And she had been swept into his hold on her, into this fascination that she'd found in him. But now, she had to take stock, she had to act. They had begun to mean something to one another, as he'd said, and it seemed that she would have to be the one to take control.

"Cole"—she hesitated, noting that her voice sounded weak because she was about to lie—"I'm not going to mean anything to you, not the way you want me to. You're looking for something else. You sound like you want a woman without a past, and I can never be that. I'm leaving in the morning, and I'm glad that we will be working together, but you have to let me go to find what it is you really want."

Cole glared at her, uncomprehending, though Carla saw the genuine hurtful flicker cross his cocoa-brown gaze. "Carla," he sighed heavily, rubbing absently at her fingers, his tone indicating that he was no longer intent on pursuing the topic. "What am I going to do about you?"

Weakened by her own turmoil, by the passionate night they'd spent together, by her denial in trying to accept any kind of future for herself, Carla removed her hand from Cole's and rose from the bed, pulling the top layer of sheet with her. "I think I'll shower and get dressed," she said, failing to propel strength into her voice. Without a backward glance at Cole, she quickly picked at some clothes, then rushed into the bathroom, craving solace.

The safe haven of the shower cubicle didn't leave her feeling any more comfortable. She began to wonder what exactly it was she'd done. But she didn't want to face giving herself an answer. Too much was going on inside, and she disliked immensely the way it was making her feel presently: light-headed, nervous, panicky even.

When she left the bathroom, fully clothed, her expression schooled carefully to mask the turbulence she held within, she was to find Cole still sitting on the bed, counting U.S. currency which he'd extracted from his wallet. A simple guess told her that it was at least six hundred dollars, then she remembered that he was expecting to visit Kingston that day to buy information. "Cole"—she marched over to him—"do you really need all that?"

"It's palm oil," Cole answered lightly, carefully replacing the twenty- and fifty-dollar bills back into his wallet. "I need it to grease someone's palm in Kingston for that information I was telling you about."

"Cole, I don't like this." Carla felt horrified. Suddenly all her kept-in feelings were beginning to intensify, more sickly than they had done before her shower. "Just call the police. Let them handle it."

"No." Cole overrode her sternly. "If Lucas has anything to do with this, then I want to be the one to catch him. I want to deal with him myself."

"Then I'm coming with you," Carla insisted bluntly.

Cole looked at her, shrugging noncommittally. He wasn't going to argue with her because his emotions were too raw to deal with that. This would be the one time he had left to spend with Carla McIntyre, and he was not going to waste it, especially when he needed her near him. "Okay," he jabbed. "We're leaving now."

What isn't known is often feared. That was how Carla McIntyre felt when she and Cole entered Kingston that afternoon. The ride had taken nearly three hours from the Trelawny Beach Hotel, and she had felt numb all the way, not knowing what confrontation they were to expect when Cole kept his meeting, as arranged.

Her feelings for him had intensified throughout the journey. She felt genuine worry for him. Perhaps it was because they'd made love, and her emotions were still causing havoc within. Or perhaps it was because she'd found something within herself that she didn't really want to admit to: the part where she now believed that she could give love to somebody.

She heard Cole beep his horn, and her sable eyes blinked alert as three street urchins ran out in front of the Toyota Land Cruiser, laughing. "Kids!" Cole ejected a breath.

Carla looked at him, detecting his features to be contorted and troubled. He was weighing how he would handle Lucas, she thought. Was that why Lucas had come into Kingston, to sell stolen coffee? Looking around her, she absorbed the city sights. Her reaction was like that of many people who were regarding a large city for the first time.

She knew it was true that Kingston had a reputation for violence, especially during the troubled nineteen seventies elections where party politics meant the PNP and the JLP tradition of loyalty both went hand in hand with murder and hysteria, and where each party's pressure group had war zones or garrisons, killing shamelessly in the name of political sympathy. Thank goodness those days were now gone, she mused, her memory reminding her that more recent elections had proved that the political anarchy was now over.

But as she now watched the hoard of people squeezed together in small spaces, she became more tangibly aware that when things tended to get a little close, hustlers could hustle, peddlers could peddle, and that a visitor even of the most unscrupulous nature had to be aware of the nuances of city life. London wasn't any different. She'd been mugged there not once, but twice, her purse carefully extracted out of her handbag while she traveled. But she'd wanted to see Kingston, and she tried to relax as the car took smooth twist and turns down the busy streets.

The city was not only Jamaica's government and administrative center but was also a place of music and art, theater, sport, and commercial trade. Her eyes began to quietly digest the numerous large restaurants as they passed by, the architecture which was a combination of old Georgian and modern high-rise, the traffic lights and pedestrian crossings, all of which amplified that she was indeed visiting a busy city.

"Where are we going exactly?" she asked Cole as he took another decisive curve which took them down a place marked Half Way Tree Road.

"Trench Town," Cole answered in response, his eyes keenly trained on the road as he approached another turn where a post office and the Carib Theater pinpointed the juncture.

"That's a ghetto, isn't it?" Carla tentatively inquired. She'd heard of it before, in a Bob Marley reggae tune, a place where the small camps of homeless people were as much a part of Kingston's core culture as the theater and fine food.

"Don't worry," Cole's voice reassured, though it was a little irritated. "You can stay in the car if you want. We're not going to be there very long."

Carla swallowed as the car ventured further, eating into Slipe Road before it veered again, and it wasn't long before the area around them became a little confusing. Dispirited faces tracked their progress: young and old with knotted hair, unkempt clothing, walking with a slow shuffle as though life appeared meaningless, took their time to move out of harm's way as Cole slowed the vehicle to a steady crawling pace, the windows rolled down to allay suspicion. Carla's heart felt panicky as she observed the clusters who were trying to make a life on the coarse streets and dwelling-stacked slums who seemed content to watch their world amble by. She could almost feel the energy of indigence exude from the eyes of those looking on, their expression distrustful, resolution implanted on their foreheads that their lives were destructive, but above all, without life.

She imagined Trench Town to be one of eruptions when the distrust was stretched to breaking proportions, and she also analyzed the culture to be one of whispers, on where the next deal was to go down or what news could ultimately spell an extraction of money. It was hard to believe that this stultifying poverty-stricken part of Jamaica—with its severely political environment and its fortresslike enclave barriers, proof that there was indeed trouble in paradise—had produced the island's two most vibrant of commodities: Rasta and reggae music. As Cole stopped the car and cut the engine in front of an old dilapidated shack that seemed condemned, unsafe for human habitation, a fear gripped the vanguard of her chest, and she eyed him in earnest before her gaze trailed to the graffiti splashed across its walls.

"We're not going in there, are we?" Her voice sounded unreal.

"Carla, I have to do this," Cole affirmed slowly, taking her hand and working it between his palms. "I'm not going to let anyone hurt you. We're just going to talk to the man in here and then leave, okay?"

Carla nodded, dumbfounded, agreeing to support him as they stepped from the car, her eyes becoming vigilant as she slowly closed the passenger door then looked around her curiously. Dressed in a white vest shirt and a white skirt, she seemed almost virginal against the slum around her. Following Cole to the scabby front door where part of the shack had crumbled, creating a dangerous hazard for passersby, Carla could hardly imagine that the place was inhabited.

She was not to know as she approached the wood-rotted step that the nearby ghetto residents had seen their fair share of shifty, nervous-looking characters pick their way up that same wooden step upon which she was now embarking and which led into the shack. Inside was dark, even though the intense sun outside was smiling across a flawless blue sky. She stepped on something and turned to find knee-high weeds growing in all directions and there were broken stones, a litter of broken bottles and garbage in a corner, a certain haven for flies, gnats, and mosquitoes. She flinched.

Cole held her hand tight as they followed the weed trail straight into the shack. A fat man, his hair tightly braided in a short, street style met them with a casually sly smile playing against his lips. Cole, too, seemed unsuitably dressed, still in the outerwear he'd worn the night before, as he approached the darkly dressed man, accustomed to his surroundings, and cast him a steadfast glare.

"Mr. . . . er?" the fat man inquired.

"Mr. Er. will do," Cole responded, his eyes narrowing. "I'm in the market for some information. I'm told you're the man who can sell me a hot tip."

"What you after?" The man smiled lazily, walking around an old table to deposit himself in a crooked, worn-out chair. The table was splotched with old paint, and Carla didn't miss the .38 caliber gun that sat at the corner's edge, nearest to the fat man in his chair.

But Cole kept his eyes fixed, noting the interior as she had done. "Shipment of coffee," Cole pressed.

"I see." The man rubbed his chin, thinking, weighing the charge. "What's your currency?"

"U.S. cash."

He eyed Carla speculatively, licking his lips slyly. "Gal in, too?"

"She's with me." Cole squeezed Carla's fingers.

The fat man eyed them both, his harsh eyes and heavy-set brows adopting a sudden menacing appeal that Carla found frightening. Then he scratched his nose and said, "Okay. What y'want know?"

"Ninety kilos, Linden Vale Estate coffee. Who brought the load in?" Cole asked.

The man smiled knowingly. "Yeah, I remember she."

"She?" Cole's eyes traveled to Carla's in amazement then back to the man.

"Worth five hundred for the name and description," the man slurred, assured his knowledge was worth the money.

Cole reached for his wallet, extracting the crisp dollar bills then placed them neatly on the tabletop. "So you can describe the girl?" He put his hand over the money.

"I'll not forget she," the fat man remarked crudely.

"Mature, short hair, around thirty years old?" Cole pretended.

The man looked confused. "No, that's not the girl me see." His eyes rolled widely. "This one have canerow hair—she at least twenty, and she have legs so long me no know where them end. Nice body, good looks. That's the woman me see. She name Tata."

Tata, Carla told herself in amazement.

"Where's the shipment?" Cole demanded, his lips tight holding in his anger. He added another one hundred dollars as a lubricant to coax out the information.

"Runaway Bay," the man offered quickly. "Leaves tomorrow on a boat named *Lady Velvet.*"

"Come on." Cole took Carla's hand in readiness to make their departure.

"If you're in the market for more information, you know where me is," the fat man volunteered. He watched as Cole and Carla left before he reached for the money he'd earned on the table.

Back at the car, Carla was to see young boys dressed in soiled rags and tattered shoes, muttering private litanies to themselves as though they were keeping demons at bay. They were washing the windscreen of the four-wheel drive, and she found the scene to be all too sad, her mind agonizing over why their mothers had chosen to have them as she reached into her bag and pulled out a U.S. five-dollar bill to place it in the hand of the one nearest to her before she quickly reentered the car.

Cole was seething as he, too, threw himself into the driver's seat, hardly glancing at Carla as he ignited the engine. He moved at a fast pace as they left Trench Town and into the throes of traffic before he spoke. "I wonder how long she's been doing this?" he bellowed. "And how?"

Carla shook her head. "Do you think her brother knows?"

"Lucas?" Cole bristled. "Of course. They're bound to be in it together. They're entitled to the family inheritance, aren't they? It's not enough that I kept them working on the estate, that I treated them as a cousin should. Greed is what's going on here," he told Carla. "They want what I've got and because of the blood bond, they feel they're entitled. I'll show them entitled."

Carla's heart reached out to Cole. It was unfair that this should be happening now, on her last day in Jamaica, that Cole should be going through so much trouble at a time when she was beginning to think it was time they talked about the marketing of Eden Lea, the reason which had brought her there in the first place—and on a more personal nature, the reasons why she felt compelled not to see their relationship through further.

Even though her senses were heightened by what had transpired in Trench Town, her mind was more trained selfishly on how she would cope once she traveled back to England. She felt out on a limb, half dazed, half drifting, and yet the potency of emotions that Cole was now going through, had its own bearing on her bereft and obscured thoughts.

Anger was what suddenly seeped through her veins. Cole had dragged too much out of her, and she'd known that she was not yet ready to open up to him, to anyone in that way. She'd once been ever intent on proving that point to herself, too, that men were to be despised, certainly to be avoided. It was an unhealthy, jaded view, but having it had protected her, though in some ways it had contributed to her low self-esteem.

Now, she noted her distance, degree, and pitch of adversity had changed somewhat. She'd found something in Cole Richmond, and she asked herself, would she be allowed to keep it? *No,* a tiny little voice in her head pressed, angry and frustrated. He belonged here, in Jamaica, and she belonged in England where her work was all she needed. Would ever need.

Troubled, she looked at Cole handling the steering wheel, suddenly finding herself venting out some frustration at him. "Slow down, Cole," she jabbed harshly. "You're driving much too fast."

"We're being followed," Cole shot back, putting the car into a higher gear.

"What?" Carla gasped, looking behind her through

the rearview mirror. Suddenly her adrenaline pumped and fear gripped her heart.

"I'm going to have to shake them," Cole temporized, determination etched in his profile. "The fat man must think I have more money."

"We should never have come," Carla breathed, watching Cole dodge traffic, her sable eyes anxiously shifting from side to side, praying that he didn't hit anyone. The street was full with people, as any city midafternoon on a busy weekday would be.

As he made a fast run, a bus approached them and sounded out a wailing plea that they move out of the way. Carla screamed as the car veered sideways, the tires screeching from brushing harshly against the pavement before it landed back on all four wheels, venturing further along the road to take them out of Kingston. She gripped her seat, one hand groping desperately at her chest in a frantic attempt to check that she was wearing her seat belt.

"Damn." Cole's voice held steel as the blast of a jeep's hostile horn alerted his senses. He steered and made a mad pace down the street, looking into his rearview mirror as he progressed along. The weaving inside and outside of traffic seemed to go on endlessly, hitting the sidewalk, skidding toward the curb, catching its balance only to go along further. Cole had his full weight on the gas pedal and kept it there as the bumper hit a pile of garbage dumped on the pavement's edge, spreading litter everywhere as bags bursted open, their contents springing in all directions. And as it roared past, barely missing a street vendor, Carla felt herself on the verge of supreme panic.

Then as tall green trees began to loom up against them, the air becoming less frantic, even seeming cooler, she felt rather than heard the engine slow its pace, knowing that the chase had finally ended. She looked at Cole murderously, her emotions heightened that he had yet propelled her into another emotional morass. "You could have gotten us both killed," she yelled.

Cole glared at her, shaking his head in amazement before he fixed his eyes back on the road. "Are you all right?"

"No."

"I'm so sorry."

"Not as sorry as I am."

He looked at her again. "What does that mean?"

"You just had to do this, didn't you?" she said violently, releasing her frustration. "It's not enough to just ask your cousin or check things out properly at the plantation. You just had to take over."

"Take over?" Becoming annoyed now, Cole protested. "I'm not the one who's stealing coffee, behaving unreasonably, trying to—"

"There are ways of sorting things out," Carla interrupted, not sure of what she was saying. She didn't really know Lucas or Tata, so she knew she wasn't suggesting how he should proceed to sort things out with them. Somehow she was tangibly aware that she was talking about them, and Cole's perception astonished her when his answer tapped into her confused mind.

"You're talking about us, aren't you?"

"Am I? Am I really?" she denied. Spots of anger colored her cheeks, and she felt uncomfortable, even fretful as she sat there in the car.

Cole shot her a fulminating look. "Talk to me, Carla."

"About what?" she jabbed.

"About what's going on in your head." Cole's voice sounded urgent.

"There's nothing going on that I can't sort out myself," Carla returned angrily. "Just don't interfere in my life."

"Interfere!" Cole was struggling to contain his anger. "I don't want to interfere, Carla. I want to be part of it."

"I don't want you to be," Carla shot back. "My life is in England and yours is here, looking after the plantation that you inherited. It's my fault. I should never have allowed my work to get me so close, but you're so good at rationalizing everything. You're attempting to make me believe in things that are not going to happen. I told you I like solitude."

"You and Mr. Solitude," Cole scoffed contemptuously almost in absurd jealousy. "And what has he taught you exactly? That you've learned the difference between being by yourself and being on your own. Or is he pampering to your solo ego, like when you told me on the beach that you didn't need anyone. I had to kiss you then to force you into believing that you needed something."

"I don't," Carla denied again.

"There. You're doing it again," Cole affirmed, throwing her a furious look. "You have hidden depths full of things you don't want to share. Perhaps can't share for the moment. But don't let me getting to know you cramp you into admitting it to yourself."

"You're doing it again, too," Carla accused him hotly. "Trying to put a perspective on things. It frightens me the way you analyze my life. Why do you do it?"

Cole's voice was filled with anguished defeat. "Because I know what you're going through," he told her, much quietly.

"No, you don't," Carla seethed.

"My mother was like you," Cole began bitterly. "So full of guilt and shame, fear and rejection. As a child,

I absorbed a lot of it. I grew up on two different energies. Knowing that I was infinitely Caribbean and yet Canadian because my mother took me there. It was difficult having a family so far away. You could say that's how my logic began. I questioned everything and everyone. There was a lot of shame when I was born. That's how things were back then. Before we left for Canada, there was a time when I was even my grandmother's son to save face from inquiring strangers. So I do understand Carla, because I have hidden depths, too. And I want to share them with you."

"Don't do this to me." Carla felt shaken. "It won't work. You're talking about . . . unconditional love. And . . . and . . . I'm already immobilized by fear that I won't get that."

"Still so full of self-pity." Cole spat the words at her. "Didn't our making love do anything for you? Didn't it make you open up to me?"

Carla's heart leapt erratically as she thought of what they'd shared. They'd exchanged hearts, and she'd shed tears at the glorious release he'd given her. *We're beginning to mean something to each other,* he'd told her. She didn't take him seriously then, and she didn't want to take him seriously now. The nightmares had returned, and that was enough to tell her that her insecurities needed to he challenged. In retrospect, she knew she needed to challenge her past. As she'd told her uncle, she needed to work her way into the best part of herself.

"What I found with you, Cole, it was special," she began in earnest. "But—"

"It seems nothing short of a crisis is going to force you to open up to me," he repeated angrily. "Remember when I told you that? I also told you that a woman who is afraid of life is a woman who is afraid of love. And you need to be loved, Carla."

Carla's sable-colored eyes grew remorseful. How could she explain to this man that her entire life had been one long ridicule of obscurity, first with Iona McIntyre and then with Darnell Farrell. He was the only one good thing that had ever entered it, but it was so cruel that they would be so far away. How could anything be reconciled with such distance between them. Unconditional love? Where would that enter into the equation? "Cole, I'm sorry." It was all she could say. All she needed to say.

"Damn it all to hell, Carla." Cole kept his eyes on the road.

The rest of their journey back to Falmouth was spent in comparative silence. Neither spoke to the other, except on occasion exchanging confused, despairing glances. Each felt like they'd lost something, lost the wild, free spirit they'd come to find. In Cole's heart, he was filled with desolation and anger with Carla for not surrendering to him. It had been like a natural inbred instinct, from the moment he'd seen her sable-colored eyes, the endowed hipline, and the breasts he'd come to know so well, to want Carla McIntyre.

And he knew he hadn't been mistaken in her want and need for him. The last time they'd made love, she'd done something inexorably primitive. She'd bitten into his neck, a slow, deep, sweet bruising bite, like a lioness, he'd told himself. And feeling primitively male, he'd bitten her back in kind, almost symbolic of his true feelings, that of a lion ensnaring its prey. They'd shared a lovebug's bite that was as deep and effectual as being wounded by it. He'd found what he was looking for, and deep down he knew that she'd found what she wanted, too. But damn it all to hell that she'd ever known Darnell Farrell.

When they'd reached the Trelawny Beach Hotel, Carla stepped exhausted from the car. It was already approaching evening time. Her watch read 7.42 P.M., and she had yet to pack that night for her departure back to London in the morning. Cole took both her hands into his and looked down into her face as they stood together beside the Land Cruiser. "I won't come in," he told her quietly. "You must have a lot of things to sort out, and you need to rest."

Carla nodded, deciding to quickly steer her mind to business. "I'll leave you the folder," she told Cole softly. "Select what you find suitable, the things you liked and let us know. I'm sure we can work together without . . . with an understanding."

Cole shook his head. "I feel like you're escaping me."

Carla trembled. "It's best this way." She removed her hands cautiously. "I have to go." She didn't look back as she walked away nor as she heard the sound of a songbird warbling overhead in the evening silence. It put her in mind of the Harry Belafonte song, 'Jamaica Farewell.' The songbird was singing her farewell to Cole. And as he watched her walk away, swallowed quickly into the interior of the hotel, the ethereal sound of the bird stirred his heart. His mouth tasted like ashes, his heart felt like stone.

TEN

You're not fooling anyone but yourself. Carla sighed heavily as she entered her apartment and closed the door behind her. She lived on the top floor of an imposing terrace of six-story converted Victorian-style apartments situated in Bloomsbury, London, near the British Museum. The prosperous-looking street was guarded by columns of old trees and was a place where she could glimpse familiar lawns and hedges. She liked the dormers, bay windows, and solid front doors with their fanlights and latticed glass and the elderly neighbors who were always informally adopted to help her feel closed in and obscure.

The world became a very small place as the deathly thud of her front door shut out the early evening echo of rush-hour traffic which sounded from the hallway passage, giving her an eerie feeling when the lock clicked, another reminder that she was now alone.

The first reminder had shook her rigid when she arrived at Heathrow International Airport in London, her mind filled with thoughts of Cole Richmond. She hadn't wanted to leave him, not really, and the circumstances in which they'd parted were not good, either. She hated leaving him so troubled and with family problems complicating his life. If truth be told, she'd actually wondered what it would be like sharing those problems with him, easing his troubles. But a nightmare dogged her, telling her that she should check herself. Was it really what she wanted?

Her dejected solitary figure deposited her leather suitcase against the native Indian-style rug which decorated her simply designed hallway. A pile of mail, over fifty envelopes of white, manila, and polyethylene, indicative of junk mail, instantly confronted her inquiring sable gaze as she began to digest and familiarize herself with the place she'd made her home.

Stooping low to the floor, her mind a quandary of emotions, she bundled up her mail and carried it diligently to the small living room across from the hallway. Turning on the light switch, she felt the cold chill of a room which hadn't been lived in for ten days. Speckles of dust became evident as the bright light shone against the small teak coffee table, the television cabinet, and bounced off the varying dried flowers in delicate vases that provided the renaissance look she'd found so inspiring. She felt sheltered in her brief moment of tranquility before she sighed again and dropped the bundle of mail into the creamy-colored sofa.

She felt tired, even yawned, her thoughts in an oasis far removed from the hubbub of life as she remembered a place called Jamaica with its beaches, hot sun, and flawless blue sky. She remembered the grove of palms, flowery coffee trees, azure waves dashing on a sandy, sun-bleached shore—all parts of a picture that had not faded in her mind or blurred against her dismal homecoming. The image which was one of wonder and fascination against the gray monotonous solitude of her apartment awoke the deeper feelings still present in her gut. In that mental state, one man was indelibly impressed on her lonely mind.

"Oh, Cole," she voiced weakly to herself, surprised

by her pounding heart. She knew immediately what was going on. She was pining for him. If she weren't careful, she told herself, she could turn into an empty husk, just like those shed from his coffee beans that no longer appreciated such delightful things as a hot steaming bath.

In her weariness, she headed straight for the bathroom, sighing irritably as the gush of water from the hot tap stayed cold. "Forget that, then," she voiced out again, wondering what Cole was doing at that precise moment. The distance which was now between them had slipped by unnoticed as she'd slept silently on the plane journey back home. She hadn't been able to eat properly, even though food had been placed in front of her, and that had earned her suspicious glances from the air stewardess, ever alert to nuances of danger.

It was air traffic knowledge to watch out for passengers that did not eat, for it could be an indication that their bodies were housing drugs. And of course, she was returning back from Jamaica, a place where such matters were taken seriously, so eventually she had been able to force down something, even though the taste turned her stomach over.

A sardonic smile played on her lips as she replayed the scene when Cole had driven them into Trench Town. If there had ever been any element of danger throughout her visit, that one had been it. That and the fact that she was now presently in danger of losing her heart to the most gentle, kindest man she'd ever known. Another sardonic smile twisted at her lips. But wasn't that what her life had been? A reaching out to her mother and then to Darnell without receiving the true genuine response she craved.

But Cole had given her a response. He'd dragged emotions out of her. Allowed her to confront herself and the things that she really wanted. She wanted love. She *needed* it. "Oh, damn it all to hell," she yelled at herself, frustrated. It was only when she left the bathroom did she realize she'd echoed Cole.

Annoyed at herself, Carla marched over to her bedroom and threw off the light jacket she was wearing. Kicking off her sandaled shoes, she sat on the edge of her bed, glancing over at the clock which read 8:22 P.M. I should call my uncle, she thought for a moment, before absently reaching for a book which lay by the clock on the bedside cabinet. *Legendary Quotations,* she relayed the title silently, remembering it had been a Christmas gift from her best friend, Paulette. I must call Paulette, she told herself as another reminder. She'll never believe me when I tell her what happened in Jamaica.

A few minutes later she was leaned against the bedpost, engrossed in the first chapter which enlivened her mind.

> And I said to the man who stood at the gate of the year: "Give me a light that I may tread safely into the unknown." And he replied: "Go out into the darkness and put your hand into the hand of God. That shall be to you better than a light, and safer than a known way."—Minnie Louise Haskins.

"Hmm," Carla yawned wearily, turning another page in the book. "God knows." Only God wasn't choosing to give her any answers right now.

After a while, the print began to blur and with a vacant sigh, her head laxly dropped against her pillow. Without quite knowing she was suffering from jet lag, Carla fell into a fast and undisturbed deep sleep.

* * *

When Carla awoke, the sun had already crept over her window and was peeping in through a slit between the drapes. She yawned, before reminding herself where she was and in doing so, slowly sat up on her bed. Her body ached and protested against being fully clothed and having slept in an unsuitable position. Her neck felt stiff, too, and she longed for soothing hands to massage away the strained nerves which pained her there.

She was blinking, trying to put her mind into focus when the telephone in her hallway began to ring. It was the only place a telephone was situated in her apartment, so she found herself walking carefully from her bed, a ragged impression of a woman who's seen better days, as she reached for the phone's handset.

"Carla McIntyre," she whimpered.

"So you're back?" her uncle's voice projected loudly. "What time are you coming into the office today?"

"Oh!" Carla sighed. "What time is it now?"

"Eleven thirty," Uncle Quayle announced.

"Okay. I'll be there by two."

"You okay?" her uncle asked. "Your voice sounds different."

"Empty stomach," Carla winced. "I slept off my jet lag, and I've only just woken up."

"Right then. I'll see you later." The phone clicked dead.

Carla grimaced as she replaced the handset, her mind immediately transporting her thoughts to Cole. Her uncle would want an update on the marketing contract. Perhaps that would be a good time to ask him to handle things. She knew enough about the Linden Vale coffee plantation to devise a strategy plan, and she'd certainly formulated enough marketing ideas on how to make the entire estate a tourist attraction. It was simply a matter of outlining the details in writing and having Cole agree to them before they could commence working with him on his campaign.

So it was quite feasible that she would see him again, a tiny voice in her head told her astutely. And how exactly would she handle that, having told him that she didn't wish him to interfere in her life and that he would be far better off without her? She would not ponder the matter now, she thought, rousing herself into action. She would wash, change, and get herself ready for work. Maybe there she would find the answers she would need.

Uncle Quayle was sat at his office desk, sifting through sheets of paper when Carla entered his open-plan office. It was a comfortable room, rich in plant life, floral pictures on the wall, pale green in decor, and very airy. Her uncle was a person who liked tranquility when he worked, and his chosen environment was an indication of how relaxed he liked to feel.

Her beige heeled shoes sank into the Persian carpet as she diligently made her way over to his desk. At a distance, her uncle was unmistakable. Quayle Wagnall's sleek, perfectly groomed short afro hair, his discreet silk tie, the pristine white collar, and lightweight suit, remarkably free of creases despite his having already worked a full half-day, were all so characteristic of his mild personality. He lifted his head as she seated herself opposite him and smiled, glad that she had returned safely. "Feeling better?" he asked, as he watched her smooth the crease in her pinstriped navy-colored skirt, which coordinated with the jacket that draped her somber shoulders, shielding her from the tepid late August weather.

Carla nodded and offered a smile in return. "I'm fine," she returned, "and I enjoyed the trip."

"So Mr. Richmond wants us to represent him?"

"Yes," Carla stated firmly. "I think before any of us can proceed, he would need to make some changes to the house on the plantation. It's called Eden Lea which has a nice ring to it. It would make a great guest house and museum for visitors. I also made several suggestions to him about advertising, visitor information leaflets, even an estate shop. He seemed to like my ideas, so I left the folder of suggestions with him so he could select what he wants."

"Did you discuss costs?"

"No," Carla admitted. "I thought I'd leave that to you."

"To me?" Her uncle seemed confused.

"Well . . ." Carla hesitated. "I'm not sure how close I want to work on this one. We seemed to have come to an impasse."

"What?"

"Uncle"—Carla dipped her head tearfully—"something happened to me in Jamaica, between Cole Richmond and I. Now I feel like I shouldn't expect anything. I'm frightened to plan, I'm too afraid to look ahead. I feel that . . . if I believe something could come out of it, something good and honest, then I'm fooling myself."

"Carla." Her uncle's smile widened. "I told you before not to give up on love. But I don't understand this . . . this mood swing. You're going to be seeing him again."

"Should I?" Carla was not sure that she should.

"Wait a minute, Carla." Her uncle's voice grew concerned. In fact, he rose out of his chair and walked over to lean his six-foot frame against the desk next to her. "There's always hope."

"Hope?" Carla scoffed, as though the very word was obscene. "There's no such thing. Hope is a word someone invented to have us all believe that there's something to live for."

"In your case, some man to live for," her uncle corrected, sporting his most compelling boyish expression which enhanced the slant of his smile.

Carla glanced at him and wanted to both laugh and cry. Her uncle could be quite comical, even when she felt in despair. He'd always made it plain to her that he wanted her to find love, and there had been times in the last year when he'd gone out of his way to introduce her to what he considered to be upstanding, nonjudgmental men who would have the patience and find the time to get to know her.

But as usual, she'd always been uninterested the moment she began to recognize the game moves or hear the promises of being given the moon and the stars. Her work had always provided her all the comfort and support she would need, but a business trip to Jamaica had changed all that. Now there was a burning heat in her stomach, a deep sensual throbbing between her legs, and her heart felt heavy, weakened by the turmoil of emotions that seemed to be making her uncomfortably impatient and yearning. She'd never felt like this before and the feelings were making her almost ill.

"You did tell me I'd come back feeling like a new woman, and I do," she ventured quietly. "So why aren't I happy?"

"You're beginning to sound like the old Carla again," Uncle Quayle mocked, folding his arms against his virile chest. Even in his forty-two years, though he could be playfully boyish at times, he seemed focused on telling her some impartial wisdom. "The new Carla, this new woman you're talking about, isn't happy because she's afraid to admit that she's fallen in love."

"Don't be silly," Carla immediately protested.

"Look Carla." Her uncle took hold of her hand. "I

made a mistake once that concerned my heart. It taught me one thing and one thing alone. The heart is treacherous. And it's because of this one mistake why your mother and I fell out, why out of our entire family, she cast me as the black sheep."

"What happened?" Carla inquired. She'd always wanted to know the story on that one.

"I got a girl pregnant," Uncle Quayle told her truthfully, his topaz-brown eyes taking on a faraway expression. "But I did the right thing. I married her," he began. "I did it because your mother told me it was the only thing to do, but I didn't love her. I was fond of her, but there were never any feelings that I would consider genuine."

"Then?" Carla's sable eyes lifted, expectant.

"I cheated on her. Not once, but several times. She found out, and it was a bad period for us both. I wanted to run away from the prospect of divorce and I did. I went to Jamaica."

"I remember that," Carla noted quickly, appreciating her uncle's heartfelt honesty. It was the first time they'd really opened up in this way, and though she felt some resentment in not knowing this history about him, she liked this new approach he had toward her. Perhaps now he was beginning to see something in her that had matured. "Mother never told me the reason why you went there but she did worry, because Hurricane Gilbert struck that year. But . . ." Carla hesitated. "I didn't know you got married. Mother never told me that. Things are so secretive in this family," she scolded, irritated. "Just how old is this cousin of mine?"

"He'll be twelve this year," Uncle Quayle admitted, somewhat sheepishly.

"What's his name?"

"Devon. Devon Ellis Wagnall."

Carla shook her head, new emotions of never knowing a cousin making her become resentful. "Do you see him?" she quipped.

"No."

"Why. And why couldn't I see him?"

Her uncle suddenly grew nervous, his expression evident that he hadn't expected this. "Your mother felt it best that I didn't," he told her.

"What?" Carla grew shocked. Just knowing how much Cole had wanted to know his father made her body tremble to think that her own mother's pragmatic, stick-in-the-mud values could be denying a boy the same thing. Her cousin Devon, whom she'd never known, could grow up feeling exactly the same way Cole did, searching for a part of himself wanting and needing to understand what was missing. Tears filled her eyes as she looked at her uncle. "Don't do this," she pleaded. "Don't let my mother ruin your life like she tried to ruin mine. Uncle, your son needs you and—"

His hand tightened over hers. "Carla. He's nearly twelve years old."

"Then there's still time," Carla implored him seriously. "You listened to a woman who made a wrong decision for you. A decision you should have made for yourself. You were young—"

"Your age at the time," her uncle wavered, shaken. "And I was being blamed by everyone. I think your mother blamed me the most because I was the kid brother who she devoted some affection toward. I've often thought that she imagined me to be the son she lost."

This time, Carla was thoroughly thrown into turmoil. "What son?" she gasped, having found her voice, a croak of a whisper.

"Oh, shit." Her uncle moved from the desk nervously. "I don't think I should have said that. Your mother never likes to talk about it."

Carla slowly turned sideways in her chair, her heart drumming madly with shock, her senses slapped rigid in disbelief. "I had a brother?" She swallowed slowly, her voice shaky, the words filled with incredulity.

"He died," her uncle told her quickly. "In an accident, when you were young. You would have to ask your mother about it."

Carla stared dazedly at the Persian carpet, even precariously following the intricately woven patterns as she tried desperately to correlate the information in her head. Distrusting her own mind—it already filled with untenable thoughts that she was in love and now to store more dubious revelations that she'd once had a brother—Carla rose uncertainly out of her chair. "I have to go and see my mother," she told her uncle weakly, the words shaking her into a perplexed state. "I don't think I'll be back today."

"Carla!" Uncle Quayle suddenly seemed equally an enigma, caught up in his own maze of haphazard emotion. "I don't know what I've just done, but don't debate your mother, not while you're feeling like this."

"Like what?" Carla quipped, bewildered and feeling her feet make mad strides to leave the room.

If she fumbled with her car key which admitted her into her Aston Martin, felt puzzled as she drove through London, it was because her life had become suddenly filled with suspense. Was this the answer she was looking for after all? Something to explain the bad dreams, her controversial past, the reason why she'd subjected herself to a sham of a relationship? Somehow, somewhere, Iona McIntyre knew why. And Carla was going to demand that there should be an end to her misery.

ELEVEN

The terraced house in Brixton, London, with its leaded windows against dark wooden frames, its small garden where a simple rosebush ornamented the front of the house, the York stone cladding which made up the wall and almost spoke majestically of it being the place where Iona McIntyre lived, was where Carla took herself when she left her uncle's office. Her mind was elsewhere as she drove her Aston Martin through the city of London, for once not feeling like a competitor in the familiar rush-hour mad race, but more a spectator observing the show that almost signified an autumnal rather than an August afternoon.

Her mood was one of distrust as she precariously knocked at the glazed glass door, expectant at seeing her mother answer it. She had no key for admittance, it having been retrieved when she had moved in with Darnell. Now, as she stood silently waiting for the door to open, her mind propelled back to the last time she'd been there.

She and her mother had exchanged harsh words then. It was the usual round of confrontation—she being accused of being too wayward, too reckless, and certainly not the caliber of character that was wanting in a daughter. It was an analogy she'd lived with all her life, this being compared to some imaginary ideal of a person her mother had conjured up in her head. Could it be that parallels were being drawn between her brother, the link she'd never understood but which only Iona knew how to find?

Her mind turned over questionably as she also thought of the nightmares she'd been having, the clues that had been playing around in her dreams since her visit to Jamaica, where the sun, sea, and sand had provided an air of nostalgia. It had been a bewildering thought, wondering whether her leaving Darnell had created the nightmares, but now she'd come to realize that there had been a degree of fog, a haziness of memories that was as vague as an unclear sky.

Her wavering thoughts were immediately disrupted as she heard a key turn in the lock and watched as the door opened slowly. Her hesitancy was evident as she peered into her mother's eyes, an image of cool, sable-colored indifference as they met hers. "Carlane?" Iona croaked, her tone slightly surprised. She pulled the door open a little wider and appraised her daughter coolly. "Where have you been? I haven't been well."

"I flew back in from Jamaica yesterday," Carla clipped, her voice restrained. "Uncle Quayle told me you've been a little under the weather."

"Well, come in," Iona ordered mildly. She turned her back, knowing Carla had followed her in, closing the door behind her before she entered the small living room.

Carla was to find her father sleeping by the fire, his gray-haired head nestled against a pillow while the rest of him was covered with a plain woolen blanket. The room looked the same as she'd left it: a hearth with a gas fire warming the interior, a dining table in the corner with a vase filled with imitation daffodils on top, the numerous pictures of family and church members lining the wall. Even the wallpaper, the usual floral speckled design her mother preferred, was a reminder of how little things had changed.

"Is Dad sleeping?" Carla inquired, not wanting to wake him.

"Yes. He's been tired all day," Iona replied, depositing her fragile fifty-three-year-old limbs into an armchair by the fire. Noting that Carla remained standing, she gestured at a nearby chair. "Sit down, Carla. I don't want to strain my neck looking at you."

Carla felt doubtful as she took the chair indicated and placed her bag neatly against her lap. She stared at her mother, watched as she shifted to make herself comfortable in her chair. It seemed she'd aged since the last time she'd come to the house, some eight weeks ago following their last confrontation. Iona had accused her of many things then—making the family name public, giving her raised blood pressure, causing her to be ridiculed by neighbors, to name but a few. She hadn't handled it then and she couldn't handle it now, yet she was determined to know about her background, about why her mother had never told her she had a brother.

"How are you feeling, Mother?" she asked, courtesy deeming that she dealt with the polite refinement of good manners.

"Old," came the stiff reply.

"Are you ill?"

"My legs are aching and there's pain in my chest," Iona began. "Much of what you did last year put it there."

Carla shifted her eyes wayward, deciding to supremely control her anger as she digested the slight dig at her temper. "You have nothing that one week with medicine or seven days without can't fix," she told her mother cynically. And as she saw her mother sit upright in her chair, her eyes fiery spurred on by her remark, she added, "Don't get up, Mother. I wouldn't want you to force yourself to apologize to me. You might sprain something."

Iona's eyes widened to really scrutinize her daughter. The time she'd spent in Jamaica mirrored across Carla's features, projecting a radiant glow in her tawny-brown complexion, a glistening shine to her short relaxed hair, a sparkle in the deep sable of her troubled eyes. And they were troubled. As an old woman, Iona felt unsure what to expect. "You come to fight?"

"No," Carla admitted. "I want some answers."

"Don't say it, Carlane." Iona held up a stern finger. "I've just about had my limit with you."

"Your limit!" Carla squealed. "What about my limit? For a long time, Mother, I have tried to walk your line. In your book, no woman can wear bright colors, use a hairpin, put on lipstick. Hell, they're not even allowed to smile. I have never understood why you have tried to keep me in a corner, as though I was supposed to move only from left to right."

"Is this how you're trying to rationalize your behavior?" Iona railed, thumping a fist on her knee. "Dishonoring yourself taking up with a man who I told you was dangerous."

"Yes, you're right, Mother," Carla stormed in return. "You like that, don't you, to be right? Well, I got played by a bad card, and it's taught me to look for an ace. But it would have been nice if you could've been there for me. For me."

"I see," Iona quipped tightly.

"No, you don't see," Carla returned just as tightly. "My whole life has been in neutral, wondering what I'd done, who I'd hurt. I'm sorry, Mother, but I can't keep fighting this war all the time. We never did see eye to eye, and I doubt that we ever shall. You have to see it from where I'm standing, this not knowing why you have a penchant for making me suffer."

"You think you've suffered?" Iona cried out, her voice pained. "What about my suffering?"

"Mother, please," Carla drawled ironically, knowing too well she stood to be contradicted, her voice croaked in tearful emotion. "I'm thirty-one years old, on the edge because on top of everything else, I've been having bad dreams that have been trying to tell me something. And I got the shock of my life today to discover at last the answer, that somewhere in my life I once had a brother. So, Mother, maybe it's time the family secrets got dug up."

Iona ejected a muffled, strained cry that evidently came from deep within her heart. "Quayle told you?" she asked, her tone suddenly weakened, even frightened of replaying her memories.

"He told me," Carla confirmed, holding in her emotions carefully. "It slipped out of course. He didn't mean to tell me. You could say we got swept up into something that led me to discover that he, too, has a son."

"I'm sorry," Iona breathed shakily, hardly aware that she was crying.

"You're sorry," Carla said, peeved, refusing to be taken in by it. "So this brother I had, how did he die?"

Iona shook her head, her face nothing but dread as she glared at Carla. "You killed him," she quavered flatly, her expression one of total despair. "You never listened to me then. You just never have. I'd say, Carlane, don't do this, Carlane don't do that, but as usual you chose to ignore me. And that's how your brother, Lonathan, died."

Carla shook her head in denial of what she was hearing, rendered to total perplexity by what her mother was saying. Her whole manner was one of insecurity as she glared wide-eyed at her mother, debating in her head the unbelievable things that she was replaying, as she listened and digested Iona's commentary.

"You were three years old then," her mother was telling her. "Lonathan was seven. He and Quayle used to play together. He was like a big brother to Lonathan. It's funny"—she chuckled ironically—"that you should be coming back from Jamaica because it was in the Caribbean where it happened."

"What?" Carla gasped.

"Yes." Iona nodded her head, oblivious to the panic which had gripped Carla's entire being. "In St. Kitts. Your father and I took you both there one summer. We were thinking maybe we should move back there. It was your father's home."

Carla glanced over at her father. He was still fast asleep in the sofa, totally unaware of the drama that was unfolding around his silent, snoring frame. "So how did it happen?" she asked, anxious to know the full truth.

"You were playing by the water's edge, a little river at the bottom of a hill where your father did live." Iona's shoulders were shaking as she spoke. "If I told you once, I told you a thousand times not to go near the water. But you were a difficult child," she spat out, her voice taking on a steely tone. "You defied me even then. Lonathan come running to me, saying you'd gone into the river. By the time we rushed down to get you out, he ran in after you . . . and"—she began to weep—"he got you out, but the current just took him away."

Carla dipped her head, groping around her innards, hoping against hope that she could find some control. "He drowned?" she floundered, her voice almost inaudible.

Iona could only acknowledge with a nod.

"And you've blamed me all this time?"

She was to receive another nod.

"You never even gave me a chance," Carla whimpered. There was a deathly silence as she tried to collect her thoughts, with only the sound of her father's quiet snoring rousing itself against the strange, strained atmosphere that rippled the air.

That was why she'd felt so troubled in Jamaica. It wasn't just coming to grips with herself after losing Darnell, but it was the essence of that loss against the tropical elements around her that had been the trigger bringing back memories she'd buried unconsciously. In that brief moment, it taught her many things. The fact that she could truly rid herself of the faithless relationship she'd had with Darnell, that she could now attempt to forge some kind of relationship with her mother. But most of all, she was to learn that by doing so, by truly resolving to herself those two extremes, she would finally be able to give herself—all of herself—to someone she loved. Someone like Cole Richmond.

"Now you know the truth," Iona muffled, her emotions finally spent.

"I wish I'd known it sooner," Carla muttered forlornly, completely numbed, her body filled with discomfort, sorrow, and utter distress. "Then maybe I could've saved myself."

"From what?" Iona asked curiously.

"From a life of anguish, deceit, betrayal. Never quite knowing what I was looking for, but knowing that there was something I needed to find."

"You just won't be blamed, will you?" Iona's anger came from nowhere. In fact, it took Carla completely by surprise. "It's your fault that your brother is dead and all you can do is sit there, not caring at all. Only for yourself."

"How dare you say that?" Carla rose from her chair, her bag falling to the floor and the distressing circumstances she'd just heard filling her with a new burden, even in its relief of her nightmare. "What about my life. Me. You said I was only three years old. I don't even remember Lonathan. If Uncle Quayle hadn't told me, I would never have known, probably. Just to hear that something appalling and tragic happened to me, to all of us, and . . . and . . . that I couldn't do anything about it . . . I feel tortured." Suddenly thinking of Cole and remembering that he'd once told her something, she said, "You can't change the past, Mother, you can only accept it."

Iona stood to her feet, too, towering an inch above her daughter, her expression menacing as she spoke. "I have accepted it though I've suffered for years. Suffered with Lonathan dying, then with you becoming dysfunctional, then with Quayle adding to my agony by getting a young girl pregnant."

"And you made him try to walk your line, too, didn't you?" Carla pounced, deeply trying to understand her mother. "It was never your decision to make, forcing him to marry that girl when he never loved her. And then to advise him not to see his own son. I've met a person who's told me what that's like, not knowing his father, and you have forced your own brother to do that to his son, not to mention that I've grown not ever knowing Devon."

Iona's rage spoke volumes of her bruised, frazzled state. "Why should Quayle see his son? Why? He could swim, but he refused to go into the river to save Lonathan."

"Mother?" Carla's voice drooped in amazement. "You're telling me that you deliberately advised Uncle Quayle not to see his own son because you were deprived of your own."

"And what if I did?" Iona admonished madly, in spite. "He deserved it."

"You're an embittered old woman if you could ever think that," Carla protested wildly. "And I thought you knew all about repentance, having forced God down me all these years."

A wail suddenly erupted out of Iona's mouth. Something Carla had said hit home finally, and her body quaked in evidence of all the self-reproach, remorse, and penitence she was releasing. It was all Carla could do but to go over to her mother and hold her quietly in her arms. It was the first time she ever recalled holding her mother, actually embracing her with all the humble, comforting warmth of a daughter.

Together they stood and shared that uncompromising ease, rest, and solace. It was the most winsome feeling Carla had ever known to at last find a conscience in her mother. She'd known only harshness, having been raised by a traditionalist who refused to spare the rod. It was having talked to Cole, having amassed two *C* words—*courage* and *confidence*—that she now felt able to confront the ghosts that plagued her life.

It was the stirring of her father which broke the communion between them. He coughed then turned restlessly before his eyes opened to see two women sharing some contrition he would not understand. "Carlane!" He was obviously pleased to see her.

Carla carefully broke free of her mother and bent to her knees to kiss her father on his cheek. "Hello, Dad," she greeted, her eyes awash with tears.

"What's the matter?" he asked.

Carla simply smiled, not quite comprehending him. Her father had reached that point in his life where he mumbled rather than spoke, and anyone would be hard pressed to decipher him half of the time. "I can't stay for dinner," she told him uneasily. "I just flew in from Jamaica last night, and I have a lot of work to do."

"Jamaica?" Her father forced himself to sit up in the sofa.

"I'll tell you about it when I visit again," Carla harangued, knowing she was already making excuses to leave. "I'll probably stop by during the weekend."

"But—" her father began.

"Carlane says she leaving," Iona interrupted, a cue to her father that she was ready to see Carla to the door.

As Carla rose to her feet and reached for her bag, still lying where it'd fallen on the floor, her mother took her hand and squeezed it gently. "This person who told you about never knowing his father, he's someone special to you, isn't he?"

Carla caught her mother's eyes. "Yes, he is," she admitted with sincerity. "And it's because of knowing him why I told Uncle Quayle to go and see Devon."

Iona simply nodded in acknowledgment. There was no judgmental condemnation of her special person, no probing into who he was or what he did. Carla could hardly believe that no verdict had been pronounced or that no examination of him had been made. It was the one revitalizing thought she was left with as her mother closed the door on her departure. That and her self-appraisal in knowing that she missed that someone special. She missed Colebert Richmond very much.

The bath did not help though the steam around her, the hot water brushing against her delicate tawny-brown skin, and the serenity of the saunalike atmosphere provided an air of soothing tranquility. Carla did not feel she could immerse in her bathroom haven and neither could she seek any comfort there.

She was a torn woman. Torn in finding the answers she needed that day, torn in her loss of never having known her brother, whose death she'd accidentally caused, and she was torn with her turbulent emotions, for they told her something potent and all consuming. She felt like she'd finally found someone she could love.

Random thoughts ran through her mind as to what Cole Richmond was doing presently. Was he sorting out Lucas and Tata about their stealing Linden Vale coffee? Or had he dived into his work, making plans for the plantation? Was be thinking of her and what they'd shared together or had Robyn succeeded in digging her claws into him?

A deep stab of regret pierced at her heart. They'd parted badly, and she hated herself for it even though a part of herself understood why she'd done it. There was that fear of rejection and of never quite admitting that she had a future. There had also been that reflexive action of knowing that she was running away from something: her nightmares, the memories of Darnell, and more importantly, herself.

But now, inspired by all those thoughts, as she began to reason with herself while the warm water bubbled against her flesh, she began to think maybe now this discovering herself should serve as a positive evaluation as to who she was. What she, as a person, meant to herself.

That simple critical judgment resolved a thought in her mind. She would call Cole. She just had to hear his voice. Maybe listening to some of his logic, some of his worldly acumen in conversation would help her finally admit that she wanted what he wanted, too. With that in her mind, Carla left her bath, her damp feet forming wet prints on the deep pile shag carpet as she reached for her towel and wrapped it around herself.

Her hair was already wet—she'd washed it earlier—so she ran a wide-toothed comb through it before she made her way into the front hallway and picked up the telephone handset. Just dialing the number caused tremors of wild apprehension to run through her limbs, and she was alert to the eager, lustful inclination the moment she heard the dial tone ringing.

God, she needed him, her body told her in pining. She needed the warmth of his breath, the touch of his strong hands, the brooding look that she'd caught in his eyes time and time again. She needed to feel herself against him again. Most of all, she needed to know once more the power of his kiss and his all consuming of her.

The dial tone rang out six times before she heard the phone pick up. There was a two-second delay that almost bespoke of an answering machine, but suddenly she was to hear a faint voice. "Hello?" it inquired.

Carla was suddenly rendered into shock. Robyn's voice was who greeted her. "It's Carla McIntyre," she uttered, forcing out her voice, trying desperately not to appear alarmed. "Is Cole there? I'd like to talk to him."

There was a slight pause before Robyn said, "He's in bed. And before you ask, I made him forget you."

Carla used everything within her system to smother her gasp of surprise. She was thunderstruck, but she kept her voice equable. "Then could you tell him that I called with regard to a few points I want to raise about his marketing of the plantation. He has my number, if he wants to reach me."

"I don't want him to reach you," Robyn reproved. "You know, he told me that I'm the best he ever had."

"Who are you trying to convince?" Carla swallowed, feeling the bite of her anger. "Me or yourself?"

"You don't believe me, do you?" Robyn spat out.

"I don't believe everything I see and only half of what I hear," Carla told her coolly.

"Well, believe this," Robyn threatened, her voice signaling the menace which underlined her tone. "Stay away from Cole or I'll call obeah on you."

"Obeah?" Carla laughed harshly, noting the word as being the Jamaican lingo for "black magic." The cult, based on manipulation of herbs, duppies, and religious mayhem enjoyed widespread acceptance throughout the Caribbean but was also an illegal practice that was very much feared there. On top of everything which was going on inside her, Carla could hardly comprehend that she could intake anything further. "Robyn." Her voice shook in withheld rage. "Just tell Mr. Richmond that I called, okay?"

She received no answer. There was just the click of the phone. Carla replaced her own receiver and slowly made her way into the living room. She sat there. For what seemed like endless hours, she just stared vacantly around the room. What she and Cole had shared was over, she thought. He had turned if off and she should, too. In that moment of disquiet where she felt that the answers to life's great questions were infrequently revealed, she seemed to sense that something in her life had changed, irrevocably, making her feel empowered.

So much history, so much time, so much affection. What was it all for? She told herself that it was all for nothing. If she were ever to find love, mutual love, a man would have to earn it, she decided. And as tears welled up in her eyes, she seemed also to derive some inner strength that she hoped would carry her through.

TWELVE

For an isolated moment Carla's brain divided into two distinct halves. One of them registered a question that had been directed at her with its respectful, subdued, inquiring tone; the other recoiled aghast as a reflection of Cole's face flashed before her timorous mind. The two halves clicked together abruptly and she blinked, her sable gaze searching the Metropole Hotel's conference suite in London where the last in a range of seminars was being held.

She'd been invited there to make a speech on behalf of the National Federation of Black Women Business Owners and of course, she'd been delighted to come and partake of the growing acceptance of enterprising women, particularly honored that she'd been selected to impart some of her tips on surviving the first year of upheavals encompassing taxation, gross dividends, and the building of assets.

It took a few disquieted seconds for her to compose herself before she was able to direct an answer to the question leveled at her. Nearly five weeks had passed since her calling Cole in Jamaica when Robyn had answered the phone and was to have behaved in a totally unreasonable manner. Her uncle, however, hadn't been fazed by the fact that she'd decided that Cole deal with him. Certain that everything was proceeding ahead, he'd already dispatched their contract outlining the details on what McIntyre & Wagnall would be offering: the terms, budget required, and service professionally detailed—and when Cole had accepted the ideas that she'd outlined, Uncle Quayle took control over getting the work done.

There was a concerted rush as everyone pressed close to express fervent thanks as she left the small platform which was faced to absorb the fifty women of varying backgrounds, as hands with the strength of approving clasps made to make some direct contact with hers.

"Thank you so much for coming and giving us a talk," the president of the Federation began, eyes twinkling in admiration. "I hope you will be joining us for the national awards dinner tonight."

"Of course," Carla mumbled. Her voice was faint with the sensation of claustrophobia threatening her system. She felt stifled and hemmed in by all the *you've got our attention* suddenly thrust upon her. But she schooled her expression carefully and tried to appear equable and unconcerned by all the demands. "I've been nominated, haven't I?"

"That's right," the president confirmed. "By the way," she added, seizing her opportunity. "We are currently raising funds for next year's program. It's a sort of conference-through-sponsorship idea, and we would welcome your long-term support."

"Where would the money go?" Carla asked absently, feeling some discomfort at being drawn into conversation with people she barely knew.

"Some of it will go toward the British awards to recognize the achievement of business and corporate black women," the secretary to the board interjected, deciding that it was her duty to explain. "Then, of course there are the European awards, the student awards, the international awards, and the award for excellence, and we also do a newsletter."

"It all sounds quite challenging," Carla smiled, trying to keep a keen interest in the subject though all she wanted to do was leave and seek some peace of mind. "Perhaps you can tell me more at the awards dinner tonight. But right now, I really should be going."

She had little luck in achieving that. A cup of tea was suddenly thrust into her hand together with a copy of the Federation's newsletter, and before long she found herself mixing among the expanse of women with no hope of finding a little breathing space. It was nearly two hours before she was able to depart from the hotel, having been coaxed after refreshments to stay for the afternoon session and listen to the panel of speakers, all women like herself who were making a difference.

When she returned home, she had hardly time to change. She ate, took a bath and redressed, trying desperately to keep her manner focused on the evening awards dinner she was expected to attend that night. No doubt she would have to digest another panel of speakers and perhaps, if she was lucky, receive an award herself. And of course, she felt grateful that she'd even been nominated. McIntyre & Wagnall hadn't yet reached its first birthday, but she had been considered a role model, someone in whose footsteps others could follow. She was an achiever, someone deserving, so why did she not feel elated?

It was just after eight o'clock in the evening when she and her uncle found themselves walking through the imposing front door along a high-ceilinged hall that opened directly into the Westminster Suite at the Marriott Hotel in Grosvenor Square, London. Large tables in white cloth and decorated with flowers facing a low-platform stage filled the room to capacity, most of them occupied by convivial groups of people seated in white-painted chairs, either enjoying pre-dinner drinks or lingering, engrossed in conversation.

A waitress was to take them to table number eleven, where Carla smoothed her off-the-rack Harrods' purple taffeta and lace designed ball gown before seating herself in one of the white-painted chairs. Uncle Quayle took one directly next to her, his tall frame dressed in a dark tuxedo suit, a white shirt sporting a black silk tie.

"Drink, Carla?" he asked, immediately reaching for the ice bucket at the center of the table where he quickly extracted a bottle of Moët and Chandon champagne.

"Yes, thanks." Carla nodded, smiling discreetly at the other members seated at their table. She recognized only two of them: a BBC news broadcaster who she'd met on a number of occasions and the head of corporate affairs to Air Jamaica Airlines. She sat, relaxed, happy to look around her, noting with interest the large Caribbean buffet and bar near the entrance, screened by mock spreading branches of three well-designed palm trees.

The image instantly put her in mind of Jamaica, and her heart throbbed and ached as she thought of what she'd left behind there. Maybe her uncle was right. She had fallen in love and didn't want to admit it.

"Here." Uncle Quayle offered her a glass of champagne and she took it, smiling lightly. "Chin up," he coaxed quickly, seeing that the smile didn't quite reach the deep sable of her eyes.

Carla straightened immediately, trying to inject determined brightness into her face. "I wonder who nominated me?" she asked him quietly, it being the first thing she could think up to say.

"Someone who knows that you're very beautiful, very good-willed, and that you've worked very hard to get where you are now. If I wasn't your uncle," Quayle joked pretentiously, "I'd be the envy of every man in sight."

Carla laughed suddenly, hardly aware that she'd done so. "You're doing a marvelous job for my soul. It's absolute balm for my sore and wounded spirit."

Quayle shook his head quizzically, his eyebrows furrowed. "Snap out of this Carla," It was an order meant to be obeyed. "So Iona told you about the accident. It happened a long time ago, and if you suggest again that I'm bolstering you up, I'm likely to send you right back to Jamaica for Mr. Colebert Richmond to sort you out again."

"That's barbarous!" Carla protested instantly.

"Is it?" Quayle asked just as quickly. "He's been asking about you every time he's called, and you haven't been bothered to phone him back. We've also finished the proofs for his leaflets and brochures and outlined a draft on the historical aspects of Eden Lea that I believe would make an interesting subject for visitors, and you have yet to tell me what you think of them. I put them all on your desk myself over a week ago."

"I've been busy," Carla shot back. "I'll get round to looking at them later. Besides I still have that copy-editing to do on that multiracial educational tape for schools."

"That shouldn't stop you from ringing Cole," her uncle pointed out. "I took your advice and called Barbara, my ex-wife, and now I'm seeing Devon again. The least you can do is take my advice."

Carla refused to answer. Instead she frowned, took a sip of champagne, and dissolved into silence. The champagne was a gesture toward the salmon which she selected from the buffet as the evening progressed. A comedienne took the stage to entertain them all as she picked at her salad and the salmon cutlets surrounded by creamy sauce. Peeved at her uncle throughout the entire time, she instead divulged in conversation with members seated at her table until the impromptu time arrived for the speakers to take their places.

Thankfully the speakers were all brief, all using earnest and worthy connotations on how black women had mobilized themselves throughout the nineties. By the time the awards were being made, Carla's expression had become bland and inscrutable. Her mind lapsed for a moment to what her uncle had said, sending her back to Jamaica to have Cole sort her out. She was thinking just how successful he'd been in having her admit that she needed to be loved, giving her the courage to face up to her past, that she almost missed the sound of her name against the raft of applause before she noted the many faces riveted on hers.

"You've won," Uncle Quayle beamed, his face illuminated. "Go get your award." He was urging her up.

It was quite a shock to Carla as she dazedly made her way to the stage. She could feel the rustle of the net beneath her dress, feel the glare of transfixed gazes upon her, but she was not prepared for whom she met when her high-heeled sandaled shoes met the wooden stage—and it was Darnell Farrell's face that came from behind the curtains, holding an intricate glass award in his hands. Carla glared at him, dumbfounded and speechless, though she was aware that a whole room of guests were gazing at her, expectant of her acceptance speech.

Darnell hadn't changed in the near over a year since she'd last seen him. His jaw, as usual, was clean shaven, his chubby honey-brown cheeks added a boyish look to his smile, and he was still heavy-set but his athletic physique seemed more tapered as she scrutinized him, realizing that he'd lost weight. As she stared, dazed, she began to see all the things that she'd once liked about him: his well-marked hairy eyebrows, an area she'd often kissed, his towering frame which had at one time made her feel protected, his wide shoulders and muscled arms that would sweep her off her feet as though she was weightless. Darnell was still as attractive as ever, but she felt no compulsion to offer him a smile or show any form of greeting to him in one way or another. In fact, Carla felt totally indifferent as she felt his arm slip around her waist and heard him whisper briefly in her ear.

"How does it feel to be nominated by an old flame?" he asked. "It got you a prize. Are you happy?"

Carla's body went into stun mode. "Did you have something to do with me winning this?" She recoiled discreetly, adopting a shallow smile to her face, her teeth clenching as she took the award from his other arm then quickly slipped out of his embrace.

"No," Darnell retorted, his eyebrows narrowing. "You have to take my word for it."

"And we both know what that's worth." Carla quipped, loathing that it was he that should be giving it to her at all. She had worked so hard to put him into the past, to keep him exactly where he belonged. Now, when she should be feeling that she had acquired some dignity and some respect in herself for what she had achieved, Darnell had to be right there like a lead weight around her neck. She felt annoyed. More than annoyed. Carla felt damned angry. "Stand back and watch a woman at work, Darnell," she told him, challenging his very presence by brushing past him and walking over to the stage's public address system.

Sweeping her gaze across the room, she took a deep breath. "I want to firstly thank all the members of the

Federation who have in some way contributed to me receiving this wonderful award," she began. "As most of you may know, I have put a lot of work into my advertising agency, and it's a great feeling to be awarded for such an effort. I'd also like to thank my uncle and business partner, Quayle Wagnall, for being so supportive when things got tough. Without him, this award I'm holding tonight would not have been possible. I'd like to end with saying something about my nominator, Darnell Farrell. If it wasn't for him, I would never have started McIntyre & Wagnall. Over time, I've come to discover that he was nothing more that a nasty, hateful, and odious little rat who never believed in happily-ever-after."

"Carla!" Darnell's voice was rich with alarm as he absorbed the audience's stunned, startled gazes.

"Are you laughing this one off, Darnell?" Carla defended madly, aware that photographers had now positioned themselves strategically and flashbulbs were exploding in her face. "Everything was always a joke to this man," she told the audience that had now dissolved into silence, faces wild in amazement, smiles curled almost comical, ears bridged for hearing everything that she had to say. "I swear, I got more support from my pantyhose than I ever got throughout my years with him."

Bangs of laughter erupted across the room, but Carla was not deterred in concluding what she'd held in for so long. "He played the game as only he can, and sisters . . ." she warned, eyeing the room carefully, her eyes zooming in on women at every angle, "if you're being played, you haven't got anything real. Darnell Farrell worked so terribly hard against all the things I wanted in my life. So if you want to be true to yourself do it without a man—because I've come to believe that when God created woman, she corrected all the mistakes she made with man."

"Lady, you're out of order," Darnell began angrily against a roar of laughter, more flash of cameras, and excited commotion that filled the air. "What makes you think God is a woman?"

"Because Adam had a navel," Carla rebuffed, her tone totally unreasonable. "And any woman here seeking equality with a man, lacks ambition," Carla went on. "Life's battles don't always go to the stronger or faster woman, but if she's sure of herself she can win a prize, and this award will always remind me that the one who wins is the one who is true to herself and the one who really thinks that she can."

A rupture of applause filled the room as Carla quickly departed the stage. Women in every space, chair, and corner rose up to give her a standing ovation. The clapping of hands seemed to go on endlessly even as she reached her chair, a smile of relief playing across her lips as a *C* word sprang to her sharpened mind: *cured.* That was what Carla felt. She was finally cured of Darnell Farrell. She'd taken him out in her own arena and dealt enough verbal punches and blows to knock him senseless.

But she would never have thought to do it in public had it not been for his pompous attitude in thinking that he could humiliate her, after everything he'd done, by nominating her for an award. What was it all for? She couldn't quite fathom as she retook her seat. Was he intending that they should get back together now that his life was falling into place?

She'd heard recently that he recorded a rap record with the Fugees and that he'd switched to a dairy product-free diet. He'd also begun working out with a new trainer for his first fight since being banned from the ring, and she'd heard that it would be in

Atlantic City with a purse of a cool two million dollars. His savagery in his last fight had cost him dearly which had left critics attacking him from every angle. As the excitement in the ballroom began to simmer down and she received excited glances and smiles of absolute elation, she began to wonder how she could ever have gotten involved with such a dysfunctional man.

His stepfather had been convicted of manslaughter and died a hopeless wreck in an American prison. Marianne, his mother, was addicted to crack cocaine and when she lost her nursing job, fell behind with the rent. He'd told her that he didn't want to go down the drain, and she'd once admired him for that. He'd also at one time earned her respect when he told her that he could never hate his mother, even though as a child she'd kept him in line with a big leather belt which was to be his discipline. For all the problems he had with her, she'd seen one main endearing quality. Before Marianne died, he'd made sure she was free of the drugs that ruined her early life by paying for her rehab in a private clinic. As Carla sat there and began to rationalize it all, she began to understand Darnell Farrell. She now knew that he could never be a person to show love because he'd never received it.

"I want to talk to you." Carla looked up to find Darnell's cool gaze boring into her.

"Wait a minute," Uncle Quayle intervened, restraining Carla by holding down her wrist to the table.

"No," Carla overrode her uncle calmly, raising herself up out of her chair. She followed as Darnell led the way through the web of tables and out into the high-ceilinged corridor. A bodyguard, to Carla's surprise, followed slowly behind and when they'd reached an area along the corridor, where no one was present except the three of them, Darnell stopped and faced her, his eyes troubled at her outrageous outburst.

"I can't believe you did that," he began in earnest.

"What would you have me say?" Carla answered, deciding she was going to be blatantly honest. "Hi Darnell. How are you doin'? This is real life, Darnell. When you screw it up for you, you screw it up for others, too."

"Well, you wanted too much," Darnell bellowed loudly.

"Too much." Carla's eyed widened. "Darnell, in a relationship there's no such thing as too much. I was the one who was capable of putting everything into it, remember? You weren't capable of doing the same."

"What's that supposed to mean?" Darnell's shoulders rose and braced himself for the attack.

"Look, here's the long and short of it," Carla quipped. "I wanted the whole deal, not part of it. It's not my idea to share a man. You didn't want that, so it wasn't real."

"I understand that now," Darnell admitted sheepishly. "That's why I want you back."

"Do you think I'm stupid?" Carla gasped, amazed. "What is this about?"

"You. Me. Us."

"There is no us."

"There could be. I needed to be clear about us and now, I think I am."

"If you needed to be clear about us, that means you must've been forcing something that wasn't there," Carla attacked angrily. "We were in neutral, but all the time you had me believe that we had something, when all the time you were thinking only of you. You took what you wanted and you gave back nothing."

"Should I say I'm sorry?"

"Your girlfriends might appreciate it," Carla instantly shot back.

Darnell flinched, his eyes darkening and his voice

filled with malice. "And what about you?" he barked savagely. "Always wrapped up in yourself, making a very small package. And the way you talked to me with your high-class education like I was a piece of furniture. You never talked to me like you were talking to a man."

"What?" Carla was shaking with rage. "Are you trying to tell me that I intimidated you? Darnell Farrell, WBC heavyweight titleholder felt threatened by a woman? What kind of man are you?"

"Right now, a sexually frustrated one," Darnell remarked flatly.

Carla's head shook in disbelief. "Said like a typical male," she snapped. "This is about *your* loneliness, isn't it? About *your* lonely bed. Well, I've come to discover that a bed isn't empty as long as you're sleeping in it. So, if it's satisfaction you're looking for tonight, Darnell, you're looking at the wrong woman to get it."

Darnell glared at her, seeming to understand something. Then he ventured uneasily, "When we met, there was a spark between us. Now it's gone because of how I've behaved, isn't it?"

"I'm not sure it was ever really there," Carla admitted to him in honesty. "You cannot expect us to pick up the pieces. You went to a dark place, and I couldn't get you back."

"I've found my way back," Darnell pleaded, his manner seeming a little impatient.

"And while you were doing that, I found love," Carla divulged finally. "And it's taught me that there was no way we have had or ever could have had a fulfilling relationship."

"Yeah?" Darnell harangued, his eyes murderous, the news taking him completely by surprise. "What's does he do that I didn't do?"

"He doesn't control me," Carla yelled. "I feel like

I can express myself comfortably with him, that he's willing to compromise and listen to what I have to say. Most of all, he's nonthreatening. I feel totally safe with him. For all your attributes as a heavyweight boxer, I never felt safe with you."

"Girl—" Darnell was about to hit back with a scathing attack when Carla turned at the sounds of approaching footsteps. Photographers and news reporters had sought them out and were heading their way. Within minutes the paparazzi had engulfed them and were firing questions from all directions. Carla couldn't move, swamped by the swarm of photographers who were clicking their cameras avidly, getting their strategic shots of her and Darnell. The bodyguard was slow to take action but when he did, she and Darnell were being ushered down the long, winding corridor and down a flight of stairs which led to a back basement and outside through an obscure door. Quickly they made their way around the building to the main road where a white limousine stood waiting. Before Carla could comprehend what she was doing, she was being ushered into the car.

"Where are you taking me?" she demanded hotly as her body almost fell into the creamy soft interior.

A slightly constrained note crept into Darnell's clipped voice as he took the seat next to her. "We're going for a drive," he told her harshly as he pulled the door shut and watched the bodyguard take the front passenger seat.

"No, we're not," Carla refused point-blank. She turned toward Darnell instantly, troubled by a nebulous feeling of disquiet. "If you have something to say to me, say it right here and now."

"You haven't lost it, have you?" Darnell sneered.

Carla sat for a moment looking at the recumbent man alongside her. "Lost what?"

"That knack for mental aerobics. I knew it would make you manipulative in the end. You were so clever and calculating, extracting my money."

"You mean I was adept in taking control to retrieve what was mine," Carla corrected smoothly. "I can't believe I was so unwise. It sounds better than admitting that I was stupid, so if you think you are going to cut any ice with me now, you can forget it."

Experiencing a distinct feeling of rebuff, Darnell took hold of Carla's wrist, his hold as tight as a vise. "Let's dispense with the formalities. You know you really want me."

"No, I don't," Carla insisted bluntly, twisting her wrist out of his hold on her. She scolded herself irritably for ever allowing herself to be ushered into the car in the first place, and as it hadn't yet moved away from the pavement where it was stationed, she opened the door quickly, her manner impatient. "I've left you, remember? Have a nice life."

Darnell refused to accept the brush-off. As he lunged forward to take hold of Carla, annoyed that her slippery motion in leaving the limousine made him fail to successfully take a hold on her, cameras instantly flashed into his face while Carla rushed back toward the hotel relentlessly. She didn't look back. She just marched back to the Westminster Suite, sought out her uncle to tell him that she was leaving, then departed with her award while the paparazzi digested her in their sick fascination.

On reaching her apartment, she went straight to the living room, feeling totally spent by her evening ordeal. She felt weighed down by every minute of her thirty-one years, the many mistakes that lay in them, and by her naivety that they should ever have happened. Her control slipped as she went back to her childhood before propelling herself back to this present moment. Blood was running high along her cheekbones, and her eyes glittered with anger and tears.

She eyed a little statuette of a country squirrel that had been given to her once as an Easter present. She marched right over to it and threw it on the ground, watching as the porcelain shattered in every direction. Next she attacked all the glass vases housing the decorative dried flowers that filled the room and added them to the pile of broken porcelain on the floor. She went over to the coffee table, finding a bottle of Dior perfume there which she'd scented herself with hours earlier. She threw it on the floor but only the bottle top cracked. Considering that it hadn't broken enough, she pounced on it again and with all her might, threw it right across the room. It landed with a satisfying thud, its contents spilling all over her carpet.

Finally, when she looked down at the mess she'd created, mute with horror at what she'd caused, she heard the slight rise in the decibel rate of her distress as her sobs filled the room with despair. She had just begun to feel like the survivor of some great holocaust when she heard a knock on her front door.

It was probably Uncle Quayle, she thought, ejecting a spasmodic hiccup. She'd left the Marriott Hotel by taxi in such a hurry, she could only imagine that he must have wondered how she'd gotten home or whether in fact she was all right. She stared around the room from beneath heavily swollen eyelids, ashamed at how she was going to explain the mess. Deciding that Uncle Quayle would understand, she made her way into the hallway, her spirit weary as she opened the door.

Her eyes widened, and she stood rooted to the spot. Suddenly the expression of the man looking at her came to vivid life. Something in her heart almost wept for joy as her red swollen eyes examined with delight the features she'd come to know so well: a rounded nose, full lips, amber complexion, and thick dark lashes. And those cocoa-colored eyes were ensnaring her completely as she digested the clean-shaven head and the beard that covered only the upper part of his lips and traveled a square line around his mouth and chin.

Could she believe that he was standing right there, looking at her? It was cynicism that came to her rescue as she cleared the chill desolation that sat on her throat and said, "I believe it's the young Mr. Richmond."

But Cole was smiling. She had instinctively known that about him. He was a man given to smiling freely, she'd once thought. And he was dressed as casually as his manner appeared: pale blue jeans, sneakers, a collarless blue shirt beneath a dark brown leather jacket. "Are you going to kiss me properly, or do I kiss you improperly?" he asked her, feisty.

Carla felt suddenly dazed. It was some time since she'd last seen him, since they'd last spoken, but there was no mistaking the grace of his athletic figure or the heart-stopping familiarity of his voice. Everything about him struck an immediate chord in her memory of the time they'd spent together, giving instant recall to the things she'd said, the things he'd told her that she now knew she wouldn't forget. Suddenly she began to wonder whether she was imagining his presence or whether he had in fact spoken at all. Without quite hearing her own self speak, she eyed him warily, her nerve ends raw. "That depends." She hesitated, still quite dazed. "Are you definitely here for real?"

THIRTEEN

"I'm here." Cole's whisper seemed to reach her through her troubled state of mind as he touched her trembling hand and caught the look of unease in her teary sable eyes. With a moan of sheer relief, misgivings, and yet so glad to see him, Carla threw herself against Cole, burying her head on his hard chest.

"How did you know that I live here?" she gasped, sagging limply into the arms that closed automatically around her shaking body.

"I wrote it down from the tag on your suitcase when you took a shower at your hotel in Jamaica," Cole explained, rubbing his hands up and down her spine. "I came earlier, but you weren't here. I began to worry whether I had the right address or not."

Carla withdrew from his arms and pulled Cole into her apartment, but as she closed the door and made to lead him down the hallway, he took her arm and hauled her back to his hard, rigid frame. Their eyes locked in a frisson of understanding seconds before Cole sought her lips. He kissed her frantically like a man deprived of something, and Carla responded to his kiss with such ardor that a great shudder of delight ran through them both, the force of an overwhelming surge of feeling leaving them helpless against its drive. Trembling and almost weightless, Carla drew back a fraction and whispered mindless against his mouth. "My bedroom's over there."

"Good. Take me to it," Cole whispered softly. There Carla drew him down onto her bed, welcoming the weight of his long, hard body against the petite frame of her own. He kissed her face, her eyes, her nose, and then her lips in fierce, almost desperate motions, his hands caressing and stroking her to fever pitch. When he unzipped her dress and pulled it from her body down and over her feet, instead of hindering him, thinking that the night's earlier events might propel through her mind, her hands instead frantically helped him strip it off and throw it aggressively to the floor.

Cole's eyes devoured the length of her, as every familiar line of her body came into focus, shadowed by the light which streaked into the darkened room from the hallway. Her pulses tripled as his usual cocoa-brown gaze darkened almost to black with a look in them that excited her to a frenzy as his gaze caught the lacy black underwear that covered her breasts and hips.

He pushed the straps of her bra from her shoulders, following his fingers with his mouth, nibbling, caressing, biting the fabric from her breasts until he caught one taut nipple between his teeth. Carla reared up against him, gasping Cole's name before he nuzzled her neck with his mouth until she subsided against him, surrendering mindlessly to the demands of his lips.

Her hands stroked restlessly over the leather that covered his shoulders before she aggressively began to pull the jacket down his arms. He withdrew from her long enough to help her remove it along with his shirt, frantically working at the buttons while she worked on the belt of his jeans until, together, they'd separated him from his clothes. Kicking off their shoes, they were rejoined again, each reacquainting themselves with the pliant curves of the other, surrendering themselves unconditionally to feather-stroke touches.

Lying at the side of him, Carla reached up and kissed Cole's eyelids, her expression dazed as she looked into the infinitely tender expression of the eyes that looked down possessively into her flushed, drowsy face. She could hardly believe he was really there, in her arms, his fingers delving into the lace of her panties to rub gently into the soft spot between her legs. With a muffled submission her mouth accepted his, rendering her helpless as she relaxed at a stroke, her free hand smoothing his hair, sliding over his shoulders and down his spine, molding him against her, while the pressure of his kiss hardened and became more urgent.

Cole's heated body was demanding her response as he again found the summit of one breast and caressed it so slowly it sent a shiver of fire through her body, making her gasp involuntarily. The response was enough to cause a muttered sound of triumph to erupt deep in his throat before his lips moved in a burning path up her neck while his experienced, clever, and educated fingers wrung from her the tremors she was finally powerless to withhold.

Despite what she'd been through that night—the despair and anguish she'd felt less than one hour ago—Carla's mind and body were now experiencing a totally different reaction as everything within her yielded and moved against this man. Cole would be her savior that night, she told herself erotically. She needed him and he needed her.

With fingers frantic, she pressed his head even closer as she wildly returned the caresses he gave her, increasing her tempo to match the thumping of her heart, the heavy breathing of her chest as shivers of excitement ran through her completely. She was engulfed by Cole's muscular body, by the tremors that communicated themselves to hers until they were both entwined in a mutual vibrant tide of feeling.

She was lost to everything but the urgent demands of her senses, knowing that they needed to be fulfilled, that she needed to be satisfied. Her hand slid down to the tiny, deep indentation of his navel, lightly, casually caressing the area, adding new dimension to their lovemaking. She found the masculine bones of his hips, the hairy skin of his thighs, her sensitive fingertips and palms tingling at the subtle friction of hair and skin.

All the while her mouth exacted its toll on his body, pulling sensual pleasure from his lips as she sought beneath his underpants and approached the fiery, expectant core of his need for her. He quivered beneath her touch and she delighted at causing such a deep response in him. She felt maddened by it and probed the area even further, her mood heightened at giving such exquisite torture.

Cole whispered words that stroked against her senses like his fingers inside her, dismantling all the barriers, pain, anguish, and frustration that had dogged her for so long. She groaned in intolerable ecstasy as she felt herself set adrift by the pleasure they were giving to one another. She belonged here, in his arms, she told herself again, even though she was sluggishly aware that she would have to confront the inevitable question: What did it all mean? But for now, there was no meaning other than the fact that they needed to please each other. They were together again, and that was enough for her to be engulfed in him, for her body to be so limp in mindless surrender. "I want to make it good for you," she whispered, lightly, playfully.

"Why?" Cole asked absently, his lips kissing a trail down her neck, knowing that this woman was already pleasing him. She would always please him. There could be no one but Carla McIntyre for him.

"Because you came all the way here to see me." Carla tormented him with her lips. "And I'm so very grateful."

"Grateful?" Cole lifted his head, the smile of seduction seeming to drop from his face. "What in the devil does that mean?"

Carla pulled away slightly from the heat and strength of Cole's body to find him looking at her warily. The silverlike plains of light which shone through the open door from the hallway illuminated his expression which, to her alarm, was filled with deep inescapable caution. Suddenly she realized that she'd said something she shouldn't and, in that moment, she felt transparent and weak. "I didn't mean that," she bridled quietly.

"No?" Cole rose from the bed, standing on his feet to look down at her as Carla positioned herself uneasily to sit on her bottom. "What am I to you, Carla?" he asked, troubled. "Someone who makes you feel good so you can be grateful?"

"No, you mean more than that," Carla protested weakly.

"Really?" Cole's tone was sardonic. "I came all the way from Jamaica to see you because I haven't been able to get you out of my mind. I haven't been able to work because I keep thinking about you, and you weren't phoning. I'm here for you, damnit. Can't you feel what's going on?"

Carla's body shook. She didn't really want to admit anything, not while there was so much uncertainty still plaguing her mind and especially while she felt she couldn't get what she wanted. "Cole, I'm scared." Her voice was belied with fear. "For once in my life, I want to get back as much as I'm giving and . . ."

"We both deserve that," Cole finished softly. He sat back on the bed and took her hands into his. "That's why I'm here. I want to prove to you that I'm still waiting to catch that lifeline you once told me about."

"Cole"—Carla hesitated—"so much has happened to me since then."

He tensed. "Like what?"

She hardly knew where to begin. "I found out something about my past which explained a lot of things. It explained the dreams. I thought it was Darnell who was causing them, but it wasn't, although I've confronted him, too. Like you said, you can't change the past, you can only accept it—and I've learned that now. When I came back from Jamaica, I found out that I had a brother."

"A brother?" Cole queried.

"I never knew about him," Carla explained. "But a terrible thing happened in my childhood, and he drowned. He died trying to save me, and I discovered this only a few weeks ago. It's the reason why my mother resented me so much. It's the reason why I clung to Darnell when I should've moved on. And I think it's the reason why I felt . . . so lost and empty."

Cole squeezed her fingers tightly. "Carla, whatever happened in your childhood happened a long time ago. And right now, your life feels empty because you're reluctant to fill it with the things that you really want. I thought you had dreams."

"I do."

"Then let them come true," Cole implored, kissing her fingertips, running a trail up one arm until he reached the curve of her shoulder.

His words felt like the highest accolade she'd ever received, to believe that whatever she wished could be turned into reality. Mesmerized, her body trembling, she sat with her eyes ensnared by his, seeing them widen and deepen with desire. She shivered with inward delight, knowing that this was the very man who invaded her dreams. Her own desire for Cole was an all-consuming one that frightened as much as it awed her. But in the recesses of her mind, she still felt wary, reminding herself that love that is forced was not worthy of the name. *It means different things to different people,* her mind replayed, remembering what she'd told Robyn.

Yet she couldn't deny the elementally charged, white-hot passion between them. Yes, she had dreams, and maybe she should take this for what it was—lust and nothing more. And when it was over, she could think of Cole with kindness, hoping that he would think of her in the same way. In doing so, she would always know that she'd accepted the courage he'd given her and accepted knowing that she'd submitted to her desires.

"It's all in the state of mind, isn't it?" she said finally. "Giving in to you and what I need . . ."

"Either that or it seems nothing short of a crisis is going to force you to open up to me," Cole declared deeply.

"You keep telling me that." Carla laughed weakly.

"I mean it, too," Cole answered her, drawing her close to his chest so that Carla was aware of his body heat that reached out and claimed her.

His seeking mouth instantly captured her lips, and she melted into his arms, weakened by the emotions which took hold, clogging her throat so that her breath felt stifled. Fiery, relentless warfare suddenly erupted between them as his arms contracted suddenly and crushed her mouth beneath his. There was a fierce exultation unlike anything they'd shared before. It ravaged her, and it was not one-sided. In her surrender to Cole, Carla realized that his submission was equal to her own. She felt Cole's heart pick up speed, felt the primitive rhythm of his body join her own, rejoiced in the aggressive way his kiss matched hers.

The taste of him saturated her senses, his primal male scent tickled her nostrils, his perspiring body tripled her pulse rate. Her body sprang to life just knowing that his human frame close to hers could be so enlivened. Ardent with the need to take and to give, she pulled him even closer to her, kissing him ravenously as their bodies fell slowly onto the bed.

Unhurriedly Cole began to slip the bra from beneath her and then the lacy panties that covered her hips. Inescapable fingers began to trace her every curve, from her throat, hovering impatient in the hollow at the base, down to her navel to a place that had her shivering and whispering his name. Carla was totally absorbed as she went under, giving in to the bliss that caught her again and again.

Her head shook from left to right, her eyes closed and then opened to find Cole's hypnotic ones boring into hers, fragmenting her senses, heightening her desire with their irresistible dark, cocoa-colored shade glistening like magic crystals. She was breathless as she forced him on his side to pull his briefs from his hardened thighs and gaze at the male physique which promised sweet, fresh seduction anew.

Cole lay perfectly still, his fingers brushing tentative strokes along Carla's arms as he gave her time to get accustomed to the feel of his body. He liked the way she touched him, the way her lips suckled the waiting buds of his nipples, knowing that only she could cause such exploding sensations to jab at his senses. She was becoming skilled and educated at working him into a frenzy, and he loved that about her. He loved everything about her.

He clutched at her wrist the moment he felt her delicate touch against the hardened rise of his manhood. God, she was getting good at this, he mused as he moaned aloud and rolled his body on top of her. He felt his skin flex against the warm satiny softness of Carla's skin beneath him. The erotic sensation was so heady and hot, he could hardly contain himself or handle his control.

"Baby, I need you now," his hoarse tone told Carla huskily. His fingers gauged her readiness for him in one swift movement, moments before he jumped from the bed and reached down to his leather jacket pocket for the latex protection that he needed.

"Hurry," Carla said relentlessly, anticipation tormenting her nerve ends.

When Cole returned and enclosed her, she was mindless with craving for him to conquer her. Lying on his back, Cole guided her onto him, filling her feverishly until the tension began to twist and tighten inside her. Carla felt like a woman driven as she took control, rocking them both over the border into boundless and fertile territory of pleasure. As wave upon wave of sensation flooded her body, she became aggressive, relieved that with Cole she could release her pent-up tension.

Her fingers clenched almost to cruelty as her dominant motions thrust hard and hungry. She saw the moment Cole forgot himself as his eyes closed and he disappeared into the abyss of her lovemaking. He was losing control, and she loved knowing that she had done this to him, that it was she who was causing the harsh sounds and grunted sighs to erupt from his throat.

Wrapped in a kaleidoscope of emotions that were as

complex as they were exhilarating, the hard dominance of her movements burned a slow fire that began to heat up deep inside her. The rising heat intensified and her rocking grew bolder until Cole's muscles and tendons flexed, and her thigh muscles hardened in sinuous might. When she began to lose her own power and control against the scalding fire, when Cole cried out her name, burned by the flames she'd torched him with, the last of her defenses ignited and kindled with that same flame until the joy and ecstasy consumed and claimed them both.

Carla's lips were warm against Cole's forehead as she imparted a gentle kiss before positioning herself next to him. Totally spent, her mouth still parched from the blazing passion that had spun her into another axis in time, she nestled her head against his shoulder. After a time spent lazily ebbing the rate of her heart while desirously listening to the slowing thud of Cole's, Carla said, "I didn't think I'd be this lucky again." She certainly felt lucky, though she was wise enough to tell herself not to expect more from their physical encounter. That was always her fear, if she were truly honest to herself, that she would never get more than that from Cole.

She heard him chuckle and liked the sound of it. "I told you, you can have more if you really want it."

"I want more," she dared to suggest.

Cole turned his head and looked deep into her face. "So you're not afraid of life after all?" He smiled. "What happened to that frightened little kitten I met back in Jamaica?"

Carla smiled back, rubbing satisfied circles with her fingers into his chest. "She's suddenly become a man-eating cat."

"Man-eating?" Cole chimed, chuckling at the suggestion. "Hmm, I like the sound of that."

"Just as long as the water is not too deep," Carla cautioned carefully.

"Now why don't I like the sound of that?" Cole answered. "Are you starting to be careful with me all over again?"

"I just want to be sure, that's all," Carla reasoned. She felt Cole's shoulders tense and realized yet again that she'd said something wrong.

"Who is this about now? Me or you?" he asked.

"Me," Carla said nervously. She paused, then added, "I saw Darnell tonight."

"Where?"

"At the Federation of Black Business Women Awards. That's where I came from before you arrived."

"That's why you were dressed the way you were?"

"Yeah. And I won an award, too."

"You did?" Cole smiled. "That's great."

"It would've been if Darnell hadn't nominated me," Carla said, peeved in annoyance.

Cole turned on his side and looked at Carla, gently stroking a finger down her cheek to her shoulder. "So, what happened?"

"Something explosive happened," Carla said, shaken. "There he was, on the stage, holding my award. Suddenly I thought this was his way of asking for another compromise, and you can compromise only so much before you lose yourself. I was losing myself when I was with him and it felt downright miserable. Tonight I finally showed him that I had gotten out from under all that."

Cole propped himself on his elbow. "What did you do?"

"What didn't I do?" Carla sighed. "I humiliated him in public, but it taught me something really important. I've learned now not to jump into something again until I am sure, that the bottom line is I can't change a person. I've also learned now that I don't want something fundamentally different from myself. With Darnell, we were worlds apart."

"And with me, you're worried because we're an ocean apart?" Cole deciphered accurately.

Carla winced. "Yes, I am."

"I'll do whatever it takes for you to feel comfortable about that," Cole declared sincerely.

"Don't promise me anything," Carla assayed quietly. "Remember what I told you about the moon and the stars?"

"And remember when I told you that I'm not that kind of guy?" Cole instantly rebuffed. "I'm jealous of this relationship you're having with Mr. Solitude, and it's time he left the scene."

"You're throwing him out?" Cola smiled wickedly.

"I'm definitely throwing him out." Cole smiled just as wickedly, certain that he knew exactly where their affair was heading. He pulled Carla close to him and dropped a delicious kiss against her lips, introducing her again to his earthy, demanding sensuality.

Carla immediately melted into him, her smile turning to one of lazy reminiscence as intimate memories flooded her mind of how good it felt to be in Cole's arms. While his hands traced the feminine contours of her breasts, she thought of the magical symbolism that had impregnated their lovemaking on the island of Jamaica. She'd bitten into his neck, and he'd bitten into hers, and together they'd looked deeply into each other's eyes, swept away by something that spoke beyond words of how they'd somehow caught each other in the way that a lion and lioness caught its prey. Such a symbolic gesture had a meaning, she thought, recognizing that her body was now behaving wildly, heedless of anything but the pleasure Cole was giving her.

The core between her legs propelled forward to

meet his fingers, and she was lost again in unhurried tension and reckless passion. Purring like a wildcat, she caught his lips and bruised them with the hard power of her kiss. Theirs was an elemental hunger that was as glorious, as heated and as untamed as a ferocious bush fire. It burned. It scalded. They needed no Caribbean sun to blaze the zeal of feeling that was intensely combustible between them both. Their heartfelt feelings were flammable enough, set alight by something Carla refused to admit.

This time their lovemaking was slow and tender, filled with gentle caresses, teasing lips, moist tongues that sent them both dizzy with desire. Carla was breathing rapidly when she descended from the highest euphoria Cole had taken her to find herself looking into the deep cocoa-brown of his gaze. Her heart belted madly as she saw the sincere, breathless expression of fulfillment on his face. She'd put that there, she told herself. She'd made him strain against his own self-control until he'd lost the battle deep and sweetly violent within her.

Without quite knowing what she was saying, she pressed a kiss against the tip of his nose and whispered, "I think I'm ready to throw you that lifeline now."

"Good. I told you I'd be here to catch it. And I'm right here for you, Carla."

Carla couldn't help but kiss him again . . .

After making love most of the night, the dawn chorus was lost to Carla the following morning. She slept right through it, oblivious of sunrise, even of the smell of coffee and bacon floating to her bedroom, invigorating her senses. Eventually she stirred and stretched, glancing idly at her clock then shot out of bed in guilt.

It was eleven o'clock, and if she remembered correctly, Cole was there in her apartment.

She swiftly made it to the bathroom, washed her face then tied a orange terry-cloth robe over her naked body before she sheepishly entered her kitchen to find Cole pouring himself a cup of coffee. "I should be doing that," she apologized coyly.

"They'll be plenty of other days for that," Cole answered, cheerfully planting a brief kiss against her cheek. "Coffee?"

"Yes. Plenty of milk and two sugars."

As Cole poured her a cup, he added carefully, "Something happen to your living room?"

Carla's face went blank for an instant, then she remembered all the things she'd broken in her anguish and frustration at seeing and arguing with Darnell Farrell the night before. Funnily those emotions had now dissipated to one of frantic need and wanting, especially when she charted Cole's virile expanse of bare muscle and amber biceps and his hairy athletic chest. His physique spoke volumes to her of how much he'd come to mean to her, and she marveled at the way her sable gaze traveled downward to the area she wanted most concealed beneath the cotton of his briefs.

"I expended some energy last night," she told Cole by way of explaining the reason why she'd broken her things.

"I thought you did that with me," Cole implied, his gaze ensnaring hers.

"Before. It was before you came." Carla flushed, recalling the way they'd shared each other throughout the night. "But"—she put her finger into her mouth then removed it to mark a wet trail down the middle of Cole's chest—"I don't mind expending some more this morning."

"Talk like that and I'll forget breakfast." Cole laughed, lodging his head in the direction of the frying pan where bacon and eggs were sizzling nicely.

"Only if you want to work up a little appetite first," Carla teased.

Cole sipped his coffee then looked at Carla, noting her serious intent. He wanted nothing more than to take her right back to her bedroom and show her again the joys of being a woman. But his stomach rebelled against the very idea. He was hungry, and his body was protesting for food. "Later," he promised, noting with pleasure that one of his hands was slowly clenching and unclenching.

"Breakfast it is." Carla was undaunted. Cole was with her and that was all that mattered. "Didn't you bring any luggage?" she asked, reaching for her cup of coffee. She didn't recall seeing him with a suitcase.

"Oh, that," Cole said, unconcerned. "It's at the hotel I checked into yesterday after I came here first and found you weren't here."

"You should have told me you were coming. I hate the thought of knowing that you came here and didn't find me. How are things back home?"

"You wouldn't believe," Cole sighed serenely.

"Not good?"

"Not good. Let's get the breakfast first."

It wasn't long before they were seated in the living room, plates in hand and knives and forks cutting into bacon and eggs and toast on the side. Carla wasn't sure quite what to expect when Cole began to talk, but she listened attentively as he began to tell her about the troubles that had gone on with him and his family in Jamaica.

"Lucas didn't know about the missing coffee." He started swallowing his breakfast. "I confronted him about it the day after you left for England, and he was taken aback. He knew nothing about the boat in Runaway Bay. It wasn't long before he began to put two and two together with Tata and the men that she'd been seeing. I warned her not to bring them to Eden Lea, but she had a little habit we didn't quite know about and was using the coffee to pay for it."

"Drugs," Carla surmised instantly.

"That's right," Cole admitted forlornly. "We discovered it when Lucas searched her room. When she came home, standing between the two of them was all I could do to stop him from beating the life out of her. She told us everything though. How she and the guys would wait until Masa Joe arranged the shipments, and then they would hijack the coffee en route to its destination and bribe our drivers to keep quiet. By the time I learned that they were hiding stockpiles of Linden Vale coffee in the caves down in Cockpit Country and then transferring the load by road to Runaway Bay where they would sell it on the black market for a price, I was quickly firing a handful of staff."

"It all sounds like fiction," Carla gasped, amazed. "Have you called the police in yet?"

"No," Cole said flatly.

"Why not?"

"We can't find Tata. She's disappeared, but I've warned Lucas that I'm giving her only two weeks to show up," Cole explained. "Lucas believes he knows one of the guys, so he's promised me he'll go and get her. I want to know exactly who's involved and where all the coffee has been going."

"Cole . . ." Carla felt her voice grow alarmed again as it had done when Cole had taken her into Trench Town to buy information about the shipment of Linden Vale coffee. "Why are you so stubborn? This isn't you. You're the man who always reasons with me and rationalizes everything that comes out of my throat. You're not thinking clearly, so let me think clearly for the two of us. Let the police handle it."

Cole smiled cheekily. "I can handle it." His voice was firm and lightly tainted with the ego of a man.

But Carla wasn't convinced, and she didn't really want to debate Cole. She was unused to seeing him like this, so steadfast in what he was doing. A part of her liked it, but the other part was tangibly aware of !he dangers involved. She'd heard of Jamaican bad men who were familiarly known as yardies. If Tata had gotten mixed up in drugs and was using Linden Vale coffee to pay for it, then it was likely that the men she frequented with were in fact yardies.

"How long are you here for?" she asked Cole quickly, her mind calculating how long she could avert the danger of him going back too soon.

"A week," Cole told her, a smile still evidently playing across his face. "Why? Have you got plans to keep me here for yourself, or am I allowed to see some more of London?"

Carla returned the smile, though a little uneasily. "We can start by checking you out of your hotel and getting your suitcase before I decide exactly what I'm going to do with you," she ventured quietly.

"You can do with me whatever you want," Cole suggested sweetly.

"Hmm. Let me think." Carla laughed.

They ate breakfast quickly, knowing that the suggestive banter was enough to put them both on the edge of sensual tension and longing. Time couldn't move any quicker when they at last gravitated toward each other, and Carla blew tentatively into Cole's ear. The sensation was erotic as he grabbed her arm and pulled her close enough to plant a kiss against her neck. Reaching out, Carla took his hand and carried it to her cheek, holding it there for a brief moment, then slowly guided it down her length. She delved into the terry-cloth robe and moved it over her breast, down her slim waist, to the flat plane of her stomach, and onto her well-endowed hips. "Do you want some more?" she whispered hoarsely.

"Do I?" Cole's hand was shaking, and his breath was rasping against his throat. His body was like a volcano about to erupt, his blood like molten lava, his mind almost unable to bear the sheer heat that coursed along his veins. With a groan of anticipation, he dragged Carla to him and rained hard kisses against her lips, her neck, her chest, his throat letting loose agonized muttering sounds of need as he swept her up into his arms and carried her back to her bedroom down the hallway.

Carla moved her body to him in surrender the moment he placed her on the bed, returning his kiss with wild crazy yearning filled with everything in her heart and soul. They rolled between the sheets, wrapped their legs around each other, played frantically like two frustrated lovers, moaning as they enjoyed and relished their sensuality. Shock waves of high delight filled the room with shouts of triumph as the prolonged and frenzied pleasure could be abated no more. Cole was at last free to reach out in voluptuous abandonment when Carla was finally carried to her point of ecstasy.

For a while they lay, almost exhausted, in each other's arms. Then just as Carla was about to snuggle into Cole, the radio-clock on her bedside came to life. She'd forgotten to reset the timer for her usual wake-up call, so the time control arrangement was not as it should be. Enchanted and happy, she reached over Cole's wide chest to push the switch that would turn off the radio, but her blood ran cold and her skin tensed when she suddenly heard the news reporter announce his latest scoop.

"WBC heavyweight champion Darnell Farrell was last night the center of a midnight brawl when sparks flew at the Marriott Hotel in Grosvenor Square, London. Ex-mistress Carlane McIntyre delivered a public humiliation to the boxer when he was to present her with an achievement award. Later they were found to be exchanging profanities outside the hotel moments before they were separated by paparazzi. It was said that—"

"Oh, no," Carla gasped, her body rigid, her mind horrified. "They're talking about what happened last night."

Cole felt her stiffen and looked over at her. Carla looked moody and again unsure of herself. Her singalong voice was filled with pain, and he could glimpse the childlike woman he'd grown to know so well. There seemed to be only one thing of which he was absolutely positive, and that was that she needed him right now. She needed his closeness and his support, his reasoning, and—most of all—his love.

The telephone in the hallway began to ring, and Carla felt her body jerk into panic. The scandalmongers were now calling, she thought, her mind still alert to the eloquent babble that spilled out of the radio, the yackety-yack and nonsensical twaddle about her life making her loathe the very sound of the news reporter.

"Don't answer the phone," Cole ordered immediately, turning Carla within his arms so that she could see him clearly. He caressed her gently, his hands expert now in knowing what aroused her the most. "There's only me and you between these sheets. The rest of the world can be damned to hell."

As he bent his head and took her lips into his, Carla knew that they would weather the storm together. She also knew deep in her heart that she had fallen in love.

FOURTEEN

Their lovemaking set the scene for a week Carla enjoyed enormously. Determined to ignore the media hounds who had plagued her at her apartment, who'd tracked Cole to his hotel, bombarded her with telephone calls and formed a daytime vigil outside her home, Carla decidedly packed a small suitcase and battled over to her car from where she drove with Cole to the reclusive hills near the city of Oxford, where a little stone cottage stood in the heart of Woodstock. The historic town was on the edge of the Cotswolds, a great, green saucer of land which contained many noble buildings, fine towns, and picturesque villages, as well as splendid scenery.

It was her turn to show Cole a little of British history as Woodstock was also on the regular tourist route from Oxford and could often be congested at peak times when visitors chose to take in the sights of Blenheim Palace, situated close by. Their visit there had been one of the highlights of her week as they marveled at the paintings and tapestries that were all part of its magnificent collection, and if a new pain was really the best way of assuaging an old one, it was knowing that the week would soon be coming to an end and that Cole would be returning to Jamaica.

They'd spent five days at the rented cottage that was

aptly named Caroline's Cottage and was now refurbished with its oak-beamed ceilings, its country parlor, the cozy farmhouse-style kitchen with a wood-burning stove, and the crackling fire in the huge stone fireplace where they'd one night made love on the rug in front of its amber-colored flames.

It was uncanny that she should feel so at ease with Cole, as though the five weeks since they'd last seen each other was merely the turning of a page in a book. A bond had grown between them which was as strong as if forged in steel, and it had a lulling effect on Carla, this innate tenderness he possessed coupled with his sharp perception of her feelings.

The weekend dawned on a clear and sunny morning, bringing with it the first day in October. She had left Cole asleep at the cottage in bed so that she could take a walk along the meandering country roads full of dog-roses and meadowsweet and a smattering of young trees which brightened her path as their copper-colored and gold leaves drooped, then stirred in a light airy breeze. Her short dark hair, too, was tossed by the wind, but Carla did not feel its chill. She felt sated and happy as she walked along, reminding herself that a giant void had been removed from her life.

After a full hour's walk, she returned to the cottage to find Cole dressed only in his jeans, his feet bare against the polished wooden floor stirring up logs in the open-grate fire. There was no mistaking the grace of his athletic figure, without even seeing his face. He was all too heart-wrenchingly familiar, and she groaned inwardly, regret that he would soon be leaving marring her soul.

"Good morning," she intoned, bright and breezy.

Cole spun round, his expressive face instantly alight with such radiant welcome that Carla felt sincerely touched. "Good morning to you, too," he responded easily. "Where have you been?"

"Walking."

"And thinking?"

"A little."

Cole's eyes narrowed perceptively. "What about?" The two words were spoken slowly.

"Nothing really," Carla began nervously. "I was just thinking what a lovely week it's been."

He smiled in agreement. "It's been great. This is a lovely part of England. Quiet, rural, with country folks. Reminds me of Jamaica without the sun."

"I don't think I mentioned this, but I stayed here once before," Carla ventured tersely, taking herself over to the freshly made fire to seat herself on the floor nearby. Cole joined her there, his fingers alighting onto her hands, and Carla couldn't help but notice his attraction as she watched the firelight playing across his face. "After leaving Darnell, I was looking through a magazine and saw an advertisement of this cottage for rent through an agency. It was great being here then, simply enjoying my own company, even more so now because I'm sharing it with you."

"That's a nice thing to say," Cole offered as though touched. "I'm glad you like my company."

"But you're leaving on Monday," Carla reminded forcing a rueful smile. "And we haven't even discussed your marketing contract with us. Did you like the layouts my uncle sent you?"

There was a tension between them now, and Cole knew it would be hopeless trying to ignore it. His stomach muscles contracted sharply as they both stared at each other, silent and tense, knowing the truth had weighted them. "I'm quite happy with everything," he said slowly. "But . . . I'd be happier with you."

"As in?"

"You being with me."

Carla dipped her head silently, allowing him to continue.

"I don't know how much your agency means to you, especially now that you've won an award," Cole began. "And I know we've known each other only a short time, less than some people who want to embark on something new. But I *know* you, Carla. With you, I feel like whatever I was looking for I've found. And we're both resourceful people. We can make it work even with an ocean between us. But right now, I just want you to come back to Jamaica with me. Get away from England for a while and see how you feel."

To Carla, the whole thing seemed so easy and yet so unreal. Cole was talking about them delving into unknown territory, forcing her to face up to that *C* word again which she'd thought she could never reuse: *commitment.* That was what Cole wanted from her, but she felt incapable of offering that deep emotional attachment tempered with the knowledge that life was far simpler her way; her way being to keep her heart in its cage, even though she knew that Cole had long since found the key and had opened the lock to free it into abandon, claiming it as his own.

Yet she reminded herself of how miserable she would be without him and how she'd missed him terribly before he magically came back into her life. And what was there for her in England anyway? An embittered mother, old memories, friends who were hard to get hold of half the time, and an uncle who had yet to build a relationship with his son. Hardly enough of what she would need to fill her life. It seemed so simple to choose an alternative.

Cole's eyes were completely dark with emotion, something in them making Carla lean forward slowly to brush a brief kiss across his lips. "I don't want to weather the storm of more rumors," she told him casually, a smile of pure invitation curving her mouth. "So just how soon do you want me to leave?"

Something like a growl sprang out of Cole's throat as he quickly jumped to his feet and drew Carla up with him. Pulling her into his arms, he twirled her around as he had done in Jamaica when he'd showed her off to the Caribbean moonlight. "You won't be sorry," he promised her decisively seconds before he sealed her decision with a long, smothering, and heartfelt kiss.

Carla was lost. Dazedly she pushed and dodged through the crowded Sangster International Airport, trying to forge a path through the Arrivals lounge as travelers of every nationality and color gave way to her vivid urgency to get through. She couldn't see Cole anywhere, though he had arranged to meet her there. He'd arrived back in Jamaica five days earlier, and she was to have taken a separate plane after they'd exchanged farewells following their week together in the little town of Woodstock.

Her eye-catching short mane of dark hair was caught underneath a plain white silk scarf which she'd wrapped around her neck to sport a "sixties" look that complemented the same glowing shade of white as her plain linen suit. She'd hoped that the severity of the style, throwing into relief her tawny-brown skin, would single her out immediately to Cole, who would be waiting to receive her into his arms.

Instead, a great many eyes, mostly male, watched her admiringly in her wake as Carla moved swiftly down the terminal, her sable gaze lit with concern, her mind trained elsewhere as strangers made courteous way for her until she almost missed the man who was waiting at the barrier. Carla caught sight of him when she was about to sigh in despair and then waved vigorously to attract his attention. At such close distance Cole was unmistakable. He was wearing a lightweight suit; the first time she'd seen him looking so pristine and proper. And all the characteristics of his personality were still evident as a smile fondly attached itself to his face. "Cole!"

He became alert the moment he heard the sound of her voice, pointedly ignoring several envious male glances and the hoard of people he nearly knocked over to get through to Carla, who flew toward him and straight into his outstretched arms in welcome. He clasped them around her gently and kissed her briefly on the lips, putting her away from him to pick up her suitcase. "Was the flight okay?" he asked joyfully.

"It was long," Carla gasped, taking his arm as they made their way toward the exit. "I slept in snatches, and the meals were awful."

"I'm glad you're here."

"Me, too," she admitted with sincerity.

She followed Cole's long strides as he led her to the car, and they both settled into it for the journey toward the Linden Vale coffee plantation near Good Hope. "Was it difficult finding the time to come?" he asked, taking the car down the road leading from the airport and heading east for the A1 and Falmouth.

"My uncle Quayle wasn't happy about it," Carla informed Cole truthfully. "But he realized my coming here would be the best way to keep the news reporters off my back. They're always chasing a hot story, and right now I'm still one of their favorite headlines especially now that Darnell is competing for the WBA title."

"It seems the only way they're going to leave you alone is if you got married." A slightly constrained note crept into Cole's clipped, normally very calm voice. Carla noticed it instantly and felt a nebulous feeling of disquiet. Perhaps he was becoming jealous of the numerous occasions that she'd raised Darnell's name and the way links were constantly being made in throwing her past and present together. But he needn't be jealous, she decided, leaning toward him, looking across into his cocoa-colored eyes, her own alight with mischievous invitation.

"Are you talking about your future or mine?" she asked affectionately.

"Maybe I'm talking about ours," Cole tossed back in suggestion. His eyes made no secret of it, either. They danced a merry dance even in keeping a fixed gaze on the road.

Carla pulled back an unruly lock of hair from her forehead which became slightly ruffled by the partly opened window of her passenger door. The cool October breeze fanned against her senses, but it in no way disengaged her from what Cole was implying. "Maybe that's not such a bad idea," she replied to her utter chagrin.

She saw the odd look of surprise flash across Cole's face, though he did not comment on what she'd said. Instead, he continued to maneuver the car along the A1 freeway where Carla charted the unhurried slice of the island's coastline, the hotels and businesses which had become the most populous midwinter playground for the wealthy.

Less than an hour later, they were driving into Falmouth, past the parish church where craft vendors with makeshift stands were selling their wares in the parking area, taking the route south toward Good Hope. The familiar terra-cotta tile roof of Eden Lea met Carla's inquiring gaze moments before the Toyota Land Cruiser pulled into the graveled drive.

Bessie was the first person to greet them as she scurried out of the main doorway, a smile lighting up her aged face while her hands embraced Carla with an affectionate hug. "You couldn't stay away from Jamaica?" she remarked kindly.

"I missed more than the sun," Carla intoned in truth.

"Well, the weather is not good now," Bessie drawled, leading the way into the house, knowing Carla and Cole were following behind. "The rainy season is coming, so I don't know if you going to like it."

"I noticed that it felt a little more humid," Carla admitted, aware that the climate felt much cooler, though the air felt weighted with condensation.

"Where shall I take Carla's suitcase, Mr. Richmond?" Bessie asked, halting her progress through the house as she stationed herself by the dining room door. Carla's memories were immediately refreshed anew by the colonial artifacts around her, serving as a vestige of when slavery had reigned among a bounty of skirmishes and varying alliances between Britain, France, and Spain.

"I'll take it to The Grove," Cole answered firmly, keeping a firm grip on the suitcase he'd removed from the car. "I'll appreciate if you can get Carla something to eat and drink though. I'll be right back."

Both women watched the tall man walk slowly through the house in the direction of the kitchen to where the rear door pinpointed a path that led toward The Grove, then Bessie turned to Carla in long-suppressed inquiry.

"So, you and young Mr. Richmond get close?" she asked, smiling ruefully at the startled expression she saw on Carla's face.

"A little," Carla answered, bashful.

Bessie laughed, walking immediately into the dining

room. "You don't need to be shy with me," she began without preamble. "I might be an old lady, but I remember what it's like to be in love—"

"Who's in love?" a familiar female voice interrupted suddenly.

Carla and Bessie turned instantly toward the door to find Robyn Morrison entering, carrying two clay pots filled with seeds, an ill-concealed disheartened expression marring her cool, unfriendly profile. Until that point, Carla had forgotten about Robyn. Even the subject of their conversation when they'd last spoken over the telephone had eluded her, overshadowed by the intense feelings she had developed for Cole. Robyn was still as Carla remembered her: fair-skinned, long dark curly hair, and some four years younger than her, she essayed in recollection. And her dark brown eyes still flickered with menace just as they'd done when Robyn had sought her out at the Trelawny Beach Hotel.

"Miss McIntyre and young Mr. Richmond," Carla heard Bessie confirm heartily.

Robyn stiffened her slim shoulders and shook her head in denial. "When did you arrive?" Her voice was bitter.

"Today," Carla clipped, now recalling fully their telephone conversation.

"Cole . . . Mr. Richmond did not tell me you would be returning," she said sternly, almost in protest.

"I'm going to get Miss McIntyre something to eat." Bessie smiled, oblivious to Robyn's hardened face. To Carla, she added, "Make yourself comfortable at the table. Would you like some coffee?"

Carla nodded before Bessie left. Alone with Robyn she eyed the woman carefully while slowly taking a seat by the Spanish elm table. Robyn remained rooted by the door, her face contorted with barely hidden anger.

"You're giving me the cut-eye?" she accused Carla hotly, finally breaking the silence between them. "Well, you can't fool me, you know. I know what you're thinking."

"Since when have my thoughts got anything to do with you?" Carla responded, taking a hold on herself and her own mounting fury. She couldn't believe that she'd begun sparring with this woman, but she felt tired and loathed the threatening behavior she was being subjected to.

"Because I'm going to make obeah come catch your thoughts and send you mad," Robyn stormed contentiously, disclosing verbally that she intended to call upon some black magic. "Me have eyes, and I see the way you look at Cole when me warn you to stay away from him because he's mine," she ranted on crazily. "Well, let me tell you this, English woman, if only to get rid of you once and for all with your childish fantasies about being in love with my man. It's Cole that I want, and I will make you pay if you don't put your little backside on the first available plane and take yourself to England where you belong."

"Are you threatening me?" Carla was riled.

"Me warning you for the last time," Robyn jabbed maliciously. Without another word, she left the room as quietly as she'd entered it, taking her clay pots of planted seeds with her.

Carla was astonished at the intensity of the girl's behavior and even more so by how fiery Robyn had been. Though she was furious by what had happened, she felt reluctant in telling Cole about her brushes of acrimonious sparring with Robyn. He would only be mildly reproving anyway, she convinced herself after some thought. Cole had much affection for Robyn, and they'd known each other long before she had appeared on the scene. It would be cruel of her to rake up any trouble between them now, especially while she would be staying at Linden Vale. She would keep this little incident to herself, as she had done the others between herself and Robyn Morrison.

It was raining. Huge drops fell heavily onto the coffee cherries, the coconut trees, the wild bougainvillaeas, snapping off the petals, bending the stalks, drumming heavily on the roof at Eden Lea, and sounding like pellets on the roof at The Grove. The plantation was veiled in a gray curtain of water that saturated the soil and sent up a pungent odor of earth and vegetation which told Carla that the rainy season had come. She stared out unseeingly from Cole's bedroom window at The Grove, hugging herself closely as scents from the plantation reminded her that she was indeed on an island.

Her nerves loosened as she felt Cole's naked body come up behind her, his arms tightening around her bare waist. It was her second night there, and she'd begun to contemplate many things as she stared out at the falling rain coming down from the darkened sky. One of them was the skeptical thoughts she was thinking about whether she could actually forge a life with Cole. Another was the fears she were still having about her past, about being hurt, and if she could ever bear being hurt again. And as the rain fell, she even thought about Quayle and the business which would be left in his capable hands. To some extent, he'd mastered how to run it anyway, and it wouldn't be so bad to have another office elsewhere, perhaps right there in Jamaica, she thought.

"You're thinking?" Cole bent to kiss her neck.

"I was just imagining myself living in a place like this," Carla temporized, leaning the back of her head contented against Cole's shoulders. The night sky was gloomy with blue-black clouds weeping copiously, but it did nothing to sway Carla's quiet euphoria. "It's a lovely retreat, finding refuge here among these hills and hollows of nature," she said.

"I felt this ancient magic of trees and wood once when the night was whispering among the branches in Africa. It made me feel that something earthy is buried in the marrow of all of us with African roots, though we will never know our true origins," Cole said wistfully.

"What was it like?" Carla asked curiously.

Cole smiled as the rain came down heavy and hard. "An elephant at the edge of the forest we were in suddenly got wind that we were there," he began. "It let out this loud scream, and instantly every sound in the forest stopped. It was amazing. The monkeys, the birds, all the wildlife—everything stopped, and the elephants stood still, listening and waiting." Cole's voice was awed. "We didn't know what it all meant. Then we heard this sound like a wild storm going through the forest. It gradually died away, but then we realized that it was the sound of the elephants moving on. I haven't heard a noise like that since. It's an experience of a lifetime to go to Africa and absorb tranquility like that."

"So it was more of a retreat?"

"Definitely."

"Would you be doing that kind of work now, if it wasn't for inheriting this plantation?" Carla asked curiously.

"Probably not," Cole admitted in honesty. "I've done all my traveling, hiking, and camping. If I hadn't inherited Linden Vale, I'd probably be lecturing somewhere or perhaps had bought some land in Canada or right here in Jamaica. Something that would be appropriate for a wife and family one day."

"Now you've got my curiosity piqued," Carla said wryly.

Cole laughed against her hair. "If a man is planning to settle down, Carla, he has to think about how he's going to look after himself and his family."

"You've thought about your future in great detail," she breathed.

"Yeah," Cole admitted. "All I need now is the woman."

He loosened his arms around Carla's waist and turned her around to face him squarely. Even against the torrid rain that was beating horrendously against the window behind her, to Cole, Carla was the most beautiful thing he ever did see, from her sable eyes to her endowed hipline which he was reacquainting himself with freely and easily. "I love you," he told her simply.

"Cole." Carla was shaken, uncertainty rippling along her veins, even though she felt that same love, too. "That's such a sweet thing to say, but I don't deserve it."

Cole's chuckle against her skin soothed her slightly. "What do you mean, you don't deserve it?" he countered softly. "You're a beautiful intelligent woman. You have a great mind and an even greater body. You're everything to me Carla: kind, gentle . . ." His grip tightened around her waist, and he dropped a kiss against her lips to prove it. "Marry me." Cole's voice was a weak whisper that held a note of enchantment that filled the darkened room. Carla was almost swept away by the secret promise hidden among the two words. A promise that meant everything she'd ever wanted that would fulfill the dreams she'd yearned to come true.

The back of her hand brushed against Cole's cheek, and her mouth opened in offering of an answer, but as she was about to tell him what was in her heart, though she did not know what words would fall from her lips, whether it would an assurance or a denial of what they both needed, the sound of a firecracker erupted and filled the air, and that was when Carla turned and saw fire.

"Cole," she gasped, looking through the window where she saw the outline of a figure running away from the house, and the red, orange, and yellow flames licking the walls outside beneath them.

"Get dressed," Cole responded quickly, already mobilizing himself by pulling on his boxers and jeans, slipping into sandals, and throwing on a jersey. Carla hurried, too, getting into her lace panties and putting on a plain cotton dress, barely finding time to put on her sandals before Cole was pulling her arm to leave the house. Smoke filled the room as they hurried downstairs, causing them to cough and cover their mouths in protest against the fumes that threatened to attack their lungs.

"Get down on the floor," Cole ordered, dragging Carla there until they were both on their hands and knees. "The air is cleaner down here."

"Is there a way out?" Carla wavered, afraid, knowing that the front of The Grove must be now completely alight. Wind had suddenly begun to howl outside, and she prayed that the rain would be enough to dim the flames, but as she looked at the window nearest the door, she could see the fire spreading its way toward them at top speed.

"There's a door at the back," Cole told her quickly, muttering unheard maledictions as be began on his knees to lead the way there. Carla followed quickly behind him, troubled as her mind replayed the image of someone running away, instinct telling her that the fire had been started deliberately.

She felt blessed relief when they reached the back door but almost squealed with anguish when Cole swore beneath his breath and told her that it was locked. They would have tried the windows except that she remembered they were protected by decorative iron security grills, as were the custom of houses in Jamaica, making any escape impossible. It meant that Cole would have to go upstairs for the key he'd left on a dresser by the bed, and she would have to wait down there until he returned. "Be careful," she pleaded in earnest as he left her side to return back upstairs to get the key. As he left, her heart became filled with trepidation at whether he would be returning to her safely.

Suddenly there was a crash which echoed from the front of the house, and instinct told Carla that the ceiling had fallen in. A scream left her throat the instant she heard it and another scream yelled for Cole at top volume. There was no sound but the crackling of wood burning and the trickling of rain which fell like a solid sheet overhead like a vertical mass of water drumming viciously against her strained nerves. She was contemplating whether to wrestle with the blanket of smoke to go in search of Cole when sounds of footsteps came toward her, and relief filled her when she realized who it was.

"Cole," she chimed, weakened by the sight of him, though in reality he was like a shadow obscured in a morass of fumes that encircled them. "You got the key?"

"Right here." He panicked, placing it quickly into the lock and pulling the door open widely to facilitate their escape. They didn't so much as walk but jumped out of the house, hurtling straight into the rainy night just as a ferocious flame claimed another part of The Grove.

They were both drenched as they fell back onto the wet ground and looked up at the house in disbelief, Carla's hair sleeked back against her head, Cole's jersey plastered against his shoulders, his jeans and her dress clinging to shaken limbs as their gazes absorbed the house being quickly reduced to nothingness.

"Are you all right?" Cole almost snarled, ignoring the heavy rain that was belting down against him, his mind already working overtime on who exactly had cause to try and get them both killed.

"I don't know," Carla admitted, thoroughly anxious, every part of her weakened by fear and anguish. The house was falling down in great chunks of burned wood and scorching furniture, the whole area looking like one huge combustion of glowing flames incandescent against the cloak of a darkened troubled sky. She couldn't believe that she was witnessing such a blaze, knowing that among the thermal heat were personal items, memories, and sentimental wares that would now forever be suffocated to oblivion.

The mere sight brought tears to her eyes. Such a waste. Such an awful waste, she thought, as the tears tumbled over and mixed easily with the rain that washed over her face. The look on Cole's face wrenched at her heart as she began to realize how much the fire could be equally affecting him. She felt a motherly urge to grab his hand and spirit him off into the sunset, away from all the inner searchings that were obviously going on in his mind. Only there was no sunset, no warm air coaxing them gently against the tropical morass. Instead, a storm was working its way down from the heavens and was making a fast trail toward them.

"This could be the start of a storm or a hurricane,"

Cole began swiftly. "Do you think you can make it to Eden Lea?"

"Yes," Carla stammered, her senses feeling the heat against her cheeks as the fire sent its rage into the wind that had begun to cascade around them. "But what about The Grove? Can't we try and do something?"

"Believe me, I'm going to do something to the person that did this." Cole's voice was enraged as he hurtled to his feet.

Carla rose, too, though with difficulty. She was covered with mud from the waist down, her feet soiled, her dress tarnished with dirt, her hands slovenly smeared with soggy debris and earth. The ground was slippery beneath her and she almost fell, but Cole was quick to take hold of her arm, his arms and shoulders curving protectively around her. By the time they got to Eden Lea, they were both thoroughly wet.

Thunder began to blend with the sound of their heartbeats as they approached the kitchen door. But as Cole made to knock and raise Bessie, aware of the rain rattling like rifle fire against the terra-cotta roof overhead, a scream shot out and filled the air above the cacophony surrounding them.

"What was that?" Carla wavered, turning to look round behind them.

"It sounds like Robyn's voice," Cole digested, bemused. "From over there." He was looking back toward The Grove, and Carla focused her gaze in the same direction. At a distance, all she could see was a landmark in flames that sent sparks flying into the stratosphere. "You wait here," Cole ordered quickly. "I'll see what's going on."

"No," Carla shot back, her suspicions on full red alert. "I'm coming, too."

"You wait here," Cole repeated.

"This is no time for arguing," Carla insisted, already following his strides toward The Grove. The climatic conditions had worsened tremendously, now compounded by gale-force winds running at high-pressure speed. She was reminded of her mother having said that the rainy season in Jamaica ran from July to October; her simple analog being: "June, too soon; July, standby; August, prepare you must; September, remember; October, all over." There would be no hope of it being all over. She'd arrived the second week in October, and if that meant anything, it would be to remember that a storm could be on its way. "Robyn could be hurt," she divulged as Cole's steps quickened. "We'd better hurry."

Until the clouds had lost their entire burden, Carla couldn't imagine the tropics letting go of their anger. Already her mind was spilling over with thoughts on whether the coastal roads had been affected by mud slides and fallen branches. If so, it meant that they, too, had to be careful of what could be threatening them ahead. Struggling against the conditions, they were once again at The Grove where the fire was still raging battle against the wind, miraculously having not died fighting against it.

On their approach, they could see a figure moving around in the night. To Carla, it appeared as though the person was dancing. She ludicrously decided against the notion, thinking to herself that she had definitely gone a little silly, but as her gaze came into focus and she heard the faint sound of a drum beating its own peculiar sound to mingle with the noise of the wind, she realized quickly that she hadn't become dazed by the storm that they were facing.

Robyn's gyrating frame was as mobile as a cheeky parrot, her hands flapping like wings under the colorful costume she was wearing, her mouth chanting an illegible chatter that to Carla made no sense. She seemed to be performing some form of a tribal ritual and calling as though to some mysterious magical force while her feet danced around herbs and roots, bark, flowers and leaves scattered and blowing in all directions on the muddy ground to mirror the legacy of ancient African botany.

If Carla was shocked, she couldn't imagine what Cole was thinking. Like her, he stood dazed in disbelief watching Robyn beat her drum and sway her body in the torrential gale-force winds, totally oblivious to their presence. Then, for one second, she stood paralyzed and let out another horrifying scream, her limbs shaking like she'd become possessed with something, and her breath strained and panting.

"Cole, stop her." Carla couldn't bear to watch. Robyn had surely gone mad, she contemplated uneasily. Or was this the black magic she was performing? The obeah she'd threatened to use against her if she were ever to get near Cole.

"What the devil is she doing?" Cole mouthed, amazed, immobilized into doing anything except look on in shock and incredulity.

"She's working herself into a trance," Carla countered, her own limbs now shaking from the gripping, relentless force of the driving rain which was now succeeding to take her breath away. Much of The Grove was now in cinders, and the firelight from it served to illuminate Robyn's trancelike features as she moved around dazedly in the wind. Then suddenly to Carla's horror, before either she or Cole could motivate themselves to take control of Robyn, something hard flew out of the depths among the burning flames of fire and hit Robyn, knocking her clean to the ground.

A sudden ferocious wind nearly knocked them both to the ground, too, and it took every vestige of strength

Carla could muster to keep up with Cole in reaching Robyn. Her eyes were closed; there were small cuts on her face that didn't look too bad, but what was worse was the ugly swelling growing rapidly on her temple. Normally a pretty girl, Robyn looked ghastly and ugly, the rain having poured over her successfully serving to wash away most of what was evidently painted on her face.

"We've got to get her out of here," Carla gasped in shock, trying to rouse Robyn to awaken. But she did not move, and Carla felt for a pulse in her throat, relieved beyond measure when she found one still there.

"I don't think we should move her," Cole instantly shouted above the cloudburst of noise. "She's probably concussed. We could do more harm than good if we try to lift her."

"Well, we can't leave her here," Carla returned loudly. "Maybe she's just fainted. She seemed close to hysterical when we got here."

"I'll go and telephone for the paramedics," Cole suggested, moving quickly. "You wait with her. I'll be as quick as I can."

At his authoritative voice, Carla acted automatically, rubbing Robyn's arms and legs to combat the effect of shock. Then, in a burst of inspiration, she ran over to one of the coffee shacks, struggling with all her might to pull two bags of coffee beans from within and dragging them over to where Robyn lay immobile. Positioning them by Robyn, she thought perhaps they would keep her body warm and shield her somewhat from the torrential winds. It seemed an eternity that she was crouched next to Robyn's body, rubbing at her limbs to keep the circulation of blood flowing. It was only when she heard Bessie's voice did eternal relief wash over her completely.

"Lord, have mercy," Bessie remonstrated in disbelief, her hand carrying a thick blanket, her body covered adequately to combat the elements, and her eyes wide with intense amazement, obviously stunned by the sight that met her. Carla guessed that it must now be nearly two o'clock in the morning and that Bessie had been awakened by Cole from her sleep. "Wha' happen?"

"It's a long story," Carla prevaricated weakly, taking the blanket from Bessie and immediately covering Robyn with it. "Someone set fire to The Grove and when Cole and I got out, we found Robyn doing some crazy ritual dance."

"Obeah!" Bessie whimpered in fear. "She's one of them. She can call on the evil spirits."

"Bessie," Carla began firmly, knowing she couldn't cope with hysterics right now. "Where's Cole?"

"He's in the house," Bessie crooned, her eyes widening, and her body visibly shaking. "Lucas bring Tata home."

"He's found Tata?" Carla could hardly believe it. Maybe now Cole could finally sort out what she'd been doing. She, too, wanted to go inside and hear for herself Tata's lame explanations as to why she thought it wise to steal Linden Vale coffee, but she felt obligated to remain with Robyn at least until the paramedics arrived—if they could arrive, judging by the extent of the wind and rain.

Ten minutes passed quickly, though it felt like an hour, and Carla could feel her hands and wrists ache with the effort of rubbing at Robyn's limbs, even though Bessie had remained with her and joined in the effort—an accomplishment for Carla because she'd had to offer empty words of comfort to the shivering older woman beside her in order to dissipate her fears of what Robyn had been doing.

"Thank heavens," she breathed in a cracked voice when she saw Cole returning and heard the familiar sound of the Land Cruiser approaching.

"The telephones are down," Cole bellowed forlornly, roughly wiping the rain from his eyes and face. "Masa Joe's going to try and get Robyn to a hospital."

"I think we should get her into Eden Lea first and into some dry clothes," Carla suggested loudly.

Cole nodded, looking around him and knowing how much more desperate the storm was beginning to rage. With some effort and careful strategic movements and all the intentions that purports the meaning of teamwork, Cole, Carla, and Bessie, with the sensible directions given by Masa Joe, were able to carry Robyn from where she lay into Eden Lea and onto a bed situated in the nearest guest room. With a strangled intake of breath, her eyes red rimmed with strain and fatigue, Carla finally ejected a sigh of relief.

"You have done enough," Bessie told Carla firmly. "Go to my room, it is at the end of the hall and change into something dry yourself. I will take care of Robyn Morrison."

"Are you sure?" Carla asked, now feeling helpless and aware that Bessie had earlier been fearful of Robyn.

"She's sure," Cole ordered. "I'll join you shortly," he added.

Carla did as she was told and went down the hall as instructed, walking into Bessie's bedroom and closing the door behind her. Her mind was trained on the fire as she looked around the cozy interior: the four-poster bed, the clutter of perfumes, trinkets, photographs, jewelry littered across an old dressing table. A dated rocking chair was situated in the corner, and two old wardrobes with every manner of towels, scarfs, cardigans, and church hats thrown either on top or hung on their handles were the main items of furniture that dominated the room.

She kicked off her ruined sandals, quickly shed her soaked dress, and removed the wet panties from over her hips. Naked, she selected the first oversized nightgown she found in a drawer by the dressing table and covered her petite body with it. It fit just like the one Bessie had lent her before, dwarfing her frame but providing all the ample coverage that she needed. Using a towel, she wiped her face clean then gingerly removed the mud from her hands, arms, and legs.

Exhausted and a little muzzy-headed from the entire event, Carla wanted nothing more than to just sleep, even though she could still hear the storm raging furiously outside. She sat at the side of Bessie's bed, her hands rubbing against her own limbs to coax her circulation back to its usual ebb, and thought she would stay awake until Cole returned. But before Carla knew it, she had lain against the bed's mattress and drifted into sleep to awake eventually to a slightly aching body and a feeling of panic.

FIFTEEN

A hand came down firmly over Carla's mouth. "It's me," Cole whispered quietly. Carla's eyes widened as he slowly moved his hand away and she stared dazedly at him, aware that he, too, had changed out of his wet clothes, though the dry ones he were in were not his style. She immediately surmised that his outerwear, a pair of blue overalls and a checkered shirt, belonged to Lucas.

"What is it?" she inquired, fearful but curious. She could still hear the rain outside, but the thunder had stopped, and her senses told her that the night had not yet paled into day. She couldn't have been asleep very long, she thought. Perhaps her body had just taken a nap.

"Tata's friends are here downstairs," Cole taunted a little angrily. "It appears she owes them some money, and they're not leaving until they get it."

Carla's mind went instantly on red alert. "Are they armed?" It seemed the most sensible question to ask. Tata's sheepish friend, whom she'd met on her first day at Eden Lea, was of the most unscrupulous nature to say the least. If he were a member of the yardies, as she suspected, she imagined that artillery was the language in which they spoke.

"One has a gun," Cole whispered carefully, his tone

neutral not to alarm her unduly. "They don't know you're up here, but they know I am. I've been told not to try anything, and one of them is outside this door right now, down the hall. I said I'd go get some money for them. Do you think you could go and find Masa Joe and tell him to get to a phone and alert the police?"

"Didn't they search the house?" Carla asked, her eyes widening, her heart skipping erratically to a perilous beat.

"They did," Cole whispered, "but Bessie wouldn't let them come in here. I told you that old people are as old and stubborn as their arteries, and she gave them the old West Indian woman act. Don't ask me how she got away with it. Maybe she reminded them of their mamas, I don't know."

"Where is everybody?" Carla knew that she didn't have much time to ask questions if she were to make her escape, but she wanted to be certain that everyone was all right.

"Downstairs," Cole affirmed, holding her hands tightly. "And don't worry. We're all fine."

"And Robyn?"

"She's still unconscious. That's why they've got one of their men outside in the hall. He's keeping an eye on Bessie with Robyn and he's probably listening for me, so let's hurry." Cole's voice lowered to a careful whisper. "I'm going to be worried about you the whole time, but you're the only one who can get us some help. You'll have to use the doors over there"—his troubled gaze shifted to the French doors situated in Bessie's room—"and run along the balcony to the steps that lead down below. I'm not sure where Masa Joe is, but I don't think they've found him. Just be careful, okay?"

"Cole, I'm scared." Carla felt it, too. Though her

senses were alert, and her pulses were racing in tune to the rain which pelted the walls and roof outside, she felt uncertain that she could make it to the shacks, especially when the elements would be against her.

"I wish it was me that was going," Cole hissed icily, his shoulders tensed in knowing that if he left he would be surely missed.

He'd been more than surprised when he left Robyn in the care of Bessie, had changed in Lucas's room, and gone downstairs to see what his cousins were doing. They'd been embroiled in an argument, and Lucas was furious. Seeing him so angry had made him come to realize just how much the plantation meant to his cousin. For all his insinuations that he and his sister were entitled to a share of Linden Vale, Lucas had never intended to take from it in the way that Tata had. He was deeply hurt and had added a good degree of rum to his system to numb the torment spurred by the entire ordeal. In his intoxicated state, he was not the easiest of communicators.

His tired skeptical brow rose as he digested Lucas's oratory in trying to get across to Tata exactly what she'd done, but Tata had been unrelenting in her shame. They fought terribly, and again he had to separate them, and just when he thought it was time, he laid it on the line on just what he expected to be the outcome from such a mess, three men had stormed into Eden Lea and caught them unawares, evidently having followed Lucas from where he'd found his sister.

Their macabre shadows loomed over their bodies as the lights flickered in the dining room, caused by the wind on their entry into the house. There had been no time to do anything or to employ any evasive action because the ambush had happened so fast and came totally unexpectedly. When one of them armed with a gun ran upstairs, his heart almost sank to his knees as his mind told him that Bessie, Robyn, and Carla were up there. He knew that Carla had fallen asleep because he'd gone into Bessie's room and seen her there, his mouth forming into a faint smile as he knew that she more than needed the rest. She had such courage, his heart smote him, thinking back to her determination in staying by Robyn.

He couldn't describe the relief that had washed over him when he heard Bessie refusing to allow the menacing intruder to enter her bedroom. She had been so convincing in her Caribbean lingo and in the manner he imagined that men had come to expect of West Indian women—arms akimbo, eyes fiery, a look that could make any man feel childlike—that he himself had been amazed to find that the intruder respected her wishes and did not dare wish to offend the old lady. Though Bessie had been instructed to stay with Robyn, the intruder searched the rest of the rooms before being told by the leader to remain rooted at the top of the stairway where he had clear view of Robyn and Bessie in the guest room. And then he had been ordered to go get some money, and that was the opening he required.

"Don't try anything," the leader had warned, making sure Cole spied the knife that he held against Tata's back. "Just get the money your gal owe me and come back down so me can see it."

He knew that Bessie kept money inside a drawer on her dresser, but Tata and Lucas had nothing to speak of. He, of course, had nothing to contribute because everything he owned had been in The Grove which he now suspected was burned to the ground by their intruders. He'd nodded silently and said he would get the money from Bessie's room, desperately trying to school his expression carefully as not to give away the fact that Carla was up there sleeping quietly on the bed. Now his heart lurched forward with pent-up fear as he looked into Carla's deep sable eyes, their gaze just as troublesome as his own, knowing full well what he was asking of her.

Carla blinked, unbelieving that this was going on. Against the rustling sound that she could hear outside, that spoke of all manner of debris flying around in the wind, was the sound of her heart pounding against her rib cage. She was trembling as Cole pressed his forehead onto her own, as he held her hands so tight she could feel the tremor in them, as his breathing became as slow belied with tension in equal proportion to the air she herself exhaled.

Flights of bewilderment rode along her subconscious where a plan or strategy seemed to elude her. The only game move she could think of was the one that meant seeing things through at all cost. She'd played that one once before, where she'd thought herself invincible, unbeaten, a survivor. And within that thought sprang another which stroked at her courage and yet caused her to chuckle in her fear. "You did say I would make a challenge for someone who wanted to be sorely tested," her voice quaked. "Now I'm the one who's being tested."

Cole's brows rose. "In what way?"

"In believing that we're going to get through this alive."

"We'll get through this," Cole promised, pulling Carla up from the bed. "Now let's see if Bessie has some money here. You look for an overcoat or something."

As he began to search Bessie's drawers, Carla sieved quickly through her wardrobe. She found an orange fleecy nightgown that looked warm. It was the only appropriate thing in there that she seemed able to wear to brave the onslaught she could hear outside.

"Hurry," Cole whispered, looking around him anxiously. He'd found what he was looking for, though it was not much. Eight hundred Jamaican dollars wouldn't be enough for the men downstairs, who were obviously expecting plenty more than that.

"I'm ready," Carla shrieked, snuggling into the nightgown and quickly slipping her worn and soiled sandals onto her feet. "Which direction do I go?"

"That way, toward the coffee shacks." Cole pointed eastward, then turned as he heard heavy footsteps coming toward the slightly ajar door. "I've been in here too long," he warned. "One of the men is coming."

"Okay." Carla nodded her head quickly, girding herself to face the task ahead as she hurriedly rushed to the French doors and disappeared through them. Before she left, Cole pulled her into his arms and kissed her briefly on the lips. "Be careful," he warned her seriously. "I want you back in one piece. I'm going to try and keep them here for as long as possible. Hurry." Cole watched her the entire time while she disappeared through the doors before he counted out the money in his hand and then took it with him as he ventured downstairs to meet the leader.

Carla could see the path ahead. As she left Eden Lea behind her and climbed up past the cluster of coconut trees swaying viciously against the wind, whose branches were falling down on a scene of tropical chaotic disturbance, she became panicked by the force of nature's high season and whether it would allow her to make a fast pace along the winding path that was hardly visible. But she needn't have worried for very long. The moment she found herself embarking on the perilous journey, trekking her way along carefully, a bright flash of lights indicative of a car loomed up and startled her, its brakes slamming heavy causing the tires to squeak in fury.

"Miss McIntyre?" It was Masa Joe. His voice came across finely spoken from the open window of the Land Cruiser, and he was motioning with his fingers that she should come inside.

Carla hadn't expected this, but she felt gladdened of his timely arrival. "Thank goodness it's you," she said hurriedly, accepting the ride as she threw herself into the car before he rode on. They left the frantic coconut trees with their dark green leaves fighting against the wind for the palm trees along the hills that were so typical of the area.

She looked at Masa Joe, charting his aging features and his stocky frame. He was still wearing the overalls he always wore when working on the plantation, and he smelled of coffee beans as he had done before on the two occasions he'd driven her back to the Trelawny Beach Hotel where she'd stayed on her last visit. He was a quiet man not given to conversation. The three pleasant remarks she'd managed to extract from him on their last acquaintance had all commented on the tropical weather which had been quite hot at the time. When she'd risked asking him about himself, he'd skirted the topic and deftly wallowed into silence in the way that reclusive people do.

His being with her now—and that he'd spoken to her voluntarily in the broad Jamaican burr that was now familiar—somehow made him appear much more approachable. He seemed nice enough, too, an amiable old innocent content on spending his days with what little toils he could fill them with.

"Are you all right?" She heard Masa Joe ask, his eyes checking over her as she wiped the trail of rain with the back of her hand away from her cheeks, eyes, and forehead.

"Yes," she answered, realizing she needed to tell him what was going on at Eden Lea. "I've been trying to find you to see if you can take me to a telephone," she began. "Robyn still isn't conscious, and there are three men up at Eden Lea holding everyone hostage. We need to get to the police."

"I know about them yardie men," Masa Joe said quickly. "I see them arrive at the house."

"Will you help me?" Carla pleaded, helpless. "Cole said if I were to see you, then I should ask you to help me get to a telephone."

"Me helping you right now," Masa Joe told her slowly, again in that soft Jamaican burr. He didn't seem too troubled by what was going on, but Carla had come to expect that of Masa Joe—this quiet reserve of character that made her feel he cared for nothing but to listen to the birds bickering at each other or watching the rise and fall of the Caribbean sun, something to be expected from an elderly and disciplined laborer, she'd once thought.

She leaned back into her seat, feeling somewhat relieved that she had been rescued from the torrential onslaught. Soon they would reach Good Hope and could drive into the village and hopefully find a telephone that would be working. Silently she prayed to God that they would. If hope really existed, if it really wasn't a word that she'd often felt somebody had made up to have us all believe that there's something to live for, the phone lines wouldn't be down in Good Hope, and she would be successful in calling the police.

But Carla was in for a stunning shock. It was such that it caused her to slowly sit up in her seat, her back rigid and her mouth slightly aghast. Her gaze widened remarkably in numbed amazement as it settled on the terra-cotta roof of Eden Lea. The house stood proudly against the weeping sky which was starting to pale, bringing forth a new day. She hadn't detected Masa Joe turning the car around, but she hadn't mindfully paid attention, either. And not knowing the road so well, his ease and control in successfully bringing her back there was easy on all accounts.

Her first reaction was that she'd been hoodwinked. Masa Joe had pulled a trick on her and she'd been such a greenhorn, duped into thinking that his outward appearance spoke of an honest man. That alone forced her second reaction which was a sense of fury. She felt at a loss trying to assemble in her head the treachery and deception that lay hidden in his character. She was trying to sharpen her wits and think up a way to outmaneuver his tactic when she felt his clammy hand take a firm grip on her wrist.

"Don't move," Masa Joe ordered her sternly, cutting the car lights and slowly pulling the Land Cruiser to a spot within a stone's throw of Eden Lea. There was a different tone in his voice now, and his eyes held a menace she hadn't seen there before.

"Let me go," Carla wailed at him, something of the same agony of spirit which had racked her in discovering Darnell's deception tormenting her troubled mind that she hardly knew how to repress it. "I can't believe you would do this to Cole," she admonished madly. "After everything he's done to help you."

"Do what?" Masa Joe's lips tilted in speculation, his free hand engaging the hand brake.

"Betray him like this," Carla accused hotly. "How much are they paying you to keep quiet? Are you in on this with Tata, too? For how long has this been going on?"

Masa Joe held out under her fiery gaze while she shot out all her questions. His reluctance to stop her or furnish any answers skipped Carla's attention entirely until she finally silenced herself in frustrated exhaustion, her head aching and her throat raw from listening to her own self speak. Masa Joe slowly shook his head, and that was when Carla registered that he hadn't moved. Instead he was looking at her like an ancient Egyptian statue who'd seen and absorbed all the ills of the world, aging in perpetual wisdom.

"I'm here to save my son," he told her at last. "Colebert Richmond is my son."

"What?" Carla demanded, her voice shaky, her senses feeling as though they'd been knocked sideways.

"His mama, Elva Mae, and I had a relationship a long, long time ago," Masa Joe clarified.

"But . . . but . . ." Carla hardly knew where to begin.

"Why didn't I tell him?" Masa Joe guessed the question on her mind. "He's a man now. He doesn't need me. I'm a fifty-nine-year-old man who could never have offered Colebert anything. I can't even read or write."

Tears welled into Carla's eyes. "But Elva Mae must've—"

"Elva Mae was everything to her father," Masa Joe explained. "Papa Peter would've despised us both if he knew it was me who'd put his girl in the family way. He was a browning, Miss McIntyre. A mulatto. In Jamaica back when I was a kid, that counted for something. Me and my folks, we were poor people and treated like trash. We just worked for folks like Papa Peter who owned property."

"So that's why Elva Mae never told him the truth about you."

"She did the right thing under the circumstances," Masa Joe admitted quietly. "She paid hard for it, too. I never did like it when she decide to leave, but she send me pictures, Miss McIntyre. Plenty of pictures."

"I'm so sorry," Carla declared, hiding the quick, unbidden flicker of sorrow in her most sincere voice. "You have both suffered tremendous pain."

Masa Joe looked at her with studied composure. "You're a nice woman," he said, his mouth hardening. "Here in Jamaica a lot of we suffer this way. You're from foreign, so you lucky that you have parents who use their sense to leave here so that when you born you're someplace where you can get an education. Jamaica can be a good place only if more educated people like you live here."

Among the gale-force winds and rain where their brief conversation sounded so silently and yet was filled with all the cracks and flaws of an earthquake, Carla understood something of what he meant. Due to Jamaica's close proximity to the South American mainland, it had become a haven for protection rackets threatening to shatter the idyllic calm of such a paradise isle. Now she and Masa Joe were caught up in the threads of that same intricate web where gangland control and manipulation reigned supreme. "Jamaica has survived many things," she assayed with mirth. "Out of many, one people, so the saying goes?"

"So the saying goes." Masa Joe nodded, girding himself into action. Beneath the features that spoke of his African heritage and the tamed veneer that seemed suddenly ready for a vicious, no-holds-barred battle, Masa Joe schooled himself to take charge. "How many men are in the house, did you say?"

"Three. Cole said three," Carla said quickly. "One's at the top of the stairs, and there are two others inside downstairs, I think in the dining room."

"None are outside. Me check that," Masa Joe divulged. "You should never leave out to come find me though. You could've got lost. When Cole come tell me about the fire at The Grove, me know something did wrong. And when me see you come down the balcony stairs and run over into the hills, I did frighten for you."

"I thought if I couldn't find you, I'd try and get to a telephone," Carla told him lamely.

"So they don't know you out here?"

"No. You neither."

"Well, then," Masa Joe began tonelessly. "What do they want so we get them out of the house?"

"Money," Carla said flatly. "Lots of it."

"Oh," Masa Joe sighed heavily.

"One of them has a gun," Carla warned, remembering what Cole had told her. She suddenly wondered if he was all right. In her heart, she trusted that he was.

"Maybe we should check things out first," Masa Joe cautioned. "Do you want to stay here?"

"No," Carla shrieked. "I'll come with you."

The air was humid and the storm was still raging when they both left the Toyota Land Cruiser and crept over to the side of the house. The pale blue of a vagrant dawn had just winked out from behind the gloomy clouds, providing ample light for them to see their way to the rear door of Eden Lea. Carla could just make out the smoldering ashes of The Grove from where she stood.

"Someone's seen us," Masa Joe's voice was alert as he gazed horrified through the kitchen window. "Come on." He pulled her hand, and Carla felt her legs slip against the water and mud that had built up beneath her feet. "This way," Masa Joe impelled as she kept up with him, unknowing where he was planning on going, though she could see that they were heading in the direction of the plantation.

Behind her there were voices that echoed against the wind, and her senses seemed to detect that someone had followed them. As they ventured ahead, she could feel the groundwater beneath her feet rising rapidly becoming more clearly discernible as they climbed higher. Then, to her shock, a loud noise rang out, and instinct caused her to crouch against the ground, aware that she'd heard a gunshot.

"They're shooting at us," her voice rang out in fear.

"We'd better keep moving," Masa Joe implored. "I know these hills, they don't. This way."

Carla trusted him and followed carefully as he charted their way up. She was not to know that Masa Joe in his years at Linden Vale had grown to know the slopes of the hills and valley in such great detail. During his time there, he'd known the slopes to suffer frequent slips caused by the net input of water from the seasonal rainfall. It would always be enough to cause a common displacement, and he was already beginning to detect the sliding surface forming discreet slices beneath his feet, the stresses and strength on the soil's surface building up into a progressive failure.

He also knew that once the peak strength of the slope had been mobilized, the soil would shed its load so that the mass would fall and establish a new geometry. He had to get himself and Carla to the top and quickly before the nature and condition of the underlying soil failed and caused the downward movement and collapse of the ground beneath them.

He steered Carla to the safest part of the plantation, a gully that had been cut through the vegetation where movement of the slope would not affect them. Another gunshot was fired as he and Carla stumbled upward, reaching the point he knew to be the most stable. "We're safe here," he told Carla slowly, his breath panting as heavily as hers. "I'm not sure how long it's going to take them to find us, but if they do, we'll have to—"

Carla did not hear him finish. As she tried to catch

her breath from the trek she'd just taken, she heard the heavy pounding sound of earth shifting around her. To her chagrin, Masa Joe pulled her down to the wet ground into the gully that he'd pinpointed on their arrival. As he did so, she was to see mud, vegetation, and debris slide in a sharplike sequence of lithologically controlled movement to feed a master slide that conveyed foliage and earth material to the ground below them. The arenaceous flow of earth material due to the copious rainfall lasted nearly two swift minutes, the shift seeming to be as characteristic in answer to the storm that was still moaning overhead.

Carla did not dare move until Masa Joe instructed that she do so, and even then she felt unsure when she saw him rise to his feet. "You all right?" was his first question as he looked about them.

"I think so," Carla said in answer. Around her looked slightly different but not vastly so. She could still distinguish where she was, and Eden Lea projected in the distance in front of her. "I wonder if the men who were following us are all right."

"If they were behind us, I don't think so." Masa Joe restrained her arm carefully, though he knew the consequences of them being under the landslide would be only minimal—at best, slight or moderate damage to a limb or two, certainly not anything that would be fatal.

"Oh, no." Carla swallowed unhappily.

"Don't worry, they won't be dead," Masa Joe consoled quickly. "They'll be knee high in mud for a good while, long enough for me to tie them up for the police."

Carla exerted a deep sigh of relief She was just deciding how they were going to get back down when she saw Cole's tall figure standing at the toe of the landslide which was being actively eroded away by the water levels. His hand waved vigorously to alert her attention, and she felt her heart rush into her mouth as she returned an equally excited wave, feeling the rush of being alive wash across her soul. Masa Joe could not get her down the hill fast enough. The moment she was within reach, she threw herself into Cole's arms.

"Carla, baby," Cole crooned, overwhelmed with emotion. His arms tightened around her, his heart beat erratically, comforting her with its irregularity.

"I'm fine," she breathed, her arms around his neck, smoothing the hardened muscles at his nape. "You?"

"I'm okay. We're all okay. Two of the men rushed out here, and we managed to catch the other one off guard. I managed to tie him up, then we heard the gunshots."

"They were firing at us," Carla confirmed weakly. "Masa Joe took us into a gully just before the landslide."

"Oh, baby." Cole crushed her to him again. "You could have been harmed. I should never have sent you out here."

Carla pulled away slightly and looked into Cole's pained eyes. "It was the only way, and Masa Joe knew what he was doing." She tried to convince him to spare the ache and troubled emotions that were tormenting him. She turned to the toe of the landslide. "The other two men are somewhere down there."

As she spoke, Lucas and Tata were making their way toward them from Eden Lea, stumbling against the force of the wind as they ventured to get closer. Masa Joe was already picking his way around the landslide, his alert gaze focusing quickly on the two men who had been chasing them and who were desperately trying to free themselves from the wet mud that bore down heavy on their limbs, restricting their movements so that they could be easily captured.

Masa Joe and Lucas were ultra-quick in tying them up while Tata stood silently watching Cole hold Carla in his arms. He was reluctant to let her go, but instead held her tightly against him while the rain began to slow above them, his head buried into her neck praising God that they were together again. When the two men had been tied securely and Masa Joe and Lucas began to march them into Eden Lea on foot, only then did Cole finally release Carla from him and look murderously at Tata, who stood forlornly, showing little guilt. "This is all your fault," he accused her hotly. "I don't want you here. You can pack your things."

Tata's eyes widened in disbelief as she tried to steady herself against the wind brushing against her cheek, making her feel as though she'd been slapped and hard. "So she's going to play the lady of Eden Lea after all?" she raged, placing her hands against her hips.

"You'd be wise to confine your opinions on my future wife to yourself," Cole shot back just as angrily.

"Future wife!" Tata laughed, ignoring the startled gaze that flashed across Carla's face. "I always did know she was after you money."

"And you were out to ruin Linden Vale," Cole reminded. "I don't know how much you've cost this plantation, but until you go into rehab, I don't want you here. Don't worry, I'll make sure you'll be looked after financially."

Tata sucked her teeth in menace. "I don't need you, cousin," she spat out.

"Well, you need your brother, and I think even Lucas will agree with me on this one," Cole shot back. Carla shivered against him from the force of the wind, and Cole looked down into her flushed face. "I'd better get you inside," he exclaimed, dismissing Tata from his thoughts.

Carla watched in alarm as Tata shrugged her shoulders aggressively as though she, too, had dismissed the subject carelessly. In the recesses of her mind, she wondered whether Tata really cared or whether she was just unmindful of the trouble she'd caused. It was difficult to gauge what her reaction meant or the seriousness of her drug problem because Tata was holding herself together quite well. Better than one would expect after the crisis that she'd put them all through.

Eden Lea was alive with noise as they entered through the rear door. She was aware that Tata had followed behind them but disappeared quickly to her room. Bessie was the first to confront them, relief and tears washed over her face. "Robyn's awake," she gasped, having rushed down the stairs, before her gaze widened at seeing the mess Carla was in. She was covered in mud yet again, soaked to the skin, and her hair dripping wet from the rain. "Good lord," she muttered, recognizing her clothes on Carla. "This was not a good time for you to be in Jamaica."

Carla smiled at how comical that sounded. "No," she agreed, snuggling into the warmth of Cole. "It's been one thing after another."

"You can say that again," Bessie remarked, her head nodding in acceptance. "It was Robyn who start the fire at The Grove, you kno'. She put gasoline in a bottle and throw it through the window."

"A Molotov cocktail," Carla snarled, peeved that her instincts about Robyn had proved correct. She knew now that she would have to tell Cole what had transpired between them. If it were not for the fact that she hadn't been looking out the window, Robyn could've gotten them both killed.

"She think the two of you burn in the fire," Bessie

explained quietly. "Me tell her though that you both all right."

Cole rubbed his hand against his forehead, disbelief marring his face as he tried to digest what he was hearing. It was all sounding incredible: the storm, the fire, being ambushed, and then the landslide, all due to Tata's deceit and Robyn's inability to control her jealousy, he quickly surmised. He was thinking all this when Masa Joe approached him and offered him a sturdy pat on the shoulder.

"Robyn make a mistake," he told Cole in his deep Jamaican burr. "And I make one, too, a long time ago." His gaze traveled to Carla, and she knew what he was about to say, and so she reached out for Cole's hand, tentatively holding it tightly. "Cole, I know this might make you angry wit' me," Masa Joe began hesitantly. "But after tonight, when we all could have get killed, I decide it was time to tell you that me your father."

"My *what?*" Cole's voice was harsh, filled with bewilderment.

"I said me is your father."

Cole's body shook.

SIXTEEN

He was hurt. Cole knew this the moment he felt the anguish and pain rip at his heart. Suddenly years of emptiness flashed through his mind: the memories that did not exist of walks in the park, bicycle rides, going fishing, or simply playing a game of soccer. If any had been there, they would have been the illusions of a boy wanting more in his life. But he had to remind himself that he was now a grown man sensible enough to understand that circumstances had prevailed to bring them both to this moment in time.

Amid the hurt that ran along his body was the uncertainty of what it would mean to him now—having a father in his life when he'd gone without one for so long. He could feel the guilt rising in him, knowing that the emotions that should be there were not. He felt no impulse to shake Masa Joe's hand, to hug him, or even show sincere acknowledgment. What he felt instead was the apathy caused by being robbed of a normal existence and of the years that had gone by with no explanation of why he should have felt so alone.

"You're my father?" he repeated, his eyes narrowing in suspicion, any other form of inquiry failing to sentence itself in his head.

"Me is your father," Masa Joe confirmed quietly.

Cole could see the uncertainty behind Masa Joe's eyes, too, but it in no way made him feel any more secure in at last finally discovering the truth about a part of himself he'd hoped to find. "What do you want from me?" he asked, the question erupting from his mouth aggressively, and when it did an immediate recollection sprang to his mind. Carla had thrown that same question at him on the second day she'd spent there in Jamaica. He remembered the suspicion he'd seen in her eyes back then, knowing that that same suspicion now reflected in his own. She'd been frightened, and that emotion was also running along his veins, even as his mind knew the answer Masa Joe was going to give because it was something he'd told Carla in offering of genuine friendship.

"I just want to get to know you." Masa Joe wavered slightly. "If you want me to," he added after thought.

Cole shook his head at how bizarre the whole thing seemed, that his reaction to someone would be something that he himself would now receive. He looked at Carla, seeing a warm smile playing against her lips, and then at Bessie, whose gaze had widened into sheer disbelief. The hallway lights dimmed above them briefly as the storm of a fresh day brought with it a new wind, a reminder of what they had all gone through only a few short hours ago.

He knew then it would not be right to make his father feel uncomfortable. He hadn't wanted Carla to feel that way when he was endeavoring to get to know her. The last thing he wanted was to have Masa Joe feel that way, too. "I'm sorry." The apology was sincere even though it felt dry leaving his lips because he recognized the pity within it.

"Cole." Carla was aware of the tension that shook the atmosphere, even though she knew the storm outside had nothing to do with it. She could hardly imagine how her uncle Quayle was going to cope in the years ahead as he would grow to learn to know his own son, but she knew that Cole and Masa Joe needed time together alone. "I think you two need to talk," she began carefully, taking charge. "Why don't we sort everything out in here first," she suggested, "then later, you two can sit down and explain whatever it is that you each need to know."

"That is a good idea," Bessie agreed quickly and nervously.

Masa Joe nodded his head in acceptance. "I'd better go change into some dry clothes," he began, "then drive into Good Hope and telephone for some help."

Carla felt Cole's fingers tighten around her hand. "You go with Bessie and put some dry clothes on," he ordered quietly. "I'm going to stay down here with Lucas and our intruders until help arrives."

By tacit consent, they all separated and, as Carla made her way up the stairs toward Bessie's room, her sable gaze following Cole as he walked over to the dining room where Lucas and the three men were occupied, she couldn't help feeling her own sense of panic. Aside from the fact that she'd lost all her belongings in the fire at The Grove: her passport, her money, her clothes, her luggage, there was the loss of something more. Trust. That was it. On looking into Cole's eyes when Masa Joe had told him about being his father, she could detect that all his inclinations about trusting someone had vanished completely.

And he'd obviously trusted Masa Joe when he first came to the Linden Vale plantation, having inherited it from his grandfather. He'd taken the old man to be a simple laborer like the others, the longest to serve under Papa Peter before working for him. She knew what it was like to lose trust in someone. Images still rode along her subconscious on how she'd never taken seriously anything a person would say. *I don't believe everything I see and only half of what I hear,* she'd told Robyn when they'd spoken over the telephone. For months it had left her not trusting herself or her judgment. So how would Cole now react when she told him that she, too, had fallen in love?

What am I faced with? Uncertainty. That's how Carla felt as she ventured downstairs and into the dining room that evening after three days filled with getting things back to normal. The three men who'd ambushed them at Eden Lea had been arrested and taken into custody in Kingston. Tata refused to accept that she needed help and in fact decidedly packed her bags, feeling that her best option would be to leave the plantation—even as Lucas tried to put his foot down, she promised that she would never return.

Cole was able to reconcile his differences with Lucas, and he chose to remain on at the plantation, accepting in kind that changes would need to be made if it were to survive the dictates of tourism in a new century. And she'd received an apology from Lucas, too, something she hadn't expected, but it was a worry to her that he hadn't refrained from drinking heavily.

The rainfall had tapered off slightly during the time she had tried to sort out her own problems. She'd contacted the British Embassy about her passport details and airline passage for the return flight to England, and Bessie had been kind enough to accompany her into Falmouth with Masa Joe to buy a collection of new clothes. The Grove had been insured, so Cole was reassuring about compensating her loss, but since his talks with Masa Joe which had gone on intermittently during the entire three days, she'd come to realize that she had lost him somewhere.

They were both staying at Eden Lea, though he'd chosen to stay in a guest room separate from hers. It hadn't troubled her at first because she knew he would need the time and space alone to get a handle on himself at having discovered his parentage through introspection and self-examination of his feelings. She herself had gone through that important stage of discovering herself by acknowledging the painful events of her past like the neglect she'd received at the hands of her mother.

Digging into her past had been tough, but she now believed that had she not faced the dynamics of her childhood: the anger, the hurt, and pain that had stemmed from her early family life and which she'd obviously taken into her relationship with Darnell because she had desperately wanted to be loved, she would not have found the ability to move forward. She had only been able to do so having resolved much of the emotional wounds. And that was the journey Cole was now taking, but he'd chosen to shut her out.

His silence was beginning to bear heavily down on her even in her awareness that he needed to acquire some self-knowledge. *Damn it all to hell,* she told herself, frustrated at her impatience as her feet took her into the dining room. Her heart stood still when she was to see Cole sitting at the Spanish elm table, silently sipping a cup of coffee. He was alone which didn't surprise her. The clock on the wall told her that it had already gone past eight thirty in the evening, and the house was silent, though she knew that Bessie and Lucas were running around it somewhere.

She had been sitting in her room for the best part of two hours, flicking through a copy of the *Gleaner* newspaper, her mind wondering whether Robyn would be all right after she'd been taken into hospital. The newspaper keenly reported on the storm that had ripped through Jamaica and the damage that had been left in its wake. Luckily it had not been a hurricane, so the trail of devastation was slim in comparison to how bad things could have been. But she'd wanted company so had left the commentary outlined in the newspaper to go in search of Cole in his room. He was not there—he hadn't answered the door when she'd knocked several times. Now she felt relief as her gaze digested his mood which seemed to be calm and inviting.

"I was wondering where you were." She smiled weakly, casting him a sharp look. Her gaze clung for an electrifying moment to the smooth flexion of muscles in his arms that came from the push-ups he did every morning, projecting his perfect health and fitness. A quick, savage fire of desire gripped her rigorously, almost squashing the caution she had developed over the last three days. She should be careful, she told herself quickly. He's lost his trust in human beings and may well have forgotten the things he'd promised her or the things he'd said.

"Are you okay?" he asked her quietly, his gaze settling on her carefully.

"I'm fine," Carla responded just as quietly, desire now tempered with the slight shock of fear. He was wary of her, she told herself quickly as she, too, took a seat at the opposite end of the Spanish elm table. "You?"

"Just thinking," Cole breathed, looking into his cup.

"About what?"

He shook his head.

Carla panicked. "You told me once that I should learn to trust you, and I thought that meant that you would trust me right back."

Cole raised his head and glared at her. Carla didn't know what to make of the menacing look in his eyes that also seemed filled with despair and confusion. "Maybe I was just dreaming," he drawled, a disdainful smile curling his mouth.

Carla shrugged, trying desperately to hold on to her composure. She'd learned that men were masters over their emotions. They never divulged them easily or freely, especially when they were unsure of them. "So everything you told me was a lie?"

"I never lied to you," Cole began harshly. "Why would you say that?"

"Because you forced me to trust you, now it's your turn to trust me," she shot back.

"I trust you."

"Do you?" she probed bitterly. "You always said it would take a crisis for me to open up to you, and it did. After the landslide and I saw you wave at me, it felt really good to be alive, but while I've been reaching out to you, you've been holding back."

"I haven't," he lied without expression.

"You have," Carla pounced with barely suppressed passion.

Silence invaded the room for five brief seconds before Cole finally spoke. "I always felt like something was missing, like I needed to find something," he began, tearing his gaze away from the coffee cup to stare at her, tears welling in his eyes. "From when I was a child, I've been searching for it."

Carla knew that feeling and felt much empathy with Cole that he had faced it, too. "Never quite knowing what you were looking for?" she asked.

"Yes." Cole nodded, surprised.

"That's how I felt before I found out about my brother," she explained, the sorrowful feeling at hearing herself say it renewing the loss she felt inside. "And I suspect that discovering Masa Joe is your father is what's making you feel like this now."

"What did you do about it?" Cole questioned, his hands reaching out across the table to take hers, holding them casually.

"I got in touch with all the things that dwelled deeply inside of me and, for the first time in my life, it helped me to know myself and know exactly what it is that I want."

"What do you want?" Cole asked, his cocoa-brown eyes darkening slightly.

Something more than the woman in your life now gets. Carla nearly smiled at the recollection of what she'd told Cole the first time he'd asked that question. But she'd come to be the woman in his life, and knowing that made her heart tremble. "I don't want to repeat the cycle," she told him. "If I have children, I want to make sure that they know they are loved. And I want their father to be a person who I know socially, intellectually, emotionally, and intimately."

Cole's grip tightened. "That's good," he acknowledged in awe. "I taught myself a lot of things, too. Like the fact that I can't possibly get to know a person until I know who I am. Finally, I know all about me and what I want."

"And what do you want?" It was Carla's turn to ask.

Cole smiled weakly. "I want to know every part of the woman in my life. Every part of her body as well as her mind. I want to be able to look into her eyes and see what they look like when she's happy or sad, when she's just thinking, or when she's mad as hell. I want to know what they look like when she's desiring me when we're about to make love. If I can see and know all those things, then I can say I know my wife."

"Your wife?" Carla breathed, uncertainty creeping into her loins again. She was right, he had changed his mind on things. Obviously what he wanted to see in her eyes was not there, and that meant he didn't want to be offered something that he didn't really want. Without knowing it, she felt herself pull her hands away from Cole's, detecting a flicker of regret in his eyes as she risked looking at him.

"The night of the fire, I told you something," Cole intoned slowly, "but you weren't very receptive. And when I told Tata after the landslide, you didn't respond there, either."

Carla's heart began to race. "About me marrying you?" Her voice was shaky. The whole room seemed to be filled with the echo of it.

"And about me being in love with you," Cole finished. "So I guess you don't feel about me in the same way I feel about you. If you want to walk away from this, Carla—"

"No," she gasped.

Cole looked at her sharply, his eyes glittering with hope.

"Cole." Carla reached for his hands again and held them like her life depended on it. She was no longer afraid of that one *C* word that had plagued her mind since her first visit to Jamaica: *commitment* was everything that she wanted now and it was time she told Cole that. "This is all my fault," she almost wept. "I should have told you three days ago that I'd fallen in love with you, and I hope it doesn't take another crisis to shake me into telling you for the rest of my life."

"Sweet heaven, Carla . . ." Within seconds, Cole had risen from his chair and rushed over to sweep Carla into his arms. The chair she'd been seated in fell to the floor with a crash as they both felt the safety of being reunited again.

Her hands fluttering against the back of his neck, her feet on tiptoes, her mouth tender and slightly swollen, Carla accepted Cole's assaulting kiss. He expelled the growl that swelled in his throat and tasted the fire like vintage wine, sweet and potent with desire. Carla never remembered how they reached Cole's room—she knew only that she was lying on the large bed in his arms against the white cotton sheets that felt cool next to her sensitized skin.

The air was dusky and damp, cool but not cold, seeming to be of the perfect temperature to absorb the fever pitch of two people in love. When Carla searched her feelings beneath the power of Cole's kiss, it was to know that the moment of sheer terror which had flowed through her in the elemental fear of a woman who felt she had lost something, was now resolved, for she had indeed found love.

Cole's touch was summoning forth a wealth of fresh, new, and intense feelings that were as potent and fiery as the ones she'd experienced before. Every stroke, every movement, every part of her that felt his feathery fingers burned under the magic of his hands.

"Cole," her voice shrieked as his head bent and his mouth closed over her lips, his tongue delving inside to tease and coax her into surrender. She shuddered and suddenly inside her body felt wild and aggressive in her need to devour and take her man.

Clothes were torn off and flown in all directions of the room until they were lying naked next to one another. Then she whimpered her need as Cole began slowly to reacquaint himself with the source of her passion. The world disappeared, her body melted, her mind had entered another dimension of time where nothing existed except a man named Colebert Richmond. And when she opened her eyes, for one fleeting moment in a gasp of delight, she was shaken to near ecstasy as his cocoa-brown gaze ensnared her again and again.

Cole would always have that power to look into her eyes and see what he wanted to see, capturing her and making her his every time. He always saw too much, she reminded herself, knowing that it was that one endearing quality he possessed and with which she'd been met on her first time seeing him that had been her undoing with this man.

It heightened her frenzy for him, and her soft hands began to chart their way around his tapered muscles, his shoulders and chest, where the masculine pattern of his flesh accepted her fingers proudly, surrendering to her completely. His body had already warmed to the rising heat, and the clear smoothness of his skin, where dark curls of hair tickled at her hands, was suggestive to her that he intended to give her what she needed.

She couldn't wait. Four days of abstinence had been too long. Cole understood as he positioned his body over her, his heart beating erratically as she moved her legs in invitation. He kissed her throat, moaning his own need for her there but waited until he caught the splendid enchanted rapture in her eyes, his lips smiling seductively as she rigorously pulled him down, onto her and into her with one deliberate thrust forward to greet him.

His filling her contracted her thigh muscles violently, such was Carla's greed to be possessed by Cole. The rhythm that rose from the deepest part of her was as wild and frantic as the African drums that had infiltrated her mind as she'd watched the folklore dance that was called the Etu. That magical night was when Cole had taken her the first time in her hotel room under the mystical glare of moonlight. She remembered how hot it'd been then, even more so now as she felt him drive deeper and deeper into her, taking her body over entirely, forcing her to a pinnacle that was as high as the moon itself.

She reached it with unbridled emotions, her voice

screaming loudly into the early hours of the night. Then she felt the sudden stiffening of Cole's body as the built-up need that was stored within him caused him to fling his head back and spill into her. Carla felt the fluent fascination that came from him deep and delicious, marveling at how womanly it made her feel.

It was only when they had settled into each other, her head nestled safely into the hollow of his shoulder, did Cole murmur a soft admission, his voice still thick with satiation. "Those dreams you were telling me about, it seems I could be sharing them with you sooner than you think."

Carla nodded, realizing that they'd forgotten to use protection. "In that case you'd have to make an honest woman out of me sooner than you think."

"I intend to," he promised.

He rolled onto his side, scooped her up, and pulled her on top of him. Carla was so light, he felt his manly acumen rise in answer to her petite femininity by showering her with a series of drugging kisses. Carla couldn't resist them as her hand circled his head and smoothed the shaven skull that felt as heated as his body, working her hands over his chiseled jawline where she felt fresh stubble intrude against the style of his beard.

When he let her go, her bones felt robbed of strength as she lay relaxed across his chest. "I don't know what I'm going to do about the company," she debated mildly. "I was thinking maybe set up a sister company right here in Jamaica and then McIntyre & Wagnall could truly be international."

"Would your uncle mind?"

"I don't think so. Uncle Quayle always wanted me to be happy."

"And your parents?"

"I'd invite them to the wedding"—Carla laughed—"but that's as far as I want my mother to interfere."

"So you really wouldn't mind living here, in Jamaica, with me?" Cole asked, a shade of uncertainty troubling his voice.

Carla raised her head to look at him. "No. In fact, I'm looking forward to working on Eden Lea with you. If our children are going to live here, then it's time we got Linden Vale into shape."

She felt Cole's soft finger tip her chin up so that she could see his face. "My man-eating cat," he taunted, planting a kiss on the tip of her chin.

"Wildcat," Carla reminded, bending her head to kiss his chest. At least that's what she thought she was going to do until she felt desire rising up in her again. Instead she ran a wet trail down Cole's chest with the powerful sorcery of her tongue, stopping when she found the small dimple of his navel, exploring it madly.

She felt the sharp dip of his stomach in answer to the pleasure she was giving him. It made her more raunchy to evoke further responses from him as he had done with her. Her possessive hand ran down his legs, discovering the flesh at his ankles, the high arch of his foot, the hardened muscles at his thighs, and the one part of him she admired the most. She kissed him everywhere in proof that she intended to know him as intimately as humanly possible. And when she was done and felt him rise ready to take her, she knew she would know him in the darkest night.

Looking into Cole's face, that held all the hallmarks of a man about to burst free from restraint, she smiled dangerously sweet. "Is the lovebug biting?"

"Baby, it's biting," Cole murmured, pulling her aggressively toward him.

Carla raised her head to meet his kiss, finding herself melting right into it. "Can I have some more?" She held his manhood tightly.

"You can have as much as you want," Cole whispered seductively as he took her lips.

Sonia Icilyn was born in Sheffield, England where she still lives with her eight year old daughter, in a small village in which she describes as, "typically British, quiet and where the old money is." She graduated from college with a distinction level Private Secretary's Certificate in business and commerce, and has worked for the City of Sheffield's Education Department. She is currently CEO of her own corporation, The Peacock Company, which manufactures the "Afroderma" skin care line for people of color. *Roses Are Red* was her first title for Arabesque.

Sonia would love to hear from her readers:

P.O. Box 438
Sheffield S1 4YX
ENGLAND
Email on: SoniaIcilyn@compuserve.com